JAMES P. SUMNER

ROACH
TIME TO DIE

BOOKS

Vinci Books

vinci-books.com

Published by Vinci Books Ltd in 2025

1

Copyright © James P. Sumner 2023

A CIP catalogue record for this book is available from the British Library.
Paperback ISBN: 9781036701451

The EU GPSR authorised representative is Logos Europe, 9 rue Nicolas
Poussion, 17000 La Rochelle, France
contact@logoseurope.eu

By James P. Sumner

Prologue

The darkness surrounding him was total. The stale air smelled damp and decayed, and he choked on each shallow breath.

His gaze darted with futility in every direction, looking for any point of reference that would indicate where he was. He had no memory of how he got there and no idea of where there even was. All he saw was the void, which wrapped around him like a blanket of silence.

He tried to move, but his movements were restricted. His hands groped in the darkness, brushing against the soft wood that encased him, leaving him with mere inches of space on all sides.

His breathing quickened. His heart began beating audibly in his chest. Each thump knocked on his ribcage, as if his heart was desperate to leave this place.

The horrifying realization struck him like a lightning bolt.

He was buried alive.

Or was he?

Was he dead? Was this prison his punishment for a life squandered? Eternal justice for years of wrongdoing? He tried to remember, to run his life through his mind like a movie.

The thumping grew louder. His breaths were getting faster. Deeper.

He closed his eyes, trying to relax. If he was buried alive, each molecule of oxygen around him was invaluable, no matter how putrid. He allowed himself to slow his breathing and his thoughts until the thumping of his heartbeat stopped ringing in his ears, leaving him with nothing but the inevitability of his new, dark world.

He reopened his eyes. He felt calm. His mind was clear. Now that he had quiet, he could think.

Except he didn't.

The audible beat continued. A distant, rhythmic knocking seemed to come from the darkness itself.

DUM… DUM… DUM…

It wasn't possible. Yet, it was unmistakable.

His breathing quickened once more, refreshed with a new wave of fear. He frantically explored his surroundings with his hands. Even with limited movement, it didn't take long. He was trapped.

So, where was the knocking coming from?

He closed his eyes again, listening.

DUM… DUM… DUM…

It was coming from beneath him and getting louder. Or was it simply getting closer? He felt the reverberations against his spine.

He felt the fear smothering him like a pillow.

DUM… DUM… DUM…

CRACK!

The wooden floor by his head exploded and splintered, deafening him. He tried to scream, but no sound came from his mouth. Cold, thin fingers grabbed urgently at his face. He couldn't move to stop them.

Another crack, lower down this time.

More splintering.

He was drowning in the noise.

Another hand grabbed at his leg.

He rocked his body back and forth, desperately trying to shake off the intruders.

2

Another crack. And another. And another.

Dozens of hands reached up from the depths below him, ripping and tearing at his body.

The wood gave way beneath him. The hands locked in their grip. Suddenly, he was falling into the abyss. He was free from his prison, but he knew whatever awaited him in the darkness was worse.

His arms flailed. His scream remained silent. The void consumed him.

Roach bolted upright in his bed, gasping for breath. The thin bedsheet was drenched in cold sweat. Wide-eyed, he looked around the small motel room, seeking comfort from the familiarity of his surroundings.

As his breathing slowed, he ran a hand over his face and blinked hard to clear the fog of early consciousness. He glanced over at the window. Slivers of pale light were forcing their way through the blinds.

He slumped back down, allowing his head to melt into the surprisingly plump pillow. He glanced at the alarm clock beside him on the nightstand.

6:37 a.m.

He took a deep breath and pulled the sheet off him. He swung his legs over the side of the bed and leaned forward, resting his elbows on his thighs. Then he arched back, stretching his shoulders and moving his head, luring out the cracks in his neck.

"Shit," he muttered, then padded across the room in search of the shower.

Chapter One

Roach walked at an easy pace along the two-lane highway that carved a path through rural Connecticut. The trees around him swayed in the early autumn breeze, allowing the sunlight to occasionally peek through and force him to squint. The songs of birds waking to a new day accompanied the rustling of the orange leaves.

Roach glanced over his shoulder as he heard a car approaching from behind. It shot past him without a care in the world. He watched it disappear around a lazy bend in the road up ahead.

On his left, a gap in the trees afforded a view of the thin grass and undergrowth, damp with morning dew. The smell of moist, fresh earth grew strong as he passed. He took a deep breath, enjoying it the way he would the smell of baking bread. The land stretched back a way before dropping off out of sight into a valley. The faint sound of a stream trickling beyond drifted over to him.

The morning sun drowned the last of the pale streaks of dawn. The view was one of the nicest he had seen in a while. Roach had been traveling for a long time. It had been spring when he'd left Topeka. He had taken nothing with him. There was nothing he needed that he couldn't get along the way. He didn't want the baggage.

His clothes were new; they maybe had another couple of days in them before they needed to be replaced. Most motels he stayed in had a laundry service, which added to their longevity. He wore a plain, black tee and dark jeans, with strong boots that were comfortable enough to walk long distances in. He carried his thin jacket. It was only just fall, and the remnants of the summer heat still lingered, even this early in the day.

Roach followed the road. The trees thickened again, forming a loose tunnel around him with a circle of sunlight ahead. He caught himself thinking of nothing at all. Relaxing as it was, he knew he needed a plan for the next few days. He had always heard Maine was nice this time of year. Heading there before it got too cold seemed as good a plan as any.

As he cleared the tunnel of trees, he crossed a bridge over a shallow stream of clear water, which led into a larger river away to his right. On the other side was a sign:

Welcome To Waters Point — Pop. 3,548.

He glanced at it as he passed, following the road as it dog-legged left. As it straightened, he saw the beginnings of civilization ahead: low buildings in the mid-distance, on either side of the road leading into town.

Roach swallowed, his mouth sticky with thirst. A moment later, his stomach rumbled, making his decision for him. He was passing through anyway. May as well stop for breakfast.

Roach had always enjoyed coffee. He wasn't a connoisseur, but he knew a good mug when he tasted one. He sipped the dark liquid, relishing the warm taste and appreciating the full, almost hypnotic aroma.

This was good coffee.

He had walked into the first diner inside the town limits of Waters Point. There hadn't been much to see on the approach. The lack of traffic explained the impressive condition of the roads. Only a few errant leaves blew across it on the autumn breeze.

The town itself was quiet. At first, he put that down to a post-rush hour slump. But as he walked past the gas station and convenience store and the post office, all open for business and seemingly deserted, he realized it was probably always this sedated. He only saw two people: an elderly couple across the street who cast a cursory glance in his direction.

The diner appeared on his left, in the bottom corner of the main intersection in town. It looked new and clean, despite its style suggesting it had stood there since the fifties. The entrance was a plain glass door on the right-hand side. Large windows allowed a clear view inside. Seeing it mostly empty was the only persuasion he needed.

Roach sat in the booth farthest away from the door. The red leather was cracked and scuffed, but it provided enough comfort to last a meal. The floor was tiled like a chessboard. A red door stood alone behind the counter on the left, with a circular window in it offering a glimpse into the kitchen beyond.

Only three tables were occupied. Two women easily north of sixty sat together nearby. Beyond them was a young couple and, at the opposite end, facing the entrance, an unkempt man wearing a long, beige coat, visibly stained.

The only sounds inside the diner were the low murmur of conversation and the occasional sizzle from the kitchen when the door was opened.

Roach stared out the window as he sipped his coffee and waited for his breakfast. The quiet town was littered with patches of trees and grass between the low buildings, all with no real structure and symmetry. He imagined that most of the residents had been here their whole lives. Their entire world was nothing beyond these five square miles.

The waitress placed a plate of pancakes and bacon unceremoniously in front of him, along with a thin, decorative jug of maple syrup.

"Thanks," he said.

"You got it," came the casual reply.

As he shoved the first bite into his mouth, he realized that was the first thing he had said to another human being in a couple of days. Typically, it had felt like wasted effort.

He ate and drank in silence. Content and carefree and alone.

The bell above the entrance sounded as the door opened. Roach looked up and saw a woman walk in. He watched her approach the counter as he chewed another mouthful. Her stride was confident. Hurried but not rushed. Her jet-black hair rested a few inches below her shoulders. She was dressed smartly in a checked dress suit. Her skin was slightly tanned. Her slim figure walked the line between glamorous and malnourished. A big, thick watch adorned her wrist. It looked too heavy for her to even lift, let alone wear gracefully.

She wasn't the type of person Roach expected to see in a place like this. From the look he noticed the two older women giving her, he figured he wasn't the only one.

Small town, small minds, he thought.

Tiring of his idle people-watching, he turned his attention back to his breakfast and began thinking of the day ahead. He knew Maine was roughly three hundred miles north. He had options. The weather was still mild enough that he could enjoy the walk whenever he wanted. He would have to find a city if he wanted to take a break and ride a bus or train some of the way.

Maybe he would see what this town had to offer first, before moving on. He wasn't in a rush to get anywhere. He was simply wandering the country and trying to enjoy the peace. By the looks of it, it didn't get much more peaceful than Waters Point.

The bell sounded again. Roach glanced over to see three men hustle through the door. Each was dressed in a plaid shirt, a beanie, stained jeans, and work boots. Two were built like collegiate linebackers. Thick, country-grown arms swelled inside sleeveless shirts. The third was a little thinner and smaller. He was also louder, laughing animatedly to himself as the group walked over to the counter.

Roach caught the gaze of the man sitting alone by the door. It was difficult to tell if he was watching them or him. Roach stared for a moment before focusing again on the three new arrivals. The mouthpiece pushed the woman out of the way with a nudge of his shoulder, strong enough to stagger her to the side. She composed herself but said nothing.

The other two men moved left. One stepped to the woman's side. The other stood in the middle of the walkway, behind her. The thinner man looked at her.

"Hey, beautiful," he said.

The woman stared ahead, ignoring him. Roach could see the eye roll from where he was sitting.

"I said *hey*," the man persisted, his tone sharpening.

9

"Hello," she replied.

The response was curt and begrudging, but her voice was like caramel.

The man turned to face her, ignoring the waitress behind the counter who stood watching, frowning with disapproval, yet rigid with uncertainty. He looked the woman up and down with a lecherous smile.

"Don't I know you from somewhere?" he asked.

The woman shook her head. "I don't think so."

One of the men behind her chuckled. "Hey, Gary, I think I've seen her on OnlyFans."

She looked over her shoulder. "You wish, asshole."

Roach looked back down at his plate, smiling to himself. *Good answer*.

Gary laughed. "No, ain't no way a prim and proper bitch like this gets anything out."

The woman looked back and sighed. "What do you want?"

Gary's smile faded, leaving a hard expression beneath cold eyes. "I want what you promised my boss."

"I… I don't know what you're talking about. Please, just let me get my coffee and leave."

"Don't lie to me, bitch!"

In a flash, Gary reached out and grabbed her arm, thrusting her back against the counter. She shrieked involuntarily as he leaned forward, forcing her to arch backward against the edge.

Roach looked up again. He swallowed his food and set his fork down beside his plate. He saw the older women and the young couple looking on discreetly, More disapproval. More uncertainty. Perhaps some fear.

Gary leered over her, pointing an accusatory finger.

"We ain't leaving here without what you owe," he said.

Behind them, Roach noticed the man by the door was watching him. He was sitting sideways in his chair, leaning back against the wall behind him. He wasn't just ignoring the scene at the counter, he seemed completely oblivious to it. His attention was fixed firmly on Roach, watching him closely.

Roach narrowed his gaze, curious and challenging. The man didn't look away.

"P-please," said the woman. "I don't know what you're talking about. Just let me go."

The confidence and swagger had gone. She was afraid and justifiably so.

Roach looked at the men again. This time, he looked properly. He studied their frames and stance. All three were strong and healthy. The confidence to do this in public with zero fear was concerning. He didn't think they were local. If they were, one of those older women would've called them a disgrace or asked what the boy's mother would think. So, they were from out of town. Like him.

This wasn't a random mugging. Gary knew the woman and wanted something from her. The woman was afraid and in clear danger.

Roach picked up a piece of bacon and took a bite, sighing heavily. He didn't want to get involved. He had chosen to roam the country alone to *avoid* conflict, not to seek it out.

This wasn't his problem.

Gary tightened his grip on her arm and began shaking her.

"That ain't happening," he said. He leaned closer. She tried to pull away but couldn't. His lips were maybe an inch from her ear, yet he still spoke loudly enough to be heard. "You pay what you owe, or we take it another way."

Roach gritted his teeth. He sat back in his booth, clenching both fists until his knuckles lost their color. He tried to remain calm. Logical. They wouldn't do anything. They were just threatening her. But they wouldn't do anything more. They were trying to scare her, and it was working, but they would leave soon. Then everyone would forget it ever happened. Except maybe the woman. But that wasn't his problem.

He looked around the diner. The man sitting alone by the door was still more focused on him than anything else. But he was sitting comfortably. He wasn't going to involve himself. The old women looked appalled by the scene but seemed content to mutter their disapproval to each other instead of out loud. The young couple were just as useless. The guy was scrawny and looked terrified. The woman he was with had her phone out, filming it.

Gary took a step back. The two guys to the left did the same. Then Gary nodded, and they rushed forward, each grabbing an arm and holding the woman in place against the counter. The waitress yelped with shock and took a step back.

Gary began pacing back and forth in front of her. Short steps. He didn't break eye contact. He looked like an apex predator circling its prey. A sickening smile crept across his face.

The woman began to struggle in the men's grip, but to no avail.

"No, please, no!" she shouted. "Help me, please!"

Behind the counter, the red door swung open and the chef appeared next to the waitress. He was an overweight guy in a stained apron. He glanced at the phone attached to the wall.

Gary shot them both a menacing glare. "Touch that phone, and I'll burn this place to ashes."

The staff believed him. They side-stepped away from the phone, choosing to watch helplessly like everyone else. Gary then turned his attention back to the woman. He looked her up and down, his smile growing.

The two men with him laughed, pulling harder on the woman's arms.

Roach watched Gary's body language. He was flexing his right hand, as if preparing to use it.

He took a deep breath.

Don't do it. Don't be stupid enough to make this my problem.

Gary lunged forward and wrapped his left hand around the woman's throat. Her eyes bulged as she forced a strained whimper from her mouth. Shock and fear. He pressed his finger against her cheek.

"I think we need to send a little message, don't you?" he leered. "One you won't forget in a hurry."

He slapped her across her face, then grabbed one of her breasts. He squeezed hard and licked her cheek. The men with him looked on, laughing. No one in the diner moved. They just stared. Entranced by the horror, like seeing a car wreck.

All right. Enough.

Roach calmly got to his feet and walked the length of the diner with measured steps, never talking his eyes off the two men holding the woman. Gary noticed him approaching and pointed.

"Hey, sit the fuck down," he ordered. "This doesn't concern you."

Roach didn't say anything.

As he got nearer, one of the men released his grip on the woman and turned to square up to him.

"Hey, asshole, are you deaf?" he asked.

Roach didn't say anything.

His expression remained emotionless and cold, betraying nothing. Without breaking stride, he drove his right boot hard into the man's groin, like he was kicking a forty-yard field goal. The man dropped to the floor, clutching himself. His face contorted with a silent scream of pain. Roach immediately delivered a solid right hook to the side of his head. He fell sideways, unconscious.

Taking advantage of the distraction, the woman yanked her other arm free from the second man's grip and tumbled to the floor. She scurried out of the way. Roach walked past her and grabbed Gary's still-outstretched hand. He snapped the finger back against its joint, breaking it like a twig. As Gary screamed with pain, Roach took a large step forward and drove his forehead into the bridge of his nose. The thin cartilage shattered under the impact. Gary stumbled back, but Roach held onto his arm. He dragged him back toward him and swung his elbow. The thick part of his forearm smashed into Gary's temple. Roach saw his eyes roll back in his head. He hit him again. And a third time. Finally, he let go of his hand and let Gary drop to the floor like a felled tree.

The remaining man hadn't moved. Roach shot him a glance. His head was tilted slightly forward, and he was staring up through his eyebrows without blinking. In that moment, as he rode the wave of adrenaline coursing through his body, he was prepared to break the man's neck and rip his head clean off.

His eyes said as much.

The first man clambered to his feet to join his friend. He hunched over, trying to relieve the blinding pain in his groin. They both stared but didn't move. Roach flicked his gaze toward the door and nodded once. Taking the silent cue, the men bent to scoop Gary up off the floor, each hooking an arm under one of his, then dragged him out of the diner without a word.

Roach watched them leave before taking a deep breath to relax. The man sitting alone by the door eyed him curiously. Roach ignored him and turned back to the woman, who had taken shelter beneath an empty table. He leaned forward and extended his hand. She took it. Her skin was smooth but cold. He helped her to her feet and stepped back to give her space.

"Are you okay?" he asked her.

She sighed. "Yes. Thank you."

Her response was short.

Roach frowned. "Are you sure? You seem—"

"I said I'm fine," she snapped. "I just… I need to go."

She pushed past him and left without looking back.

Roach remained there for a moment, confused by the reaction. Everyone in the diner was staring at him, equally stunned to silence. He took that as a sign he was done with breakfast.

Something caught his eye on the floor as he headed back to his table. Something shiny that didn't belong. He looked down and saw the watch. Figuring it must have slid from the woman's wrist in the chaos, he scooped it up as he passed. It was as heavy as it looked and seemed expensive. The black face had white numbers on it, and the hands had small diamonds at their tip. It was gold with a silver or platinum trim—he wasn't sure which. He turned it over in his hand. There was an engraving on the back, which he assumed was personal. He put it in his pocket as he reached his table. He grabbed his jacket, left a twenty-dollar bill trapped under his plate, then headed for the door.

He ignored the stares of the other patrons but couldn't avoid the gaze of the man sitting alone opposite the entrance, who watched him with a raised brow and a half-smile. Roach held eye contact until he turned toward the door. He stepped outside and looked around. No sign of the woman or the men who attacked her. He glanced in all directions before deciding to head left.

Roach sighed, frustrated.

So much for this being a quiet town.

Chapter Two

It had taken him a couple of hours to see most of what Waters Point had to offer.

He had begun by turning left at the diner's intersection, which led him along one of two parallel streets. He headed up one, then back down the other. The circuit revealed little of note. A couple of hardware stores, a sports bar that wasn't open yet, a café, a few run-down houses with chain-link fences around the front yards, and the bridge across the river that led to the next town over.

Back at the intersection, he took another left, sending him north. This part of town was busier. There was a mid-sized grocery store with a parking lot a quarter full. Across from that was a gas station and a small movie theater. Larger convenience stores competed for customers, with angled parking spaces out front on the wider road. Farther on, a church stood alone on the left, and beyond it was a sign that indicated the way out of town lay ahead.

As he headed back to the intersection, Roach shrugged on his jacket. The fall breeze had picked up, blowing dust and leaves lazily around his feet as he walked. The people he passed looked at him quizzically. None of them wore jackets. He figured the locals were accustomed to the weather.

The third time he approached the intersection, he took another left, sending him east. He found himself on a straight road with several others branching off it to the left and right. It seemed a bigger part of town than anything else he had seen. There were more bars. A few motels. A couple of old factories were tucked away behind the main row of buildings, but besides them, seemingly every other store was either coming soon or established inside the last three years.

He followed the road until he reached an incline bordered by tall trees. At the crest, he found a single building with a picturesque view of a cove and lake behind it. The approach was on a rise, and a sign at the base said it was an auction house. Beyond it was a steep drop away to the bay below.

Roach found his mind wandering back to the diner. The woman had seemed almost offended that he had intervened. He was confused. He was also frustrated with himself for not being able to let it go. The entire time he was exploring the town, he was quietly hoping to run into the her again, so he could make sure she was okay and return her watch.

He reached into his pocket and took it out, checking the time. It was now well after midday. The gnawing of fresh hunger in his stomach outweighed any thoughts of moving on. He put the watch back in his pocket, lingered on one last look of the view, then turned to head back. There were plenty of places to eat on the east side of town. Hopefully this time, he could finish his meal in peace.

He walked back on the opposite side of the street. The first streetlamp he passed had a flyer stuck to it. A picture of a missing young boy. Roach slowed to read it. The boy's name was Michael. He was eight years old. It had a number printed beneath his picture, asking anyone to call if they had seen him or had information on his whereabouts. Roach shook his head, saddened and frustrated, then sped up again. He walked on another fifteen minutes or so before coming up on a pawn shop. The storefront was dark blue. The paint had chipped and cracked away with time. He slowed his pace to glance through the window at the wares displayed there. He stopped when his gaze came to rest on a baseball card. It stood on a small tripod stand, like an easel, encased in thick plastic. The image was of Ted Williams, mid-swing, wearing a vintage Red Sox uniform.

Roach smiled to himself, momentarily lost in recollection. He had few pleasant memories of his father, who had left when he was nine years old. The man was a cruel drunk, and as the oldest child, Roach took the brunt of his alcohol-fueled wrath. But before that, he had watched baseball with him. Every Sunday, he had listened as his father told him stories of how *his* father collected baseball cards and tried to get them signed at the games. His prize possession was a Ted Williams card that the player signed for him when the Red Sox visited the Cardinals. It was lost in a fire when his father was a boy. He figured it would've been worth something nowadays. Seeing the card in the window reminded him, for a brief moment, that one of the monsters from his past hadn't always been a part of the darkness.

As he turned to continue walking, he caught his reflection in the glass. He saw movement behind him, across the street. He saw a man watching him. The same man from the diner earlier. He was being discreet, but he wasn't invisible. Roach's jaw muscles pulsed with tension. He took a long, deep breath, then set off walking.

Behind him, the man crossed the street.

Roach carried on. His mind was racing with questions. That man had seemingly showed interest in him earlier. Or had he? Was he being paranoid?

After a few minutes of deliberation, he decided to test his theory. Without warning, he jogged across the street, picking his gap in the light traffic. He took a few steps, then stopped in front of a small restaurant, pretending to read the menu in the window.

He watched the reflection and saw the man cross back over behind him.

It isn't paranoia if they're really after you, he thought.

Another heavy breath steeled his nerves and calmed his mind. He set off again. On the other side of the road, there was a side street coming up that led toward one of the small factories. Again, Roach moved without notice. He strode across the street and turned the corner, out of sight from the main road.

Behind him, the man followed. His hands were dug into the pockets of his long coat, holding it close around him. His shoulders hunched around his neck. He quick-stepped across the street, slowing his pace before rounding the corner.

Roach stepped out in front of him from a doorway, startling the man and forcing him to stumble back a couple of steps.

"Why are you following me?" he asked bluntly.

The man hesitated. His eyes narrowed as he looked Roach up and down, as if debating what to say. His inquiring gaze came to rest on Roach's dark, unblinking eyes.

"I was curious," he said with a sigh.

His voice was rough with smoke, deep and graveled.

Roach studied him. He was about the same height. Maybe a little older. Long overdue a shave. He was dressed in old clothes that gave off a faint odor of whiskey.

"About what?" he asked.

"About why you helped that woman."

"She looked like she needed it," said Roach with a shrug. "Didn't see anyone else rushing to her aid, so I stepped in."

"Well, aren't you the hero?"

"No. I just like being able to look myself in the mirror at the end of the day."

The man stepped to the side, as if preparing to walk away. He moved level with Roach and looked him in the eye.

"Word of advice for you: this isn't the place to make waves or draw attention to yourself."

"Noted." Roach leaned closer. "Word of advice for *you*: I'm not the kind of guy you should follow."

The man smiled. "Noted."

He walked past Roach and didn't look back. Roach watched him for a few moments, then turned back to continue his search for lunch.

Chapter Three

Lunch led to a drink. One drink led to two. Roach grew complacent and settled, and before he knew it, the afternoon was almost over. Relenting, he found a decent bed and breakfast on the west side of town to stay the night in. He showered while waiting for their in-house laundry service. Then, as evening descended, he headed for a bar.

Outside, the night air was cool but refreshing. The streets were quiet. The traffic was almost non-existent. The leaves on the trees rustled in the light breeze. Crickets chirped in the undergrowth. And most importantly, no one followed him.

The bar was busy without being crowded. Roach sat on a stool at the bar, away from everyone, cradling a glass of whiskey as he stared up at the big screen mounted on the wall behind the bar. It was showing a recap of the day's sports. He couldn't hear it over the noise of the world around him. The captions were on, but he wasn't interested enough to read them. He was content to simply stare at the screen and drink, lost in his own thoughts.

Music played from a jukebox, competing with the sounds of overlapping conversation and pool balls intermittently clacking in the corner behind him.

It had been a strange day. Not how he had imagined it playing out. Still, he had stayed in worse places than Waters Point. He would move on tomorrow, keen to forget the whispers of responsibility still echoing in his mind. He had looked for the woman and couldn't find her. There had been no sign of her attackers either. It was no longer his problem.

He focused on his drink and the mindless distraction of the TV. It helped him ignore the judgmental glances from the locals. His stalker was right: in a small town like this, anything was news. Especially when it concerned someone new. But he wasn't going to be around long enough for it to bother him, and good luck to anyone who said anything in the meantime.

Lost in his thoughts, Roach didn't notice the woman enter the bar. He didn't see the attention she drew. He didn't see her approaching.

"I'm sorry about this morning," she said.

Startled, Roach turned to look at the woman from the diner. She wore a three-quarter length jacket over a loose high-neck sweater. Her fitted jeans were tucked into flat knee-high boots. She looked like a model for a designer's winter collection.

She smiled, sheepish and apologetic. She was a far cry from the woman he had met that morning.

"What do you have to be sorry for?" asked Roach, making sure to never break eye contact.

"I was shaken and rude to you after you helped me." She glanced away, pursing her lips with shame. "I never properly thanked you."

Roach waved her words away with a casual shrug. "Not necessary, but you're welcome. I'm just glad you're okay."

Her smile returned. "Can I buy you a drink?"

Roach finished the one he had and pushed the glass away from him. "Sure."

The woman caught the attention of the bartender and pointed to the empty glass. "Two more of that, please."

He nodded and set to work.

She turned to face Roach and extended her hand. "I'm Vanessa."

He shook it gently. "Roach."

"That's an odd name…" she said, frowning.

"It's more of a nickname. It grew on me."

The drinks appeared in front of them. Vanessa took hers and raised it toward him. Roach returned the gesture, then they both sank the shot in one.

"You didn't have to step in and save me," she said. "You could've been hurt."

Roach shrugged. "Those assholes weren't a real threat to me. Besides, it was the right thing to do. Anyone would've done the same."

"Except no one did. No one except you."

He didn't reply. Gratitude made him uncomfortable. He simply signaled to the bartender for two beers. He figured if Vanessa drank whiskey, she would probably be okay with a beer. The bottles appeared in front of him moments later, and he slid one across to Vanessa, who had taken the seat beside him.

"Who were those guys, anyway?" he asked before taking a swig.

Vanessa held the bottle, distracted by the condensation dripping down the neck. "I… I don't know. They weren't locals. Everyone around here knows everyone around here, y'know."

Roach nodded. "Small town mentality. I get that."

She looked up at him. "You're obviously not local either."

"What gave me away?" he asked with a gentle smile.

She grinned. "You're nice."

"I wouldn't go that far. The men who attacked you certainly wouldn't agree."

She fell silent again, turning her attention back to her bottle. Roach watched her. Her vacant stare was laced with hesitation. Perhaps even fear.

"What did the police say about this morning?" he asked.

Vanessa swallowed and shook her head. "I didn't tell them."

Roach frowned. "Really? Why?"

She sighed. "Honestly? After it happened, all I wanted to do was go home and forget about it. I didn't want to deal with all the questions and paperwork and whatever else."

"Would one of the other customers not have reported it?"

She gave a faint smile, humorless, laced with disdain and regret. "I doubt it."

They fell silent. His gut told him there was something she wasn't saying, but he wasn't about to push. He was happy to let the conversation play out at her pace.

"Where are you heading, anyway?" Vanessa asked finally. "No way you're planning on hanging around here..."

"It wasn't my intention, no," he replied. "I'm staying the night. Moving on in the morning. I've heard Maine is lovely this time of year."

"Oh, yeah, it's beautiful." She took a sip of her beer. "Are you traveling alone?"

Roach raised his eyebrow curiously, tensing at the question.

She saw his expression and her cheeks flushed. She smiled, trying to hide her embarrassment. "Sorry. I don't mean to pry, I'm just… not great at making conversation."

He relaxed. "It's okay. Me neither. And yes, I am."

"And what exactly do you do for a living, Mr. Roach?"

"It's… just Roach. And, right now, I don't do anything. I guess I just want to take some time for myself. Recharge the batteries. See a little bit of the world."

"Like a sabbatical?"

He shrugged. "Yeah. Something like that."

"Well, there isn't much to see around here, I'm afraid."

"Oh, I don't know. It's been pretty interesting so far."

Vanessa looked at him for a moment, then broke into a soft laugh. Roach smiled, feeling himself ease more into the conversation. It was harmless and pleasant. It wasn't often he enjoyed company. He figured he may as well make the most of it while he was there.

"Okay," she began, "when you're not traveling alone and doing nothing, what do you do?"

Roach took a deep breath. "Nothing too exciting."

"Oooh, mysterious!"

"Not quite." He took a sip of his drink. "What about you, Vanessa? What do you do when you're not buying drinks for strangers?"

She laughed and reached out, brushing his hand with hers.

"Don't get the wrong idea," she said. "I've never done this before."

"That's what they all say," he said with a wry smile.

Vanessa laughed and shook her head. "Stop! To answer your question, I don't work myself. My husband owns the auction house. He's... kind of a big deal around here, I guess. I sometimes help him out with the accounting, marketing, et cetera. But mostly, my time is my own."

Roach nodded along. "Must be nice having the freedom. Does your husband not mind you buying me a drink? Most men wouldn't approve."

She sighed. "Honestly? He doesn't know. I'm not hiding it or anything. He's just out of town, and we haven't spoken today."

Roach frowned. "You haven't told him what happened this morning?"

"No," she replied, shaking her head. "He's away on business. I... I wouldn't want to distract him. I'm fine anyway, really. Thanks to you."

"It was honestly no trouble."

Vanessa shifted on her stool, turning to face him. She crossed her legs and leaned forward, resting her elbow on her knee. "Okay, listen... Roach. It took a lot for me to leave the house again today, but I came out and hit every bar in town in the hope I would bump into you again. And not just to thank you."

He took a long, patient breath, frustrated by his own instincts. He remained facing the bar as he took a long pull of his beer.

"What can I do for you, Vanessa?" he asked.

"I want to offer you a job."

He glanced at her. "Like I said, I'm not looking for work right now. Sorry."

"I want... I *need* you to protect me. I'll pay you whatever you want."

He turned to look at her. He saw soft, brown eyes misted

with desperation. Her demeanor had changed. The confidence had gone, replaced by a fear he didn't fully understand.

She reached out and placed a hand on his forearm. "Please."

Roach let out a terse sigh. "Protect you from what? Or... from who?"

"I... I think people might be coming after me."

"Like those assholes this morning?"

She nodded silently, glancing at the floor.

"I can promise you those guys won't be back, Vanessa."

She looked back up at him. "But others will be."

Roach took another sip of his beer. His grip tightened round the bottle. The cold numbed his fingertips. He was beginning to feel uneasy. For a start, she said *will*, not *might*, which meant she knew more than she was telling him. He didn't want to get involved. He stared ahead, cursing his decision to stay in town for the night.

"Can't your husband protect you?" he asked her finally.

"No. He's... he's hardly around, and when he is, he may as well not be. His work is his life. He wouldn't care."

"I find that hard to believe. What man wouldn't want to protect his wife? Especially if she was in danger."

"You would be surprised..."

Roach rolled his eyes and smiled regrettably. "Probably not. Look, Vanessa, I'm sorry you're dealing with... whatever you're dealing with. But I'm not your guy. I'm not a bodyguard, and I'm not looking to stick around anywhere right now, let alone a backwater town like this. I'm sure there are plenty of services you can hire that would do a better job than me."

Vanessa held his gaze for a moment, then pushed her half-empty bottle away and got to her feet. Her body tensed as she took a step back, putting some distance between them.

"It's okay. You're right. I'm… I'm sorry. Forget I said anything, okay?" She pushed the stool toward the bar with her foot. "Thank you again for this morning. Good luck with your sabbatical."

She turned to leave, but he reached out to stop her before she could take a step.

"Hey, Vanessa, wait a second."

She spun back around, a spark of hope in her eyes. Roach dug his hand into his pocket and took out her watch.

"You dropped this earlier," he said, holding it out to her. "I was actually looking out for you today, so I could return it. I was going to hand it into the sheriff's office on my way out of town. Figured they could get it back to you."

Vanessa's expression hardened. Roach couldn't tell if it was due to disappointment or renewed fear. It certainly wasn't the reaction he was expecting.

She reached forward and pushed his hand back to him. "I appreciate your honesty, but it's okay. I want you to have it. A reward for saving me."

Roach pointed at the empty shot glass. "You rewarded me with whiskey. *This*… this is too much. It's clearly an expensive watch—worth way more than what I did for you. Besides, I'm not sure it would fit on my wrist."

He smiled, trying to lighten the mood and relieve some of the tension. But it didn't. Vanessa glanced past him. In the split-second her gaze was torn away, he saw the color drain from her face. She swallowed hard and looked back at him.

"I should go," she said urgently. "Please, keep it, Mister… Roach. I'm not sentimental about it. You should sell it. Put the money toward your travels."

Roach went to speak, but she cut him off.

"Please. I insist." She smiled weakly. "Goodbye."

She turned and headed for the door, walking gracefully despite her pace. Roach watched her go, then looked over his shoulder to the far corner of the bar. He didn't see anyone. He frowned, then looked back at the watch in his hand. He shook his head, put it back in his pocket, then returned to his drink. He took a deep breath and sighed, running his thumb absently over the label, where it had begun to peel away from the condensation.

"What a weird day," he muttered to himself.

Chapter Four

Roach stood outside the pawn shop, staring at the baseball card, still in its case on its stand. The breeze was heavier than yesterday, and it tugged at the collar of his jacket as it carried the fresh smell of fall around town.

He had slept like the dead and woke up feeling more refreshed than he had in a while. No nightmares. No lingering frustrations from the day before. He was ready to move on. He had checked out of his bed and breakfast and decided to take a final walk around town before heading north. The handful of locals he had seen so far eyed him warily as he walked by. Residual doubt from yesterday's gossip, he figured. He didn't give them a second thought.

He found himself distracted once more by the baseball card, unable to forget the memory it had shaken free. As he stared at it, he took Vanessa's watch from his pocket. Maybe he would take her up on her offer and get it appraised. Maybe he could buy that baseball card.

He cast a habitual glance up and down the street. Seeing nothing that concerned him, he pushed the door open and headed inside. He was greeted by a wave of warm, musty air. Inside was small, with each wall stocked high with heirlooms and memorabilia. Roach looked around casually, unable to ignore the sense of claustrophobia the place gave him.

Facing the door was a glass counter, with more wares displayed inside. Standing behind it, leaning forward and reading a newspaper, was the owner. He was a portly man with graying stubble on his jowls. His cheeks had a permanent red tint. He wore a sweater vest over a polo shirt. Behind him, beads hung over the doorway leading to the back.

He looked up as Roach idled toward him.

"Mornin'," said the owner with a courteous nod.

"Morning," replied Roach.

"Not seen you in here before." He stood straight, spreading his palms out on the counter in front of him. His gaze narrowed slightly. "You new in town?"

Roach offered a small smile, recognizing the tension for what it was: more of that small-town hospitality.

"Just passing through," he said calmly. "Saw that Ted Williams card in your window…"

The owner relaxed and smiled. "You a baseball fan?"

Roach shook his head. "Not really. But my father was."

"I hear you." He extended his hand over the counter. "John. John Ramsey."

"Roach," he replied, shaking it firmly.

"That's a… funny-sounding name you got there."

"It's a nickname. I got used to it."

Ramsey chuckled. "Fair enough. So, you want to take a look at that card? I'm sure I could give you a good price."

"Yeah, maybe. But first…" He reached into his pocket,

took out the watch, and placed it on the counter between them. "Can you tell me what this is worth?"

Ramsey let out a low whistle. "Looks like a fine piece. Why are you selling?"

Roach shrugged. "It was... an unwanted gift. Figured I'd see what it's worth. Maybe start a baseball card collection."

Ramsey reached to his side and grabbed a loupe. He placed it over his right eye as he held the watch up to the light.

"Well, let's have a look..." he muttered.

Ramsey studied every angle of the watch, front and back, occasionally murmuring to himself. After a couple of minutes, he placed the watch back on the counter and looked at Roach.

"Don't quite know how to tell you this, my friend, but what you have there is a fake."

Roach frowned. "Excuse me?"

"That," said Ramsey, pointing at the watch, "is fake. It's a damn good one, I'll admit that. But it's not real."

"I don't understand. The person who gave it to me... they do well for themselves. No way they wouldn't have the real thing."

Ramsey shook his head with a sigh. "I don't know what to tell you, buddy. I've had this store thirty years. Seen all sorts of things pass through. I usually can spot a fake from a mile away."

"Usually?"

He nodded. "As I said, this one's good. No denying that. On first glance, it looks like the real deal. But up close, if you know what to look for, you can tell. I'll show you."

He held the watch up between them and ran a finger around the circular edge of the face.

"If this were legit, it would feel smoother," explained Ramsey. "This has been shaped using, I would guess, a bench grinder. Maybe a sixty-grade abrasive pad." He looked up at Roach and saw the blank expression on his face. He smiled. "Like building a house of cards with a crane."

Roach nodded slowly. "Right."

"It does the job, but it's not perfect. Pieces that sell for serious money... *they're* perfect. Also, see here..." He flipped the watch over and tapped the small engraving on the back. "Like I said, this is a damn good fake. Almost indistinguishable from the real thing. But there's one thing that gives it away."

Roach leaned close and squinted. "Is that not a personal engraving?"

Ramsey shook his head. "That's where the manufacturer information goes. You craft something this beautiful, you want people to know you did it. But this... this isn't any manufacturer I've ever heard of."

"Could it be one you *haven't* heard of?"

Ramsey smiled. "If it was, it wouldn't be worth anything anyway, real or not."

Roach took the watch back and stared at it. It looked expensive to him, but he believed Ramsey.

"You'd find something like that being sold for a couple o' hundred bucks on the beach of a European tourist trap," said Ramsey. "And even that's a stretch. Sorry, pal."

"No problem." Roach put it back in his pocket. "Explains why they gave it away, right?"

Ramsey chuckled. "I guess it does. You still want to take a look at that card?"

"Maybe later. Thanks for your time."

"Don't mention it."

Just as he was about to walk away, a woman appeared from the back. She reversed through the beads and turned to reveal a mug of coffee in each hand. She smiled at him before looking at Ramsey.

"Here, this'll keep you going," she said.

"Thanks, sweetheart," said Ramsey. He looked at Roach. "This is my wife, Helen."

She had curly, dark hair and a kind face. She looked younger than her husband, but that was likely due to her being slimmer. They both looked as if they were approaching sixty.

Roach nodded to her and smiled. "Nice to meet you."

She returned the gesture but said nothing.

"Thanks again for your help," said Roach.

"Any time," replied Ramsey.

Roach headed for the door.

Behind him, he heard Ramsey's wife spark up a conversation.

"Did you hear about that attack last night?" she asked. "Just awful."

Roach stopped, his hand hovering over the handle. He looked back over his shoulder. "There was an attack?"

Both Ramsey and his wife stared at him.

"A woman was mugged last night," said Helen. "She's in the hospital."

Roach ambled back toward the counter, intrigued by the news. "That's terrible."

Helen nodded. "The sheriff hasn't released any information yet, but Cherie—" She looked at Ramsey. "You know Cherie. From Pilates. Neil's wife." She turned back to Roach. "She said she had heard it was Thomas Pope's wife."

Ramsey shook his head solemnly. "Damn shame. She's always so nice, despite how some people treat her."

They both looked at Roach, as if expecting some input. He shrugged. "I'm sorry, I don't know who that is. I'm not from around here."

"Thomas Pope's a big deal around here," explained Ramsey. "Owns that auction house up by the cove. Generates a lot of revenue which gets pumped back into the town. Nice guy."

Roach felt a chill on his face as the color drained from his cheeks. His stomach began somersaulting with nerves.

"His wife... is her name Vanessa?" he asked absently.

Helen frowned. "Yes. Do you know her?"

Roach took a breath and refocused. "Hmm? No, I just... heard the name mentioned in the bar last night. Wondered if it was the same person."

Ramsey and his wife exchanged an uncertain glance.

"Yeah, that's her," said Ramsey.

Roach nodded. "Well, I hope she's okay. I guess when something like this happens in a small town, everyone feels it."

"We sure do."

An awkward silence fell on the store. Roach flashed a polite smile.

"Well, I should be going. Take care."

"You too," said Ramsey.

Roach turned and hurried out of the store without another word. He looked up and down the street, then turned left, heading back toward the main intersection in town. He needed to find the hospital.

Chapter Five

The hospital was roughly halfway between Waters Point and its neighboring town to the west, a little farther than Roach had explored yesterday. It was small, only two stories high, and painted a brilliant white that was blinding when the sun hit it.

It had taken Roach less than an hour to walk there, and that included the time it had taken to stop for flowers. He had spent most of the walk trying to decide if the guilt he was feeling was misplaced. He felt responsible for Vanessa getting hurt. She had asked him for help, and he had said no.

As far as he was concerned, what happened to her was on him.

He carried his jacket in one hand, the flowers in the other. Only a couple of cars had passed him on the straight, dusty highway that continued over the bridge a half-mile beyond the hospital, all the way to the next town over.

He headed across the small lot outside and toward the main entrance. The doors weren't automatic. Roach pushed one open and stepped through, lingering momentarily as he passed under an air conditioning unit mounted above. The blast of fresh, cold air was a welcome reward for the steady pace he had maintained on the way there.

He scanned the lobby to get his bearings. There were only two corridors: straight ahead and left. The front desk stood on his right, dominating the space. Two receptionists were stationed behind it. One was talking on the phone. The other hovered in front of a filing cabinet with her back to him.

The thick soles of his boots padded out a dull, rhythmic click on the stone-gray linoleum floor as he walked over. The receptionist on the phone hung up as he approached the desk. She saw the flowers and flashed him a courteous smile.

"Morning," she said warmly. "Can I help you?"

Roach nodded a greeting back. "I'm looking for Vanessa Pope's room. I believe she was brought in here last night."

The nurse placed her hands on her hips and narrowed her gaze, taking a small, defensive step backward. Her expression hardened as she looked him up and down.

"And you are?"

Roach's eyebrow twitched upward, surprised by her sudden abruptness.

"A friend," he said. "I heard what happened and came to see if she was okay."

"Well, she's resting right now."

Roach tilted his head slightly. Impatient. Defiant. "Then I'll leave the flowers on the nightstand."

The nurse took a deep breath and sighed. "Room nine. Down the hall, right, then left."

"Thanks."

He walked away, following her directions until he came

to a seating area in the middle of a small vestibule. A horseshoe of cheap, plastic chairs faced him. Around the walls were three doors, each one leading to a private ward. Room nine was on his right. Two deputies stood outside it, talking quietly to each other. Another man was pacing back and forth by the seats. He looked up as Roach appeared and immediately stepped toward him, cutting him off.

"Can I help you?" he asked.

Roach looked at him. He had a short, military-style buzzcut and a handlebar mustache. He looked older than he probably was. His face was etched with tales of a tough life. His uniform was clean and pressed. The sheriff's badge pinned to his left breast said his name was Bushell.

"I just heard about Mrs. Pope," said Roach. "I came to see if she's okay."

Sheriff Bushell gestured to his hand with a subtle nod. "With flowers?"

"I couldn't find any grapes."

The sheriff's expression didn't change. "And how do you know Mrs. Pope, exactly?"

Roach sighed. He knew he had to be careful what he said and quickly decided it was best not to mention he had shared a drink with her shortly before she was attacked. He knew that wouldn't look good. He had nothing to hide, but he also didn't want to answer too many questions.

"I don't, really," he said. "I was grabbing some breakfast yesterday morning when three guys started harassing her. I stopped them. When I heard what had happened after that, I thought I would check on her."

Bushell eyed him warily, then relaxed, content he was telling the truth. "How thoughtful. I'll make sure she gets your flowers. I'm sure she'll appreciate them."

"I'd rather give them to her myself. That's not a problem, is it?"

The sheriff straightened and ran his hand over his mustache. "She's resting. I wouldn't want you waiting around. I'm sure you have things to do."

Roach shrugged. "Not really."

"Uh-huh." The sheriff's eyes narrowed slightly. "You're not from around here, are you? You are a drifter?"

Roach shook his head. The suspicion in the sheriff's voice was notable. "Not really. I'm just… taking a sabbatical. Seeing a bit of the world."

"That right? So, where you heading?"

"Maine. I've heard it's nice this time of year."

"I've heard the same." The sheriff let out a taut sigh. "You staying in town?"

Roach shook his head again. "No. I already stayed one night, which is one night longer than I intended. I was just leaving. Wanted to call in on my way."

Bushell rested his hands on his hips and frowned. "You're traveling a little light, aren't you?"

"I don't like luggage," Roach shrugged. "I buy new clothes when I need them. I can get everything else from a hotel."

Bushell eyed him warily for a moment, then shook his head. "Huh. Whatever. Listen, do me a favor, would you? Stick around another night. Just in case I need to follow up with you about anything."

"Couldn't you just call me?"

The thin line of the sheriff's mouth formed an almost imperceptible smile. He raised an eyebrow. "You got a cell phone?"

Roach's expression mirrored Bushell's. "No."

"I figured. People on… *sabbatical* usually don't. All I'm

asking is that you wait until Mrs. Pope wakes up and I question her."

Roach shifted his weight between his legs, rocking anxiously on the spot. He was beginning to think coming here was a mistake.

"I already told you everything I know," he said, sounding more frustrated than he intended to. "Information I volunteered, I might add. Can't see how I could be any more use."

The sheriff relaxed, sensing Roach's tone. "This is a small town, Mister…"

"Roach."

He raised an eyebrow. "Right. Well, I've lived here my whole life. We don't have much trouble in these parts, so any we *do* get, I take it seriously… and personally. Consider it a favor to me."

Roach fixed him with a hard stare. His frustration was beginning to boil into anger. "Why would I do you a favor? I don't know you. I already helped one person in this place, and it apparently didn't do them much good. I just want to move on."

Over by the door, the two deputies turned to face them, each resting a hand loosely over the guns holstered to their hips. Roach watched them in his periphery.

"Y'know," mused Bushell, "you seem keen on not sticking around. That could be considered suspicious, to a cynical man."

"Are you a cynical man, Sheriff?"

"I'm a *law* man, Mr. Roach. And I'm good at my job. I'm asking you to stick around for twenty-four hours."

"Are you asking nicely or formally?"

"For now… nicely."

Roach glanced at the deputies, whose gazes were boring

into him from across the room. For a fleeting moment, the urge to punch the sheriff was overwhelming. He was trying to be nice, and he somehow wound up the subject of an informal interrogation. It made him angry. There were people out there who deserved the attention. People like the ones who put Vanessa in the hospital. Not him.

But he would probably think the same thing about someone else if the roles were reversed. He knew his involvement would look strange because he was from out of town. It was why he didn't mention the drink with Vanessa to the sheriff.

Finally, he relented, letting out a heavy sigh.

"Fine," he said. "One more night."

The sheriff nodded. "I appreciate that. Thank you. Where were you staying?"

"The bed and breakfast on River Street. About a quarter-mile west, off the main road."

"I know it. That's Ron's place. He's a good guy. He won't mind putting you up another night, I'm sure."

"Great."

"It's just for the night," said Bushell with a heavy breath. "You don't see me before morning, you're free to leave."

"Right." Roach held the flowers out until the sheriff took them. "Make sure Vanessa gets these."

He turned and walked away, not caring to look back. He crossed the lobby without looking at the desk. He was in no mood for more judgment from strangers. He pulled the door open and stepped out, greeted by a warm gust of wind. He glanced to his right, along the road leading to the bridge. It would be so easy to just leave right now. He didn't want to get involved, and no one would ever find him.

"Didn't the sheriff just ask you to stay?"

The voice startled him. He spun around to see the man

he had spoken to yesterday leaning casually against the wall, one leg tucked up behind him. A cigarette hung loose between his fingers, half-smoked. He was dressed the same as he had been the last time Roach saw him.

"What did I tell you about following me?" said Roach.

The man pushed himself away from the wall. "And what did I tell you about drawing attention to yourself?"

"How am I doing that, exactly?"

"By showing up to the bedside of a woman married to the wealthiest man in town, holding flowers. People will start talking…"

"I don't care what people say. I'm just leaving."

"So, you're not going to stick around for another day like you were asked?"

Roach frowned. "How do you know?"

The man shrugged. "Just a hunch."

"Right." Roach fixed the stranger with a hard stare. "This is the third time I've seen you in the same place as me. I don't believe in coincidences. The universe isn't that lazy. Maybe it's time you started talking."

The man looked Roach up and down. He saw the tensed jaw, the stern gaze, the stiff posture. He took a final drag of his cigarette, then flicked it away and nodded.

"Fine. But not here." He turned and began walking back toward town. "Come on."

Roach watched him for a moment, then took another look around.

"Shit," he muttered.

He cracked his neck, then followed.

Chapter Six

The two men sat across from each other in a booth, in a quiet corner at the back of a small pizzeria on the north road. It was a family-run place. The sign outside said it had been there since the fifties. The surface of the table was chipped and faded and stained, but it was clean. Incredible smells emanated from the kitchen, behind the opposite corner. One waitress was visible behind the service counter. The rest of the staff were in the back.

They were the only customers.

They had chosen one of the few booths not by a window. It was away from the kitchen and service area. It was close to the restrooms, but there was no one there to use them. It was about as private as they were going to get.

Between them was a large pizza. Double pepperoni with olives. They each had a slice on a small plate in front of them, with a large glass of Coke beside it. The man opposite Roach wasn't discreet about pouring whiskey into his from a flask he kept in the inside pocket of his coat.

"So... talk," said Roach. "You haven't said anything since we got here."

The man shrugged. "I ordered the pizza."

Roach took a deep breath and clenched his jaw, making the muscles pulse with frustration. "Do I look like I appreciate a smartass?"

"Honestly? You look like you need to get laid. But I reckon that's an issue for another time."

Roach picked up the saltshaker that rested next to them on the table and held it up by the end for the man to see. "Ordering a pizza doesn't buy you as much grace with me as you might think. I don't even like olives. So, you're going to start talking, or I'm going to beat you to death with *this*."

The man's gaze flicked between the saltshaker and Roach's unblinking, ice-cold stare. Then he nodded.

"Fair enough." He took a bite of his slice and took his time eating it. "My name's Valentine. Hank Valentine. I'm a private investigator from Pittsburgh."

Roach put down the saltshaker. "A little far from home, aren't you?"

"Tell me about it. I'm working a case. Or I *was*. There's a young boy, Michael Turing. He was taken from outside his school in Harrisburg almost a year ago. He was only eight years old."

"That's the kid on the flyers I've seen around town," said Roach.

Valentine nodded. "Put them up the day I got here. It's a long shot, but you never know."

"So, what happened?"

Valentine sighed. "The local police hit a dead end. Too busy barking up the wrong tree, trying to prove Michael's parents were somehow involved."

"You don't think they were?"

"No. Statistically speaking, yes, it's usually a family member in these situations. But not this time. Michael's father is Leon Turing. He's a prominent investment banker. His wife passed away shortly after Michael was born. He remarried a few years later. The stepmom is clean. She loved Michael like he was her own. It was the parents who hired me. They're desperate to get their son back. I also think it's a move to help clear away some of the bad press they're getting."

Roach nodded. "Okay. So how did you end up in the middle of fucking nowhere?"

"I spent months poring over every shred of evidence there was. Security footage from outside the school showed an unmarked van parked across the street. Police dismissed it as just another van, so I did too. I figured they had already looked into it, ya know? But as time went on, progress slowed, then eventually stopped. It seemed like they were giving up. I didn't trust they were taking it seriously anymore, so I went back over everything from the very beginning. I had a buddy of mine run the plates on that van from the security footage. Turns out it was registered to a dummy corporation, and I've been keeping an eye on it ever since. Traffic cams spotted it at a gas station not far from here a couple of days ago. It was heading this way. I haven't found it. Not that I expected to. But this was the last place it was seen, so I stuck around here hoping to get lucky." He shrugged. "I haven't."

Roach stared at him. "You know if someone's missing longer than forty-eight hours, they're usually dead, right? It's been a year. The kid's probably gone."

Valentine took a terse breath. "Yeah, I know. But the parents paid upfront. I feel obligated to see it through.

Figured it would give them some hope. Or closure. Which-ever comes first."

"Okay, Hank. Let's say I believe you. Why the interest in me?"

Valentine took a long gulp of his spiked drink. He closed his eyes briefly, relishing the taste, then grabbed another slice of pizza.

"Someone new arrives in a place like this, they kinda stand out," he explained matter-of-factly. "I decided to keep an eye on you."

"So, what... you think I kidnapped a child?"

Valentine shook his head. "Not anymore. You didn't exactly strike me as the kidnapping type when you got up to help that woman yesterday. Before that, though, I *did* think it was a little suspicious that you happened to appear right around the same time that van was rolling through."

Roach stared at Valentine as he absently tried to push a piece of pepperoni from between his teeth with his tongue.

Valentine smiled. "So, I looked into you."

Roach's body tensed. "And how did you do that, exactly?"

"I have friends, believe it or not. Your description and nickname make for interesting search terms."

"Right. And what did these friends of yours find?"

"Not much."

"Good."

Valentine smiled again, wider this time. "But I asked them to keep digging anyway."

"Why?" asked Roach, sighing impatiently.

"Because nobody has nothing to find."

Roach watched Valentine relish every second of the conversation, resenting him more with each mouthful of pizza.

"Your information makes for a real interesting read... William."

Roach shuffled upright in his seat. His lips tightened into a fine line. Out of the corner of his eye, he noted the position of the saltshaker.

Valentine grinned. "Yeah. Turns out you're a bit of a celebrity, aren't you?"

Roach glanced around the empty restaurant, then leaned forward. "Keep your voice down," he hissed. "I'm not a celebrity. I'm not *anybody*. I'm just... trying to keep to myself."

Valentine leaned close and spoke with a courteous whisper. "See, in my experience, people like you are either hiding *from* something, or running *to* something." He sat back and made a show of looking Roach up and down. "You don't look like the running type."

"Don't talk like you know me. You don't."

"Oh, I know all I need to know about you, *Roach*. The question is, what are *you* hiding from? All that business a few years back... you were right in the thick of it. The way I see it, this country owes you a debt of gratitude it can never repay for the things you did."

Roach sighed. "If everyone would just leave me alone, I'll gladly call it even."

"And that's what confused me." He casually pointed a finger at him. "That, right there. This whole *wandering loner* thing you have going on. I don't get it. So, I kept digging."

"Of course, you did..."

"You're like an onion. So many layers. The prison sentence for involuntary manslaughter when you were too young to drink. The short career as a foot soldier for a small-time criminal outfit. And then... you hit the big leagues, didn't you? Tristar."

Roach leaned forward again; his words seethed out through gritted teeth. "You should be careful saying that name out loud nowadays."

Valentine waved his comment away casually, then took another swig of his drink. "Ah, no one's listening. Besides, they may have been grade-one assholes, but they did one hell of a job training a wayward mercenary like you, didn't they?"

Roach sat back and pushed the pizza away from him. His appetite was gone. He shook his head. "That isn't me."

"Really? Should we ask your sister and see what she thinks?"

Roach slammed his palm on the table and pointed a cautionary finger at Valentine's face. "I've had just about enough of this 'show and tell' routine of yours. You don't know me. But mention my family again, and you'll soon find out why I'm hiding."

The two men stared at each other across the table. A tense and palpable silence descended.

Valentine looked away first.

He calmly took a gulp of his drink and grabbed another slice of pizza. He took a bite, seemingly oblivious to the death stare across from him.

Content the point was made, Roach relaxed. He sat back and finished his drink.

"So, I was right," said Valentine after a few moments.

Roach sighed. "What?"

"You *are* hiding. But not from someone else. From yourself."

Roach glanced at the surface of the table, his eyes drawn to a drop of pizza sauce that had splashed beside the plate.

"This is all some... self-imposed exile, isn't it?" he pressed.

Roach looked at him. "Now, why would I do that?"

"If I were to guess? Despite all the good you do... or that you're *capable* of doing... you can't seem to forgive yourself for the shit you did in the past."

Roach held his gaze for a moment, then shook his head. He let slip a small, humorless smile. "My sister would love you..."

Valentine shrugged. "I know people. It's what makes me good at my job."

"Yeah, well, I dislike them. That's what made me so good at mine."

"Hating the world made you good at saving it?" asked Valentine, frowning.

"I didn't..." Roach sighed. "Jesus... look, here it is. I tried to do the right thing once, and someone died. Since then, I've done a lot of bad things for a lot of bad people. I tried to leave that life, and those closest to me got hurt. Whenever I try to make amends, karma kicks my ass. I would argue that I deserve it. So, the simplest option is to just... leave the world behind. I can't be responsible for hurting anyone if there's no one around."

Roach took a deep breath. That was the most he had said to anyone in months.

Valentine nodded, finished his drink, and scratched idly at the thick, graying gristle on his chin and throat. Finally, he asked, "You wanna know what I think?"

Roach shook his head. "No."

"Tough. I think this isn't the first time you've had that conversation. I think that little speech you just gave me was rehearsed. Or, at least, repeated." When Roach didn't respond, Valentine winced slightly, regretting his directness. "Your sister?"

Roach nodded quietly, avoiding eye contact.

"What happened?"

"We... disagreed on what I should be doing with my life."

"Let me guess. She thought you should still be out there, fighting the good fight, and you wanted to walk off into the sunset?"

Roach looked up at him. "Something like that."

"Listen, I know you might not like it, but you and your sister... what the two of you did during Orion's takeover a couple of years ago... that's the stuff of legend. You know that, right? You can't hide from that."

"I'm not."

"But you *are* hiding."

Roach sighed. "It's like I told you. I'm just done. Whenever I pick a cause to stand for, people around me get hurt. Besides, honestly... most people simply aren't worth saving."

Valentine shook his head and smiled. "Well, ain't you just a ray of sunshine?"

"Are you saying I'm wrong?"

"Me? Not at all. I've seen enough of what humanity has to offer that I'm inclined to agree with you. I'm guessing your sister didn't?"

"No. She wanted to continue the fight. Make sure every single person responsible was exposed and held accountable. Make sure the truth got out, so people really understood what happened. She said she couldn't understand why I wanted no part of that. We fought about it. I walked away. She stayed in Topeka, chasing another *Pulitzer*. We haven't spoken since."

"And when was that?"

Roach shrugged. "About five months ago."

"Jesus. Sorry, man. Never easy arguing with family. But that doesn't change the fact you're full of shit."

Roach frowned. "Excuse me?"

"Look, you can tell yourself whatever helps you get through the day. But you can't fool me. Your reasoning is flawed."

"How's that?"

"What did Vanessa Pope want with you last night?"

The question caught Roach off-guard. He frowned. "How did you—"

Valentine smiled. "I've been following you, remember? Tell me what she said."

Roach took a deep breath, which came out as a reluctant sigh. "She wanted to hire me to protect her. She thought she was in danger."

"And you said no, right?"

He nodded silently, trying not to look away.

"Uh-huh. Bet you gave her that whole speech about not sticking around... heading north... not your problem. Am I right?"

Roach didn't say anything.

"And now that she's in the hospital, you blame yourself."

Roach raised an eyebrow. "Are you saying I'm wrong to think it's my fault?"

Valentine frowned and shook his head. "Oh, no. What happened to her is *definitely* on you."

Roach's eyes went wide. "Wow, thanks."

Valentine shrugged. "What? You want me to lie and make you feel better? You knew she was in trouble, and you did nothing."

"I did something yesterday in the diner."

"But you weren't there last night, were you? When it mattered. And look what happened."

Roach stared at him. His breathing was noticeably faster than before. His expression was darker. There was something in his eyes. Not hatred or anger. Disappointment, perhaps.

Roach narrowed his gaze. "What's this really about?"

Valentine relaxed. He reached inside his coat and retrieved the flask from his pocket. He took a gulp without trying to hide it.

"I think there's something rotten in the state of Denmark," he said finally. "And I think she's involved in it."

Roach nodded. "Okay. Why?"

"Because of her husband."

"That's... Thomas Pope, right?"

Valentine nodded. "He essentially runs this place. His auction house brings in a lot of revenue around these parts."

"I've heard."

"From what I can tell, nothing much happens around here without his knowledge or approval. Good or bad."

"So, you think he's up to something?"

He nodded again. "That dummy corporation the van I tracked here belongs to... it's part of the Pope Investments and Holdings Group."

Roach was taken aback. "Wait, you think your case is somehow linked to Vanessa's husband?"

"I don't know, but I don't like coincidences any more than you do. I show up in town, and a few days later, Mrs. Pope is attacked twice in the same day. Maybe it's a stretch to think it's all related. Maybe it isn't. But nothing about any of this sits right with me."

"I can see why. But what does this have to do with me?"

"I'd wager you suspect something isn't right with Vanessa Pope too. Don't you want to know what it is?"

"No," replied Roach. His tone was flat.

Valentine raised an eyebrow. "Really? Even after what's happened?"

"You mean, even after your guilt trip."

"I mean… I'm asking for your help finding the people who put Mrs. Pope in the hospital. I want to ask them why they did it before the sheriff's department gets a hold of them."

"Why?"

"You met the sheriff, right?"

Roach recalled his brief encounter with Sheriff Bushell earlier. It wasn't a fond memory.

He nodded. "I did."

"Edward Bushell is a home-grown boy. Real stickler for the rules. Guy doesn't want to see anything bad happen to his town."

Roach nodded. "So, you think Thomas Pope is up to some illegal shit, and you think the sheriff is keeping it quiet to protect the town's reputation?"

Valentine shrugged. "I think it's possible."

Roach frowned. "And you've managed to learn all this about a no-name town you only arrived in a few days ago?"

"I told you, I'm good at what I do."

Roach fell silent. He looked around the quiet restaurant. The waitress behind the counter was paying them no heed. The place was still deserted. Hardly anyone had passed by outside.

Finally, he sighed and looked back at Valentine. "I'm just trying to mind my own business and stay out of every-one's way."

Valentine smiled faintly. "Uh-huh. How's that working out for you so far?"

"Not great."

"So, play the cards you've been dealt," he said, leaning forward and resting his elbows on the table. "Clear some red off your ledger if that's how you want to look at it. You can tell yourself you want to leave the world behind, but if I was a betting man, I'd say, when it came down to it, you're not the type of guy to walk away from someone in trouble. Not when you can maybe do something to help."

Roach didn't say anything. He stared blankly at the table.

"The sheriff asked you to stick around for twenty-four hours, right?" asked Valentine.

"Yeah."

"Where are you staying?"

"The bed and breakfast on River Street."

Valentine nodded. "I know it. I'll come and get you first thing in the morning and show you everything I have on this town. Then you can decide if you want to stay and help me out. If you still don't want to get involved, I'll wave as you walk away. No more guilt trips."

"Fine. Nothing else to do anyway."

Valentine smiled. "That's the spirit." He got to his feet and pointed to the empty plate in the middle of the table. "Thanks for lunch."

Roach looked up at him, confused. "I thought you paid?"

Valentine simply smiled wider, then turned and headed for the door.

Roach watched him go, reeling from everything he had just heard and unsure how he had found himself caught up in any of it.

He looked at the plate and picked up a discarded olive, which he held up to his face between his finger and thumb. He studied it absently for a moment, then tossed it back onto the plate and reached for his wallet.

"Goddammit…"

Chapter Seven

Roach sat on the same stool in the same bar with the same drink as he had the night before. The TV mounted behind the bar was showing a local news channel. The reporter was talking about some event the mayor was attending out of town. A picture-in-picture clip showed him standing with a bunch of people in suits, shaking their hands, smiling like a true politician, and looking like a deer in the headlights.

The place was a little busier. He recognized a few faces. Judging by the glances people kept throwing his way, he figured they recognized him too.

His conversation with Valentine over lunch had left him with a lot to think about. His usually clear mind was clouded with indecision and guilt, and it left him feeling uncomfortable. To clear his head, he had taken another walk around town. He had checked back into the hotel. He had bought himself a fresh set of clothes. He didn't like the idea of carrying luggage, but he had to admit he liked his old outfit and begrudged either trashing it or donating it to a goodwill. Undecided for now, the old clothes were left folded neatly on a chair in his room.

He had resisted the urge to visit the hospital again. He had also resisted the urge to leave and put this whole place behind him, although he didn't yet fully understand why.

He stared blankly at the surface of the counter as he cradled his whiskey in one hand. It was made of dark wood. Varnished to a shine but long overdue some maintenance. The grain was faded and scratched in places. There were small patches of stains, where drinks had been spilled and not been cleaned up in time. He picked up a coaster, paused a moment to study which beer it was promoting, then twirled it absently in his hand, lost in thought.

"Don't worry, man. It might never happen."

Roach looked up, startled. The bartender was standing in front of him, smiling. He wore a black polo shirt with the bar's name and logo printed over the breast. He was clean shaven with a time-worn face. His smile was genuine.

"What do you mean?" asked Roach, confused.

The bartender pointed to him. "I mean that thousand-yard stare you're giving my bar. You think I don't know what a man with a lot on his mind looks like?"

Roach relaxed. He flicked his eyebrows and flashed a quick, humorless smile. "Fair."

"The name's George," he said, extending a fist toward him.

Roach bumped it politely. "Roach."

"Huh. Nice. So, you wanna talk about it, or…"

"I thought barmen only did that in movies?"

"What can I say? I'm a walking cliché," he said, shrugging casually. "Truth be told, everybody knows everybody around here. Conversations tend to be on a bit of a loop sometimes, y'know? Someone shows up who doesn't live here... well... a change is as good as a rest, right?"

Roach smiled again, warmer this time. "Appreciate the offer, but I'm good. Just keep bringing me whiskey, and I'll be fine."

George pointed at him, making a gun with his finger and thumb, and made a clicking sound with his mouth. "Bury your shit with alcohol. Got it."

Roach raised his glass. "If it ain't broke..."

George chuckled and walked away, leaving Roach to his thoughts once more. He took a gulp of his whiskey and took a deep breath, appreciating the amber fluid as it burned its way lovingly down his throat.

He wasn't sure what to make of Valentine. He had no reason to doubt anything he had told him. He certainly wasn't shy about speaking his mind. His missing child case was rough. Perhaps that's why he had a hip flask with him.

The guilt trip had irritated him, although he wasn't sure if that's because Valentine was out of line, or because he was right. Maybe Vanessa *would* be okay if he had agreed to help her when she asked. He glanced at the empty stool beside him, where she had sat twenty-four hours ago.

He finished his drink and signaled to George to pour him another. The bartender happily obliged.

To hell with the guilt. This wasn't his problem, right? If Valentine wanted to kill some time in the middle of nowhere, that was up to him. But Roach was just passing through. This had nothing to do with him.

Roach had been on the road almost six months. He had yet to wander into anywhere that made him want to stay longer than forty-eight hours. Waters Point was no exception. He didn't care that people silently judged him. He wasn't sorry for helping Vanessa yesterday morning. He didn't like the sheriff, nor the fact he was coerced into staying in town another night. He figured Valentine would be entertaining as a drinking partner, but he had no real urge to find out for sure.

He sighed and took a gulp of his new drink.

All he had to do was stay on this stool until the bar closed, then get some sleep. In the morning, he could leave, hopefully without seeing anyone in the meantime.

Another drink was placed in front of him. Roach looked first at the generous measure he didn't ask for, then up at George.

"I don't drink that fast," he said.

George's face wore a grave expression. The friendliness from minutes ago had given way to a mix of concern and sympathy.

"Thought you might need it," he replied. "Those, ah, those problems you didn't want to talk about... they got anything to do with you helping out Thomas Pope's wife yesterday?"

Roach frowned. "How did you..."

"Small town, remember? Anyway, the fella you chased away... he just walked in with a couple of friends, and they've been eyeballing you ever since."

Roach took a deep breath, weary and frustrated. He glanced over his shoulder and saw the man from the diner, Gary. His two friends were new.

Roach looked back at George and shrugged. He gulped what remained of his current drink, then reached for the new one.

George patted the bar with his palm. "Do me a favor? Take whatever this is outside. I don't want to have to clean up after you, okay?"

"I'll do my best," said Roach, nodding.

George walked away as Gary and his two companions approached the bar. Roach ignored them, choosing to focus on his drink. He glanced into the mirrored surface of the liquor stand behind the bar in front of him, watching their movements. The two men moved left. One rested against the bar at Roach's side, a few feet away. The other lingered behind him, keeping roughly the same distance.

Gary appeared on his right, sneering at him. His nose had a thin bandage across it. There was bruising around his eye sockets.

"I was hoping to see you again, asshole," he said. "I owe you. My friends and I here are gonna—"

"Let me stop you right there," said Roach, who continued to stare at his drink. "I promised the bartender that if there was any trouble, I'd take it outside. Save his bar from getting messed up. So, before you make any more idle threats that we both know you can't carry out, let's take this outside, hmm?"

Gary frowned, then burst out laughing. It was loud and arrogant. "Are you... are you kidding me?"

Roach finally turned his head to look at him. "No."

The icy stare silenced Gary's laugh, but it did little else to deter him.

"You shouldn't have gotten involved in things that don't concern you," he said.

"You shouldn't have put your hands on a woman," countered Roach.

"Who the fuck do you think you are, asshole? Saving damsels in distress like this is the goddamn 1800s or some shit."

"It wasn't just about saving her. I don't like cowards."

"Excuse me?"

"You heard me. Three grown men intimidating a

woman who's by herself. Makes you a coward. No way I was letting that stand."

Gary leaned forward and looked into Roach's eyes. "I'm gonna make you sorry you ever set foot in this town."

"Too late for that…" Roach huffed. He gulped the last of his whiskey, holding onto the empty glass. "Why'd you do it, anyway?"

Gary frowned. "Do what?"

Roach stared at him. "Why did you go after her? And why did it need three of you?"

"That ain't your business, asshole. Now, you said you wanted to take this outside… so, let's go."

"Well, wait a second. I get up and follow you, how do I know your two friends won't jump me from behind?"

Gary shook his head, his expression contorted with disbelief. "Are you serious? Look, I give you my word we won't beat the shit outta you until we get outside. Happy?"

"Not really," said Roach. "I don't know you. Your word means nothing to me. Tell you what. The count of three, I stand, then your friends move behind you before I follow you out."

He sighed. "Whatever. You're just delaying the inevitable."

Roach nodded. "You ready?"

"Sure."

"One…"

Roach swiveled on his stool and slammed the empty glass into the side of Gary's head. As he was falling away, Roach got to his feet and kicked the stool away behind him. He spun around as it connected with the legs of the guy standing closest to him and lashed out with his left hand, landing a stiff jab to the nose. Before the guy could react, Roach grabbed the side of his head and slammed it down toward the bar. The guy's face connected with the thick, polished brass rail attached to the bar's edge. His cheek instantly split open, leaving a splatter of blood on the point of impact.

The second guy stepped back, seemingly hesitant to get involved.

Roach watched him, trying to decide if he would have the balls to attack him. But he didn't think so. He had lost the color in his cheeks. His stance was wide and uneven. He kept glancing around him, seeing how many people were watching.

He was too scared to do anything.

Roach turned back just as Gary was winding up his right hand. He side-stepped the punch and drove his fist into the side of Gary's ribcage, knocking the wind from him. Roach wrapped his hand around Gary's throat and held him in place as he launched his forearm into his already broken nose. Two shots in quick succession. The first started the nose bleeding again. The second shattered it for a second time, causing instant swelling around the eyes and cheeks. Roach released his grip, and Gary slumped to the floor, unconscious.

A noise from behind drew his attention. As he turned, he glimpsed the frozen looks of shock on people's faces as they stared at the carnage unfolding. The second guy was charging him.

Guess he found his balls, thought Roach. *Maybe I'll hide them again*.

He lashed his back leg forward, driving his boot hard into the approaching man's groin. He stopped dead in his tracks, his eyes bulging in their sockets. His mouth was open, silently screaming in pain. Roach stepped toward him and grabbed his head with both hands. Then he brought his knee up and smashed it into the man's face. Once. Twice. Then he pushed him away casually, letting him fall away to the floor and land in a crumpled heap next to Gary and the other guy.

Roach stood for a moment, breathing hard. He looked over at the bartender, who was watching with the same look of disbelief as everyone else. He simply shrugged.

"Sorry."

Just then, the door flew open. The sheriff burst in, weapon drawn. He was flanked by the two deputies who were with him in the hospital earlier.

"That's enough!" shouted Bushell. "Hands where I can see them."

Roach sighed and held his arms out casually to the side.

Bushell nodded to the deputy closest to him. "Cuff that sonofabitch and get him out of here."

Roach stared at the deputy as he headed for him. He was young. Early thirties at a push. It was doubtful he had seen much action. Probably watched a lot of cop shows on TV. He produced a set of handcuffs from behind him and reached for Roach's arm.

He didn't resist.

The cuffs were awkwardly locked in place, then Roach was frog-marched away, past the sheriff and outside into the cool, night air.

The sheriff holstered his gun and stared at the pile of bodies by the bar. There was almost total silence around the room, except for a low, monotonous moaning from one of the guys on the floor.

Bushell shook his head. "Goddamn…"

Chapter Eight

The sheriff's office looked more like a storage room. There was one window, which wasn't on the exterior wall. The air was warm and stale due to a noticeable lack of an AC unit. The fluorescent light buzzed and flickered overhead, bathing the room in a sickly yellow ambience.

Roach sat quietly on a rickety wooden chair, facing the desk that dominated the square room. His hands were cuffed behind him. He hadn't been there long. Maybe a half-hour. He was focused solely on his breathing, keeping it slow and steady, so as not to succumb to the growing frustration curdling inside him.

He heard the door behind him open. Bushell walked in and took his seat behind the desk. The sheriff looked tired. Dark rings sat beneath his eyes like tattoos of fatigue. The collar of his tan shirt was unfastened, and the sleeves were rolled up, displaying his defined and excessively hairy forearms. The sheriff placed a small baggie containing Roach's belongings on the desk between them. He then leaned forward and clasped his hands together. He fixed Roach with a hard stare.

"So, are you going to tell me what the hell happened back there, Mr. Roach?" he asked.

Roach took a slightly deeper breath and stared back at him, holding his gaze. He didn't say anything.

"Did you know the men you were assaulting?" he continued.

Again, Roach didn't speak.

The stalemate lasted only a few moments.

Bushell nodded to himself. "Y'know, while you have the right to remain silent, it doesn't always do you much good. In fact, right now, it isn't helping you one bit." He paused, waiting for a reaction that was never coming. "Where did you go yesterday, after we spoke at the hospital?"

Roach sighed and looked away. The irritation he felt was evident in his expression.

"Look, you—"

"I wasn't assaulting them," said Roach flatly.

The sheriff raised an eyebrow and scoffed with disbelief. "You beat the shit of those men. In front of maybe thirty people."

"I was defending myself."

"That wasn't self-defense, Mr. Roach. That was fucking combat. You tore those men apart."

"They came in and headed straight for me. Threats were made." Roach shrugged. "You threaten me, you get what you get."

Bushell sat back in his chair, resting one elbow on the arm as he absently stroked his chin.

"Do you consider yourself a smart man, Mr. Roach?"

"Yes. Although, I do sometimes make bad decisions."

"Such as?"

Roach looked the sheriff dead in the eye. "Such as hanging around a backwater town longer than I wanted to as a favor for someone I don't even know."

Bushell held eye contact, unfazed by the glare that had forced many a man to shrink. "Well, this backwater town was doing just fine before you showed up. Now, there have been two violent disturbances in as many days, and you've been at the center of both of them."

"Vanessa Pope wasn't attacked because I was eating breakfast. That would've happened whether I was there or not. But I can promise you it would've been a lot worse if I wasn't. And tonight was simply revenge for me getting involved yesterday."

The sheriff frowned. "How so?"

"One of those assholes was the same guy who put his hands on Vanessa yesterday. Gary."

"Is that supposed to make it better?"

Roach shrugged. "It's supposed to show you the two instances are related, and neither of them were my fault."

"Maybe. Maybe not. Either way, you were involved both times, which makes me think you might be the catalyst for it all."

Roach huffed with frustration. "That's what I get for trying to help, I guess."

"You want a medal?" The sheriff smirked.

"I want to be left alone."

"Well, for now, I'm afraid that isn't an option for you."

Roach looked away. He tugged resentfully at the cuffs as he tried to understand how he went from a peaceful walk along a quiet highway to sitting in handcuffs in the space of forty-eight hours. He tried to do the right thing, against his better judgment, and it had done nothing but backfire on him ever since.

Then something occurred to him.

His mind drifted back to what Valentine had said to him earlier. He thought there was something shady happening in the town. He suspected the sheriff was involved somehow. If Roach had unwittingly landed in the middle of it, arresting him would certainly get him out of the way. He was a drifter with no ties to the community. No one would miss him or question his disappearance, especially after what happened in the bar.

Roach looked back at the sheriff. "Have you at least brought those three assholes in for questioning as well?"

Bushell shrugged and shook his head. "No. Why would we? When we got there, you were wailing on them something fierce. They looked like victims to me. We let them leave to get medical attention."

Roach screwed his face. "You see a three-on-one bar fight, and you assume the three are the victims? Did you even question anyone else who was there?"

"My priority was getting you the hell outta there before anyone else got hurt."

"Jesus…"

Bushell emptied the baggie out onto the desk in front of him and arranged the contents out in a line. There was a wallet with some cash inside, an expired I.D., and an old Zippo lighter.

He picked up the I.D. and looked at it for a moment before nodding toward the door.

"I have one of my deputies running a background check on you," he said. "Tell me what he's going to find."

Roach smiled. "And ruin the surprise?"

"Don't try to be funny. It doesn't suit you."

"So I'm told…"

The two men stared at each other.

Bushell took a long, tired breath. "Why are you here, William?"

"Because you arrested me."

He rolled his eyes. "Why are you in my town, smartass?"

"I told you this morning at the hospital." Roach sighed. "Remember? It was right before I agreed to stay in this shit-hole to help you out."

"Right. Right. Your *sabbatical*."

Roach nodded.

The sheriff placed the I.D. on the desk and rested back in his chair. "Well, that would suggest you have a job you're currently not doing. What would that be?"

Roach shook his head. "I guess you could say I'm free-lance. I'm just… taking some time away from everything. Trying to see some of this beautiful country of ours. That's not a crime."

"No. But vagrancy is. So is assault."

"I'm not a vagrant. I'm on vacation. And it's not assault if it's self-defense."

"So far, the only person who says you were defending yourself is you."

Roach glanced away, allowing himself a moment to quell the rising frustration within. He knew this was a delicate situation, and the last thing he wanted to do was make things any worse for himself.

"That's because you haven't asked anyone else," he replied. "Nor have you spoken to the other guy who was present at both incidents. His name's Gary. He probably has a concussion, along with a severely broken nose, but I'm sure he could answer your questions. But you don't care about him, do you?" He raised his eyebrows accusingly. "To a cynical man, that could look like you don't want to know the truth."

Bushell tilted his head and narrowed his gaze. "Meaning?"

"Meaning... right now, it feels a lot like you're looking for any excuse to come after me."

"That's a little paranoid, wouldn't you say? Guilty conscience, Mr. Roachford?"

Roach looked away. Valentine's words echoed through his mind as he pictured Vanessa lying in the hospital.

The sheriff got to his feet. "I think we're done here. It's late. You'll spend the night in a cell. Tomorrow, we'll process you and send you over to county. Then you're someone else's problem."

"Are you serious? I didn't do anything."

"That's for a judge to decide." Bushell looked out through the window and beckoned with his hand. A moment later, the deputy who had cuffed Roach appeared in the doorway. "Henderson, take Mr. Roachford here to cell three. Give him a blanket."

The deputy moved to Roach's side. He uncuffed him, then placed a hand under his arm and guided him to his feet, before marching him out of the office.

"Sweet dreams," the sheriff called after him.

Roach didn't look around. He knew if he did, he would give them a genuine reason to arrest him.

Chapter Nine

They came for him once more in the darkness. Claw-like hands with decayed, peeling flesh sprouted from beneath like corrupted plants. They broke through his coffin and pulled him into the infinite abyss below, tugging at his face and body with hateful urgency.

His contorted expression screamed silently for help, but he was alone with the demons that consumed him. He began thrashing his limbs, desperate to break free from the thousand deathly grips. Rotten faces flew toward him in the darkness. Skulls with eyes as dark as his world, their jaws locked open with horror, swirled around him. These banshees made no noise, but their faces somehow shone in the eternal black.

Fear gripped him, wrapping its icy tendrils around his rapidly beating heart. His whole body shivered as it was pulled taut in all directions. For a moment, it felt like he was floating, not falling. For a moment, he simply existed in this inexplicable prison, spread-eagled and vulnerable, surrounded by demons.

He could almost smell the hatred on them.

A ghoulish figure hovered next to him and ran its bony finger over his cheek. Its touch felt like death itself, yet it stared into his eyes almost lovingly. Flecks of dust began to dance around them, like ash caught in a breeze. Then it grew denser, swarming the figure's head like piranhas. Slowly, the dust began to settle on its face, layer upon layer, gradually taking the shape of a person.

His eyes grew wide. It was a face he recognized. Someone from his past that fate had deemed would glance into his life. The person now staring back at him felt familiar and strange at the same time. He felt comfort in the darkness, but also a sense of guilt which he couldn't place.

For a moment, he became lost in the soulless eyes of the specter floating beside him. A wave of calm washed over him, providing fleeting reprieve from the fear.

Something tugged his other arm, distracting him. He looked around to see a second demon staring at him. Its dark skull was surrounded by more ash. Then the cloud consumed it, gradually attaching itself to every contour, revealing another face.

He was confronted with more foreign familiarity.

He looked back and forth between the two figures. Countless others flocked around him. All the while, hands poked through the darkness, pulling him down toward nothing.

Then the faces screamed. The wail was high-pitched and deafening. The confusion he felt gave way to a renewed sense of terror. They swooped forward, smothering him, turning his world even darker than it already was. He gasped for breath, panicking as he felt the oxygen melt away.

He was drowning in the void…

Roach twitched awake. His eyes snapped open, wide with the shock of sudden consciousness. He was lying on a low camping bed, his arms folded across his chest, his shoulders hunched, searching for warmth. He looked down to see the thin blanket discarded on the stone floor.

He let out a long sigh. The pillow under his head felt damp. He looked around, momentarily confused by unfamiliar surroundings. Then he saw the bars of the cell and remembered everything.

He swung his legs over the side and sat upright, rubbing his eyes and stretching. He had slept in worse places, but no examples were immediately forthcoming. Through the bars, he could see only two other cells in the small room. Neither was occupied. A small window high on the back wall allowed a rectangle of early sunlight to beam through.

The sound of raised voices and commotion drifted into earshot. He frowned, trying to focus on the words coming from somewhere within the station house.

"Is he back here?"

He recognized the voice.

"Hey," said another. "You can't just come marching in here and... Sheriff?"

Sheriff Bushell's voice boomed out, easily more distinguishable than the other two. "You're out of line here, and I *will* arrest you if you don't—"

The door to the cells burst open, and Hank Valentine appeared on the threshold. Roach stared at him, both surprised and intrigued.

Valentine marched inside, with the sheriff and Deputy Henderson close behind.

"I'm this man's lawyer." Valentine turned around to face the two officers. "You have no grounds to detain him, and you will release him at once."

Bushell stood with his hands on his hips; his mouth twisted into a disapproving line. "Is that a fact? Well, Mister..."

"Valentine."

"Well, Mister Valentine, your *client* was arrested for assaulting three men in a bar last night."

Valentine looked at Roach and raised an eyebrow. Roach simply shrugged back.

"I find that hard to believe," he said, looking back at the sheriff. "I would like to review the witness statements you took at the time."

Bushell fixed him with a hard stare and sighed. He didn't say anything.

Valentine nodded. "You don't have any, do you? That means you only have my client's testimony on file, and you're choosing to ignore it. Given he is innocent until proven otherwise, you have nothing to justify imprisoning him."

Bushell relaxed and folded his arms across his chest. "Our priority was to defuse a violent situation and protect the public. We didn't have time to—"

Valentine looked at Roach. "Did these fine officers read you your rights before they arrested you?"

Roach shook his head. "No."

Valentine sighed. "Sheriff, I'm sure I don't need to tell you that if you neglect to read someone their rights, you not only invalidate their arrest, but it makes everything they said to you during their detainment inadmissible in court." He shook his head and chuckled. "Boy, you fellas sure screwed the pooch on this one, didn't you? Now, release my client before I file a lawsuit against this office for wrongful arrest and dereliction of duty and wrap you up in so much red tape, your grandkids will be shuffling the papers."

Deputy Henderson wavered on the spot, uncertain how to act. He looked at the sheriff for guidance. Bushell gave him a barely perceptible nod. Henderson sighed and walked toward Roach's cell, fumbling with the bulky ring of keys he took from his pocket.

Roach got to his feet and stood patiently in front of the door, like a lion at feeding time. Henderson pulled the door open. Roach stepped out and glared at him.

"Go and get my things," he said flatly.

Henderson scurried out of the room, being careful to avoid the sheriff's disapproving gaze as he passed.

"This is horse shit," muttered Bushell.

Valentine pointed at him. "No, Sheriff. This is on you."

He headed for the door. Roach was close behind him. The sheriff leaned close as he drew level.

"I'll be keeping a close eye on you, Roach," he said quietly. "You should leave town before you get yourself in any more trouble."

Valentine stopped in the doorway and looked around. "Are you threatening my client, Sheriff Bushell?"

The sheriff's eyes didn't leave Roach's. "Just offering some friendly advice."

Roach looked at him. "You can shove your advice up your ass. I wanted to leave. It was you who insisted I stick around. Now, you want me to go. Well, I think I'm gonna hang around a little while longer. I'm starting to like it here. If I were you, I'd stay out of my way."

Bushell's gaze narrowed. "Are you threatening a police officer?"

Roach shook his head and smiled. "Just some friendly advice."

He stepped past Valentine and out into the main room of the station. Three desks were haphazardly spread out in front of him. He didn't break stride as he passed Henderson and snatched his belongings from his hand. He walked right out of the station, pushing the doors open with enough force that they smacked against the wall outside.

Roach looked up at the fading pink sky and took a deep breath. Whether it was after one night or one year, the first free breath you take when you get out of jail always felt different. He looked around the deserted street. His stomach growled with discontent. His back ached from a poor night's sleep.

He sighed, trying not to let his frustrations govern his actions.

Valentine appeared at his side. "You okay?"

Roach nodded. "Yeah. Thanks for that."

"Don't mention it."

"How did you know they didn't Mirandize me?"

Valentine shrugged. "Educated guess. Now, come on."

Roach frowned. "Where are we going?"

"To get you showered and fed before we go and speak to Vanessa Pope."

He set off walking in the direction of town. Roach took a deep breath, then followed.

Chapter Ten

Roach walked in through the open door of Vanessa Pope's hospital room. He had showered, eaten a large breakfast, and drank three mugs of coffee, so he was feeling more human and sociable than he was a couple of hours ago.

Vanessa was lying in the bed, propped up by a stack of pillows behind her shoulders. She was staring blankly at the corner of the room when he entered. She turned to look at him as he entered and smiled weakly.

Roach raised his hand, giving her a casual and awkward wave. He smiled back, but he wasn't confident he had managed to hide his guilt behind it. Vanessa's face was partially obscured by a large bruise, which covered her left eye and cheek. There was no obvious swelling, and the coloring wasn't deep. Roach figured it was the back of the hand that hit her.

She looked tired but comfortable. The room was basic, but it had everything the doctors and nurses needed to do their job. An IV stand rested in the corner opposite the door, unused. A glass of water stood alone on the nightstand next to the bed. A medical chart hung over the foot of it.

Valentine stepped inside the room, moving to stand beside Roach. When Vanessa saw him, her smile vanished instantly, replaced by wide-eyed fear and panic.

"Oh, God, no!" she shouted. She looked at Roach. "Get him away from me, please! Don't let him hurt me!"

Roach frowned. He looked at Valentine, who wore the same confused expression he did.

He took a step toward the bed, holding his hands up with his palms facing her. "Vanessa, relax. You're safe. Hank's a friend."

She shook her head rapidly. "No, no... he's following me. He was in the diner. Then, he was in the bar the night I... the night I was hurt. He must have something to do with it."

Valentine went to speak, but Roach held a hand up to him, silently asking him to wait.

"Vanessa, he isn't here to hurt you, I promise," said Roach, firm yet gentle. "He's a private investigator working a case in town. He was actually following *me*, not you."

Valentine cleared his throat and stepped forward, careful to keep a respectful distance.

"It's true, Mrs. Pope," he said. "I was keeping an eye on our friend here. You just... happened to be near him both times. I want to help you, same as he does."

She alternated her skeptical gaze between them, then rested her tired eyes on Roach. "Is that true?"

He nodded. "It is."

"Why was he following you?"

"Mostly, I think he was just bored."

Roach flashed a smile, which seemed to relax her. She adjusted herself against the pillows and rested her hands on her chest. She smiled back. Her teeth seemed to glow against the darkness covering her face. Her beauty still shone through the bruising.

Roach moved closer and perched at the foot of her bed. "Vanessa, I'm sorry I wasn't there to protect you. I should've agreed to help you when you asked. You were clearly in trouble, and I—"

She reached out toward him. "There's no need to apologize. I shouldn't have asked you in the first place. You already did so much for me, and this isn't your problem to fix." She glanced away. "Honestly, I'm surprised you're still in town."

Roach flicked his eyebrows. One corner of his mouth curled into a small smile. "That makes two of us."

"But seeing as you are… would you maybe reconsider my offer?"

Roach glanced back at Valentine, who was watching quietly from the corner of the room, resting against the window. He said nothing. His expression didn't change. But Roach heard the guilt trip loud and clear.

"Vanessa, I need you to be honest with me," he said.

"W-what do you mean?"

"I mean, these attacks on you aren't random, are they?"

She said nothing, which Roach interpreted as confirmation.

"Why are these people after you?" he urged. "Who are they?"

"I… I don't know."

She swallowed hard and stared down at the bed sheet. Her eyes danced in their sockets.

She was lying.

"Gary, from the diner… was it him who attacked you the other night?" asked Roach.

She nodded. "Yes. He wasn't alone."

Roach glanced over his shoulder at Valentine. "Probably the same guys who came for me last night."

Vanessa looked up at him and frowned. "Wait, what? They came after you?"

"Yes," said Roach, casually. "Gary brought two new friends to help him get revenge for me saving you."

Her mouth fell open a little. "Oh, God… are you okay?"

"I'm the one here talking to you, aren't I?"

She shook her head to herself and glanced away, as if ashamed.

"This is all my fault," she said quietly.

Roach sighed, growing impatient. "Vanessa, what aren't you telling me?"

"Nothing," she implored.

He fell silent for a moment, then asked, "Does this have anything to do with your husband?"

The color drained from her face. Once again, she looked away, but not before casting a dubious glance at Valentine, which Roach saw.

"Vanessa, do you trust me?" he asked her.

She nodded. "Of course. How could I not?"

"Well, to trust me is to trust Hank. He stuck his neck out for me when he had no reason to, and he's been nothing but straight with me. Right here, in this room, you are safe. I promise. You can talk freely. It will stay between us."

She held his gaze for a moment, then gave Valentine an apologetic smile.

He smiled back. "Listen, after what you've been through the last couple of days, I can't blame you for being suspicious. I don't trust many people, and I certainly don't give that trust away easily." He pointed at Roach. "But this guy is the real deal. He wants to help. We both do. But to do that, we need to know what's going on."

Vanessa sighed and shimmied herself upright in bed, pulling the cover up over her chest to hide the hospital gown she wore.

Before she could speak, another man appeared in the doorway. Behind him were two large, thick-set guys wearing expensive suits.

"Vanessa?" said the new arrival.

Her head inched forward as her eyes widened. "Thomas?"

Roach got to his feet and stepped to the side, casting a wary glance toward Valentine.

Thomas Pope moved to her bedside, ignoring everyone else in the room. He wore a slate-gray suit with the jacket open, which revealed a slightly overweight frame. Underneath, he wore a shirt with no tie. His beard was full; the balance between white and dark had long shifted. Beneath it, his skin was smooth—a result of discreet plastic surgery that hid his years. It was impossible to guess the age gap between him and his wife.

He took her hand in his. "I came as soon as I heard. Are you okay?"

She swallowed again and nodded. "I'm… I'm fine."

"Why didn't you call me the moment this happened?"

"You were away with work," Vanessa said, looking away sheepishly. "I… I didn't want to worry you."

Pope shook his head. "Hey, hey, it's okay." He reached forward and placed his finger and thumb on her chin, gently turning her head back to face him. For a split-second, she flinched at his touch. "This is more important than my work. *You're* more important."

He smiled. Timidly, she smiled back.

Then he took a breath, got to his feet, and turned to face Roach. "I'm sorry. You are?"

Roach held his gaze, giving away no ground or emotion. "A friend of your wife's."

"Is that right?" Pope's gaze narrowed and never left Roach's dark, cold eyes. "Honey? Aren't you going to introduce me to your... friend?"

Vanessa's breath shook as she inhaled. "The night I was attacked... the same people had come for me that morning, in the diner. This man saved me."

Pope's expression softened, and a smile creeped across his face. "Well, why didn't you say so? I owe you a debt of gratitude, Mister..."

He held out his hand. Roach looked at it. A gnawing feeling in his gut told him the last thing he should do was touch that man's hand. Nothing about him felt right. But the two men in his periphery reminded him that not shaking it would do much more harm than good right now.

"Roach," he said, shaking Pope's hand firmly.

Pope laughed. "Is that some kind of nickname?"

"Yes."

"Well... Roach. Thank you for helping my poor wife."

They were still shaking hands. Pope's smile remained, but his grip was getting noticeably tighter. As Roach looked into the man's eyes, he began to see his gut was right. There was more to Thomas Pope than the façade standing before him. He was a businessman and likely unaccustomed to not getting what he wanted. The handshake... the muscle at the door... the politician's smile. He was a bully who got his way through intimidation.

Roach had come across men like him before. He had never met one he liked.

"Now that I'm back in town, you don't need to trouble

yourself worrying about her anymore," continued Pope. "I'll take her home, where she'll be safe."

Roach's instincts were screaming at him. He didn't believe for a second that Vanessa would be safe with this man. He felt the men by the door tense.

He broke eye contact for a heartbeat, casting a silent cue at Valentine, who didn't hesitate.

"Actually, Mr. Pope, your wife isn't ready to be discharged just yet."

Finally, Pope relinquished his grip of the handshake. His smile faded slightly when he saw no reaction on Roach's face. He turned to face Valentine, looking him up and down quizzically.

"And you are?"

"Dr. Valentine."

Pope continued to study him. The long trench coat that hadn't been cream-colored for at least a decade. The brown suit beneath it, with the untucked shirt and loose tie around the neck. The unshaven face and dark, sunken eyes.

"You don't look like a doctor."

Valentine didn't miss a beat. "It's my day off. I came in to check up on Mrs. Pope, as I was on call when she was first brought in. We look after our own here, Mr. Pope. You should know that."

Pope held his gaze, wavering slightly as he adjusted his approach. "Of course. Thank you. So… how is she? When can she come home?"

Valentine sucked in a deep breath and paced idly into the middle of the room. He rested a hand down on top of the chart hanging over the bed rail. "Physically, she's healing well. But there's some internal bruising around her ribs that we'd like to monitor a little longer. Not to mention the shock and mental trauma of what she's been through.

We can reassess her tomorrow, but for now, we don't want to take any unnecessary chances."

Pope stared at him. The smile had gone. His jaw pulsed beneath his beard.

"Yes, fine. Of course. Whatever you think is best." He looked at Vanessa. "We'll have you home soon, my love. I'm back from my trip now." He turned to leave but lingered in front of Roach, locking eyes with him once more. "And I'm not going anywhere."

He marched out of the room, pushing between the two men in the doorway, who quickly turned and followed.

Roach watched them disappear, then looked at Valentine. "Way to think on your feet, Doc."

He shrugged humbly. "Thanks. But we should go in case Thomas decides to question the oddly dressed medical professional with the front desk."

"Agreed." Roach looked at Vanessa, who had sunk back down in the bed. "We'll come back later, okay? We can talk more then. For now, get some rest. If anyone comes by that you don't like the look of in the meantime, buzz for a nurse. Any trouble, they will call the sheriff. Okay?"

She nodded meekly. "Thank you. Both of you."

Roach smiled and left the room. Valentine followed, and they walked side by side along the corridor.

"You see the look on her face when the husband walked in?" he asked.

Roach ground his teeth. "I did."

"What are you going to do?"

"What do you mean?"

"Are you going to take her job offer?"

Roach didn't say anything.

The two of them made it outside. The sun was high as midday approached. The temperature drowned out the breeze once again. They stood together in a moment of silence. Then Valentine stepped to move in front of Roach.

"You really think the sheriff will come running if shit goes sideways here?" he asked.

Roach nodded. "Yes. Regardless of where he fits into all this, I suspect the safety of Thomas Pope's wife will be a priority."

"Good point. Okay, we should split up."

Roach frowned. "And do what?"

"Hit the town. Speak to the locals. See what the general opinion of Mr. Pope really is among the residents of this town."

"And how are we supposed to do that?"

Valentine shook his head and gestured with his arms, as if that was a stupid question. "Wander into the local stores. Grab a lunchtime drink in a bar. Get talking to people. See if you can get a feel for how things really are around here."

"What use will that do?"

"Okay. Here's a little crash course in being a P.I. for you. Typically, what you see and how it is are two different things. You want to get to know a place, you get to know the people."

"Right."

"I'll take the west side of town. The stores, the residences. You take the east—bars, factories, et cetera. I reckon you're more likely to connect with the blue-collar crowd."

Roach shrugged casually. "Whatever."

"We'll meet up in the sports bar across from your hotel in a couple of hours, see what we've found out, then come back here to see Vanessa again."

"Fine."

Valentine walked away without another word, leaving

Roach standing alone outside the hospital, at the side of a quiet road, surrounded by trees and fields. He took a few deep breaths, taking in the smells of the outdoors, relishing the peace. Then he set off walking, trying to figure out how he was going to force himself to be nice to people.

Chapter Eleven

Roach wasn't a complicated man. He kept things simple because life felt easier that way. His thought process was basic, logical. His principles were primal, steadfast, and uncompromising.

His morality was self-taught at a young age. He grew up watching his alcoholic father take his frustrations out on his mother. It changed him. It showed him the world wasn't a nice or fair place. Good people were often punished for doing the right thing, and bad people seemed to always be able to do what they wanted without reproach. To help himself understand, he broke down his experiences into straightforward, binary categories. Right... wrong. Good... bad. Yes... no.

What his mother went through was wrong. Nothing would ever justify what his father did. He was a bad person, and he was never made to answer for what he did. Roach's newfound approach to life made sense and had stuck with him ever since.

That's why he found his decision easy to make.

He hadn't said anything to Valentine when he had asked earlier, at the hospital, but he knew he was going to stick around and help Vanessa the moment he walked into her room and saw her in that bed. His desire to turn his back on the world could wait. When he saw her lying there, bruised and beaten and afraid, he saw his mother, all those years ago, sitting on the kitchen floor, trying not to cry as she comforted him and told him it wasn't his fault.

Whatever's going on, Vanessa didn't deserve what had happened to her. Just like his mother never did. He wasn't about to let someone get away with doing something so wrong. It was that simple.

Also, something didn't sit right with him about her husband. Yes, Pope was an asshole, but it was more than that. He was a bully, and his own wife was intimidated by him. After refusing to help Vanessa once, there was no way Roach could walk away from helping her again.

He cleared his mind and walked along the street, heading toward a bar he had seen on the corner of the road leading to one of the factories in town. He passed another streetlamp with one of Valentine's flyers stuck to it. He glanced at it as he walked by.

He shrugged his jacket on but left it open. It flapped lazily in the cool breeze. The town was so quiet, he could hear birds in the surrounding trees. A handful of people walked by on either side of the street, paying him no heed.

Then a thundering mechanical splutter shattered the idyllic silence. Loud pops of air spewed from an exhaust like gunshots. Moments later, a car appeared next to him, driving on the wrong side of the road to coast at Roach's side. It immediately slowed to keep pace, making no secret of it.

Roach stared at it, let out a heavy sigh, and stopped dead in the middle of the sidewalk. The car rolled on for a few feet, then stopped, mounting the curb slightly as it pulled over. The driver's door opened, and a man climbed out gracefully. He wore a thin, red silk shirt and black jeans. Gold-rimmed sunglasses rested on his olive face. He strolled toward Roach, then stopped a few steps in front of him and removed his glasses. Dark eyes stared without fear.

Roach looked the new arrival up and down. He was a couple of inches shorter, but he could easily see the slim, wiry frame was deceiving. The man's shirt waved in the breeze, brushing the chiseled body beneath. There was a lot of power there.

Roach then looked at the car.

"Nice ride," he said.

The man nodded. "It is."

His accent was foreign, yet his pronunciation was flawless.

"It's the Charger, right?"

"The SRT."

"A *Hellcat*. Impressive."

The man tilted his head and smiled. "You know your cars?"

Roach shrugged. "I'm not an expert, but I used to have a Challenger. The SXT."

"Oof," he replied, forming a tight circle with his mouth. "That's a beast. You still got it?"

"No. Sadly, I forgot where I parked it one day."

The man frowned. "Really?"

"Yes. There was… a lot going on at the time. So, you want to tell me why you're following me?"

"Because I want to talk to you."

"I was always told not to talk to strangers."

"Well, who I am isn't important, so you'll have to make an exception."

"Whatever."

"I wanted to see if you would do me a favor."

Roach shrugged. "Get to your point and I'll tell you."

"Fair enough." The man smiled, wide and fake. "I need you to leave town—right now—and never look back."

They stared at each other in silence for almost a full minute.

Finally, Roach nodded. "Okay."

The man raised an eyebrow. "Really? Just like that?"

"Sure. I was just passing through anyway."

"I appreciate your cooperation. Thank you."

"No problem." Roach paused. "One question."

"Shoot."

"Why?"

The man's smile faded, taking his patience and friendly demeanor with it. He shifted his weight on the spot and glanced around again.

"Because I'm asking you to," he said flatly.

"And why would you care whether I'm here or not?"

"Because I would rather an outsider didn't involve themselves in business that doesn't concern them."

"Which would be… what, exactly?"

The man sighed. "What part of *doesn't concern you* did you not understand? You've made some waves since you hit town. We can't have that. You stepped in to help Mrs. Pope, and it was appreciated. But it's time for you to go."

Roach nodded and smiled to himself. "Let me guess. You work for Mr. Pope?"

"You catch on quick."

"So, he sent you to threaten me?"

"He didn't send me. My job is to deal with things *before*

they become a problem for him. And this isn't a threat. I'm simply asking you for a favor."

"The favor being I leave town?"

He nodded. "That's right. I'll even do a favor for you in return."

Roach flicked up a skeptical eyebrow. "Which is?"

"I'll let you."

Roach cracked his neck and squared up to him. The two men stared at each other in a silent battle of wills. Behind them, sirens grew louder until two police cruisers appeared, speeding past them. Both men glanced at the convoy. Neither said anything until the sirens had faded out to silence.

"Well, I've given it some thought, and I'm afraid I can't do this favor for you after all," said Roach finally. "You see, Mrs. Pope has asked me to serve as her personal security guard for a few days. She's understandably shaken after the assault. I wasn't sure if I wanted to hang around here that long, but after meeting you... fuck it—I think I'll take her up on the offer."

The man took a step forward, adjusting his gaze slightly to maintain eye contact. "That would be a very bad idea."

"I don't think so. I think Mrs. Pope is afraid, and I think she needs all the help she can get. If her husband doesn't like it, he's welcome to take it up with me himself."

The man's jaw pulsed with frustration. "Do not test me."

"Or what? She's nothing but a business asset to him anyway. You certainly don't give a shit about her. Say whatever you want, but we both know you're only here to fix your boss's pride. You ask me, she's better off without any of you."

The man shoved him, forcing him back a few steps.

Then he jabbed the air between them with a threatening finger. His face twisted in an instant, contorting with a sudden rage. "You don't have the first fucking clue what you're talking about!" he snapped. "Vanessa should be at home. I work for the family, and I'm all the protection she'll ever need. Do you understand me?"

Roach narrowed his gaze. He forgave the shove. He was far more interested in the man's reaction. "If that's the case, where were you yesterday when she was assaulted twice?"

His expression hardened. His jaw clenched. "I was with Mr. Pope, helping him protect his business interests."

"Right. See, you *say* you serve the family, but really, you just do whatever he tells you. I doubt he allows *Mrs. Pope* to make it anywhere near your list of priorities."

"Enough!" The man was breathing heavy with adrenaline. He stepped close to Roach and pressed a finger against his chest. "I came here looking for a civil conversation. The next time I see you, there will be no civility... no conversation... no favors. I will simply tell you to leave."

Roach leaned toward him. "And if I don't?"

"Then I'll make you." He stepped back, locking eyes with Roach once more. "You have until sundown to get your shit from your hotel and fuck off."

He turned and walked away before Roach could say anything.

Roach watched him climb back inside the car and slam the door. The engine exploded into life, growling like an untamed beast. Tires spun and screeched, kicking up smoke that drifted across him, then sped away. The few people walking nearby turned to look disapprovingly.

Roach didn't move until the car was out of sight.

He was angry about being threatened. He was also

concerned by Pope's insistence on him leaving. It left him numbed with frustration and questioning whether he was right to have handled that as diplomatically as he had.

By his standards, anyway.

Chapter Twelve

Roach walked into the sports bar he had frequented the previous two nights and saw Valentine sitting in a quiet corner, across from both the entrance and the bar. It wasn't busy. A couple of small clusters of men were huddled together, enjoying their lunch.

He gave a casual wave to George as he walked by, who was cleaning glasses behind the counter. He sat heavily in the chair opposite Valentine, who immediately slid a whiskey across the table to him.

"How did it go?" he asked.

Roach rolled his eyes and slammed back the warm, amber drink. "Not great. I was approached by someone on behalf of Thomas Pope. He told me to leave town by the end of the day and suggested it would be unwise not to."

"Jesus. Who was this guy?"

"No idea," shrugged Roach. "Bit shorter than me. Strong frame. He was Chinese, but he had an American accent."

Valentine straightened in his chair. His expression hardened with concern. "That was Ricky Chen."

"Is that supposed to mean something?"

"He's a real piece of work, from what I can tell. Thomas Pope's heavy-hitting right hand. If he made the trip to see you personally, you've made the big leagues."

"The guy had a real short fuse, no doubt about that." He looked questioningly at Valentine. "So, seriously, how do you know so much about this place? You've been here... what? Two days longer than I have?"

Valentine smiled. "I told you. I talk to people. More importantly, they talk to me."

"Why?"

"Because I'm approachable."

Roach frowned. "You're saying I'm not?"

Valentine chuckled. "I'm saying you have a look permanently etched onto your face that says people will spontaneously combust if they get within twenty feet of you."

He raised an eyebrow. "Is that an option?"

"Christ..." Valentine rolled his eyes, then leaned forward, lowering his voice. "Listen, Roach. Thomas Pope basically has free run of this place. Bushell is either blind or bought. Hell, even the mayor won't say anything to him. He's either doing pointless PR appearances or hiding in his mansion while Pope's money pays for everything around here. Have you looked at this town? I mean, *really* looked. There isn't any middle ground. Places are brand-new or fifty years old. Pope's influence here is on display like a goddamn art gallery."

Roach glanced away, thinking back to his various strolls around the place since he had arrived. He couldn't recall much, if anything, that looked old.

Valentine watched Roach's expression, seeing him arrive

at the same conclusion he had. "Exactly. His business grants allow the town to renovate and maintain everything from the buildings to the homes to the goddamn sidewalks. That means the local government doesn't need to find as much money to keep this place running, which keeps taxes lower for the residents."

Roach nodded. "Okay. So, do people like Pope… or do they fear him?"

Valentine shrugged. "Mostly, I think people around here just keep their heads down and try not to question a good thing. But personally, I think the fact he's taken a personal dislike to you should be cause for concern."

"Honestly, my only concern right now is for his wife. I don't understand where Vanessa fits into all this. Why would her husband be pissed at the guy who saved his wife from an assault?"

"You only saved her once."

Roach shot him a glance. Valentine sat back and held his hands up defensively.

"Hey, I'm not trying to guilt you. I'm just saying. No one saved her the second time. The guy might be an asshole, but you find me any man who wouldn't be angry at seeing his wife like that." He shrugged. "You're the easiest target for him to project that anger onto."

"Maybe. But you saw how she was when he arrived. She's afraid of him."

Valentine nodded. "Yes, she is. Which means maybe my other theory is correct."

"And that is?"

"That Thomas Pope is up to his eyeballs in illegal shit, and his wife knows something she shouldn't."

Roach thought about it. "She did tell me she helped out with the accounting and advertising every now and then…"

"Maybe he's trying to buy her silence with a luxury life-style. Maybe he's worried that isn't working. Maybe he intimidates her in other ways."

Roach frowned. "Are you saying you think her husband is behind these attacks on her?"

Valentine shook his head. "I don't think he would do that, no. But her fear does suggest some form of threat or abuse. Also, you saw the size of his bodyguards, right?"

Roach nodded.

"Well, did you see his hands? Clean, smooth, mani-cured... suggesting he doesn't like to get them dirty. So, he employs people to do his intimidation work for him."

"People like Ricky Chen..."

"Exactly."

Roach leaned back and folded his arms across his chest. "Huh. Maybe you actually *are* good at what you do."

Valentine smiled. "Gee, thanks."

Roach looked over his shoulder, toward the bar. When he caught George's attention, he signaled for two more drinks. They sat in silence until they appeared.

"So, what's your story, Hank?" he asked finally.

Valentine took a welcome sip of his drink. "I already told you."

"No, you told me about your case. I'm asking about you. Why are you so committed to figuring out whatever shit this backwater town is dealing with? There's almost no chance it's related to your missing kid."

Valentine let out a long sigh. "I don't have much going in my life outside of my job, all right? I... throw myself into it to distract me."

"Okay. So, what happened?"

Valentine eyed him warily over his glass. "Nothing happened. I just like my job."

"Right. In my experience, people with nothing in their life but their job usually went through something that cost them everything *except* their job. Come on. You know all about me. I'm in this thing now, whatever the hell it is. I think I have a right to know who I'm working with."

Valentine smiled. "You saying we're partners? You didn't strike me as the type…"

Roach shook his head. "I'm saying we're on the same side. Doesn't make us partners. Don't get excited. But if you want me to keep trusting you… keep vouching for you with Vanessa… tell me what you're really still doing here."

Valentine threw his head back and groaned reluctantly. "Ugh. Fine." He took a gulp of his drink. "In my younger days, I was a cop. On my way to becoming detective. I had a good life. Nice house. Beautiful wife. Great kid. The whole nine, y'know. I was working this case… spent six months undercover with a gang of drug traffickers. They weren't exactly a cartel, but they were making a name for themselves… moving up the food chain. It was going well, but then someone tipped them off about me, and I was made. I came in from the cold and was relocated for my protection until they were taken down. Problem was, the case fell through a few weeks later. Lack of evidence. The gang wanted revenge. Took them a couple of years, but they found me."

He paused to take another sip of his drink.

"What happened?" Roach asked softly.

Valentine grimaced. "When they came, I fought them off as best I could. Killed most of them myself. But not before they killed my little boy."

Roach failed to hide his shock. "Holy shit. I'm sorry, Hank."

Valentine waved his sympathy away. "It was… it was my

fault. The shot was aimed at me, but it was wayward. These guys were mid-level drug dealers, not Marine snipers. I should've just taken the bullet. I doubt it would have even dropped me. But my instincts kicked in, and I dove out of the way. I didn't know my son was standing right behind me. He died instantly."

The silence hung over their table like a dark cloud. Roach felt a pang of guilt for pushing to hear Valentine's story. He knew there was nothing he could say to make anything better, so he chose to say nothing.

Valentine finished his drink and pushed the glass away. He rested back in his chair and drummed his fingers on the table. "After that, my wife and I were never the same. I blamed myself. She never said anything, but I know she blamed me too. I started drinking. Was kicked off the force. Didn't take long for my wife to walk out on me. I spiraled for a few years after that. Then... an old friend came to me, asking for my help. He was a P.I. and wanted some advice on a case. I helped him out, and in return, he helped me get my act together. I cleaned myself up, got my license, and I've been doing this gig ever since. Turns out, I ain't half bad at it."

Roach looked down at his own glass, then at Valentine's. "You sure it's a good idea to keep meeting in bars?"

Valentine smiled. "I said I cleaned myself up. Never said I quit drinking."

"Right." Roach frowned. "So, you're an alcoholic?"

He shook his head. "No. An alcoholic is someone who can't kick their habit."

"That's your second whiskey since I got here, and it's only lunchtime."

Valentine reached inside his coat and pulled out his flask. He tipped some of its contents in the empty glass, smiling. "Fourth, but who's counting. Point is, I never quit anything in my life, and I'm not about to start with Jack Daniels."

Roach raised his glass. "Whatever works for you."

"So, do you still trust me... partner?"

"I do. I'm going to stick around and protect Vanessa. I feel better knowing you're watching my back."

"Damn right. But, ah... have you given any thought as to how you're gonna do that, exactly? It ain't gonna be easy with her husband trying to run you out of town."

Roach thought for a moment, then shrugged. "I'm going to do the best I can while you figure out what the hell I'm protecting her from."

Valentine got to his feet. "Well, according to Ricky Chen, you've only got a few hours before life gets real goddamn complicated for you, so we'd best get moving."

"Where to now?"

"Thomas Pope is unlikely to revisit his wife in the hospital today, so it's time we went and got some answers."

Valentine walked to the bar to pay his tab, then headed for the door.

Roach finished his drink and followed.

Chapter Thirteen

The dull clack of their footsteps on the gray linoleum drew glances from the few people sitting in the hospital waiting area. The smell of cleaning products stung their eyes. The nurses standing at the front desk stared disapprovingly as Roach and Valentine walked by, but both men ignored them.

They navigated the corridors with begrudging familiarity, slowing as they rounded the last corner in case anyone was waiting. The vestibule outside Vanessa's room was empty. The two men exchanged a nod of relief. Roach knocked on the door, then stepped inside.

Vanessa was still lying in bed, gazing absently at the corner of the room. She looked over as the men entered, smiling briefly.

"You shouldn't be here," she said. "If Thomas finds out..."

Roach smiled back. "He won't do shit. How are you feeling?"

She shrugged. "I'm okay. Tired and sore, mostly." She

lowered her voice. "I think I'm going to be discharged soon."

The men exchanged another glance.

Roach sat lightly on the edge of the bed. "You don't seem happy about going home, Vanessa."

Vanessa glanced away, blinking a single tear down her face.

Somewhere deep inside, buried beneath his resentment for humanity, Roach felt his heart break.

"Does your husband hurt you?" he asked.

He silently cursed his own bluntness the moment the words left his mouth.

Vanessa looked first at Valentine, then at Roach. "No. No, nothing like that."

"Then what is it? Why are you afraid of being near him?"

She tried to speak, but the words caught in her throat.

Roach sighed. "Vanessa, look... I'm happy to stick around and keep you safe. I blame myself for you ending up in here. I should've agreed to help when you first asked me. But if you want me to do this, I need the truth. I can't protect you if I don't understand what I'm protecting you from."

She looked away, her lips forming a tight line of indecision. She glanced at Valentine.

"I told you," added Roach, seeing the look. "He's on our side and he can help. Your husband might not hurt you physically, but I can see you're scared of him. I need to know why."

Vanessa wiped away the tear and sniffed back her emotion. "If he finds out I said anything to you, he'll..."

Roach frowned. "He'll what? I'm not going to tell him. Hank?"

Valentine was standing at the foot of the bed, a respectful distance away. He shook his head. "My lips are sealed."

"See? Besides, he already doesn't like me. You talking to me isn't going to make things any worse."

Vanessa tilted her head with confusion. "What do you mean?"

Roach waved away any concerns. "It's nothing. I had a little visit from someone who works for your husband. He told me to leave town tonight. He also suggested it would be unwise to ignore his request."

She swallowed. "Who was it?"

"A guy named Ricky Chen, according to our local expert over there." He gestured behind him at Valentine with his thumb.

Vanessa's eyes went wide, and the color flooded from her cheeks. Her mouth hung open. Then she looked away, rolling her eyes almost regretfully.

Roach studied her body language and reaction, thinking back to Chen's own reaction earlier, when he suggested Vanessa was meaningless to her husband.

Roach raised his eyebrow. "You know him?"

She nodded slowly. "Yes. He... uh... he works for Thomas. His head of security."

"You know, considering your husband is a successful businessman and the patron saint of this shithole, he has an awful lot of security. What *exactly* is his business?"

Vanessa caught her breath before any words could escape.

Valentine stepped toward the bed, knocking the frame absently with his hand. "Not all of his auctions are legal, are they?"

Vanessa shook her head. "No."

Roach glanced at Valentine. His theory was right.

"And you've seen something you shouldn't have when you were helping out with the accounts, right?" he continued.

She nodded without a word.

"Does your husband know?"

"Not for sure," she replied. "But I think he suspects something."

"And he's worried you'll say or do something that would get him in trouble. Is that why he buys you expensive things? To keep you quiet?"

Vanessa's mouth contorted with the effort of holding back the tears, but some escaped down her cheeks regardless. She nodded, putting a hand over her face.

Valentine's theories had proven solid, but they were missing something. Roach wasn't sure what, exactly. Not yet anyway. But Valentine wasn't the only one who saw things.

"Except he doesn't, does he?" said Roach.

Both Vanessa and Valentine looked at him, confused.

He looked into her eyes, searching for any sign of deception, but he saw nothing except innocence and shame.

He narrowed his gaze. "You don't know, do you?"

She glanced at Valentine, but he simply shrugged.

"Know what?" she asked.

"That big, expensive watch of yours. It's fake."

She shook her head. "No. That's impossible. He wouldn't... he's too proud. He—"

"It's fake, Vanessa. I had it appraised, exactly like you told me to when you gave it to me."

The revelation stunned her silent. She sat upright in bed and brought her knees up to her chest beneath the blanket, hugging them for comfort.

Valentine leaned forward and rested his palms over the

bedframe, on either side of her medical chart. "What did you see in his books, Vanessa?"

"Records of offshore accounts," she said. "More money than he ever told me he had. Strange transactions."

"Strange, how?"

"High value. Much higher than anything sold via the auction house. There was no obvious pattern to them."

"But you saw one anyway?" asked Roach.

Vanessa shrugged. "Not really. What jumped out at me was that they always came in the day *after* an auction."

"That doesn't sound strange," observed Valentine. "Surely, that's just transactions being processed from auction sales?"

She shook her head. "Transactions are processed the same day as the purchase, not twenty-four hours later. Also, the values are way above anything sold at auction. I think the most expensive thing that ever sold was an antique shotgun, which went for around a hundred thousand dollars."

Roach nodded. "And these transactions were…"

"…anywhere between five and ten times that," she said.

Roach and Valentine glanced at each other.

"Okay. That's weird, for sure," said Valentine. "It isn't evidence of guilt, though. It's also not knowledge that would put you in the kind of danger you've been in."

Vanessa looked away again, wiping the tears from her face.

The cogs turned inside Roach's head as he began to piece together the larger picture. He thought about what she had told them. What she had seen. He didn't think her stumbling across some questionable accounting was justification for the level of fear she clearly felt. There had to be more to it. Something she wasn't telling them.

Then it clicked.

"That isn't why she's afraid…" he said quietly.

Valentine frowned. Vanessa looked at him, concerned.

Roach looked her in the eye. "How long have you been sleeping with Ricky Chen?"

Valentine took a step back. "What?"

Vanessa appeared outraged. Her mouth fell open with shock. Her eyes bulged, although her gaze resisted meeting his.

"What?" she protested. "What do you… no! No! That's not…"

Roach sighed patiently. "He's head of security for your husband. He's an employee your husband presumably trusts. He's around your home a lot, I suspect. He's confident, probably good at what he does. I have no doubt he's capable in a fight. The consummate professional. Yet, when you came up in conversation, he lost control. Called you Vanessa, not Mrs. Pope. That's a little too familiar for the hired help, wouldn't you say? And just now, when I mentioned he had paid me a visit, you didn't look scared… you looked conflicted."

Tears began to flow freely from her eyes. She placed her hands to the side of her head, resting her elbows on her raised knees. "No, please… it isn't like that. It isn't…"

"Holy shit," said Valentine, rubbing a hand over his face. "You're not just sleeping with him… you love him, don't you?"

Vanessa broke down. She buried her head in her arms. Her shoulders shrugged with her uncontrollable sobbing.

Roach got to his feet and stepped away, sensing the respectful thing to do was to give her some space. He leaned against the wall by the door. Valentine moved next to him.

"Do you think he knows?" he asked quietly.

"Her husband? Unlikely." Roach glanced over at

Vanessa. "He's clearly more concerned with me being around. Probably more worried about the idea of *me* sleeping with her than anyone else. Men like him don't like feeling threatened. Especially on their home turf, and *definitely* not when it jeopardizes their possessions."

Valentine flashed a wry smile. "Guess I'm not the only one who notices things."

"I have my moments."

"We still have a problem to deal with…"

Roach nodded and moved back toward the bed. "Vanessa, unless you're going to report him for illegal activity, there's no reason not to go home with him. I understand you're worried he might find out about you and Ricky, but I suspect that would be more Ricky's problem than yours. I still don't know what you need me to protect you from."

Vanessa wiped her eyes and looked up at him.

"I knew the men who attacked me," she sighed.

"Jesus Christ… this just keeps getting better," muttered Valentine.

Roach ran a hand over the coarse, three-day growth on his face. "Okay. Who were they?"

"They work for one of Thomas's business partners. Someone called Decker."

"Are they targeting him through you?"

"No."

Valentine sighed. "No… they're targeting *you* specifically, aren't they?"

Vanessa nodded. Her mouth once again twisted in a thin line to hold back her tears.

"Why would they come after you?" Roach asked her.

She looked away, ashamed. "They have a deal with Thomas that earns them a cut of the auction house profits.

I don't know the nature of it exactly. When I saw the profits were much higher than he was admitting…"

Valentine sighed. "You went to this business partner, hoping they would go after your husband."

Roach rolled his eyes and sighed, coming to the same conclusion Valentine just had. "Which would leave you and Ricky free to be together…"

"I was going to," she sniffed. "I set up the meeting with one of their contacts. Said I had information about Thomas they would want to know. But I… I got scared at the last minute and changed my mind. Then people started coming after me to get the information I have. They must work for Decker."

"And you can't tell your husband why you're in danger because then he'll know you were about to betray him…"

"And he would start looking for reasons why," added Valentine, "which would lead him to you and Ricky Chen. Goddamn, what a mess…"

"I'm so sorry I got you involved in this, Roach," Vanessa sobbed. "This is all my fault. These people will keep coming, and I can't tell Thomas. That's why I asked you for help. I just… I don't know what to do."

An eerily calm silence hung over the revelation. It was Valentine who broke it after a couple of minutes, tapping Roach's arm with his hand.

"So, what do you think we should do?" he asked him.

Roach frowned. "You're asking me?"

"Yeah. You have the edge here. I know your history, remember? Me… I just drink and watch people."

Roach paced toward the door, thinking hard. Then he spun to face the room.

"Okay, Vanessa, here's what needs to happen. You need

to go home to your husband like nothing is wrong, and you need to tell him you've hired me to protect you."

"He... he won't like that," she said.

"I don't care. But, honestly, I don't think he will have an issue with it."

"Really?" asked Valentine.

Roach nodded to him. "Think about it. This guy's a rich and powerful businessman. He has a lot of high-level security for himself, but not so much as one bodyguard for his wife." He turned to Vanessa. "It's clear your husband doesn't value you. To him, you're a trophy. If he doesn't care enough to protect you himself, even after the attack, would he really care if you arranged your own security?"

Vanessa looked away, dejected by the harsh truth. "I guess not..."

"Exactly. Besides, before the day is done, your boyfriend will try and make me leave town. If that happens, I will need to defend myself. Not only will that blow any chance you have of staying safe without telling your husband what you did, but those situations rarely end well for the people attacking me. If it gets to that stage, things will get worse for everyone."

Vanessa nodded timidly but said nothing.

Roach turned to Valentine. "I need you to look into this business partner and figure out who we're dealing with here."

He nodded. "Of course." He looked at Vanessa. "Where is this Decker located?"

"Norwich," she replied.

"That's north of here, right?"

"Yes. But—"

He held up a hand and smiled. "That's all I need to know."

Valentine retrieved a cell phone from his pocket as he headed for the door. He paused at Roach's side and handed it to him. "Give me twenty-four hours, okay? This is a burner phone. My number's saved in it. Keep in touch."

Roach took it with a grateful nod. "Watch your back out there."

"You too."

He left the room with renewed purpose in his stride, leaving Roach and Vanessa alone.

"Now what?" she asked him.

Roach sighed. "Now, I take you home, and we talk to your husband."

Chapter Fourteen

Vanessa was reluctant to discharge herself from the hospital, but having Roach with her offered a modicum of comfort. She was in no condition for walking, so she had asked the front desk of the hospital to call a cab. Roach was surprised they even had a taxi service in Waters Point, but the cab had arrived within ten minutes. It was a clean, jet-black minivan with a hand-painted logo on it: WP Shuttles. The driver nosed to a stop by the entrance. The van's tires crunched on the thin, dusty gravel. The man who got out looked retired. Sixty was behind him. The thin skin on his face as haggard with fatigue. But he opened the door for Vanessa and helped her inside, which earned him points with Roach.

The ride was comfortable and smooth. Neither of them spoke. Vanessa was content with staring at the floor of the minivan. Her hands were clasped meekly on her lap. She looked like a child on her way to the principal's office.

Roach settled for watching the town pass by out the window, lost in his own thoughts. He had too many things swirling around his head, so the quiet time was welcome. Over the last two days, he had been so busy trying to figure out what was going on and how he could fix it, he hadn't considered just how quickly things had escalated for him. He still had no clear idea of what he had found himself involved in. All he knew for sure was Vanessa wasn't safe, and he didn't trust anyone else to protect her.

The center of town came upon them. The cab driver navigated the quiet streets with the comfort of someone who had lived in the town their whole life. Roach imagined the driver could make the journey with his eyes closed and still not hit anything. They took a right, heading north from the statue, which Roach had come to realize was the center of Waters Point.

Thomas Pope lived on the northwest side of town, on a private estate roughly a half-mile behind the church. There was a near-blind turn on the north road for it, just before it merged into the highway that continued north to the city.

As they took the turn, Roach felt Vanessa tense on the seat beside him. He glanced over at her. He felt she was still hiding something from him, but he knew it wasn't the time to push. Regardless of how much of this was her own fault, she was still in trouble she didn't deserve, and he couldn't help but feel sympathy toward her.

"You okay?" he asked her softly.

She looked over at him and nodded. "I'll be fine. I'm just…"

"Scared?"

"A little, yeah."

"Don't be. You have to act like nothing is wrong. Otherwise, your husband is going to ask questions you don't want to answer."

She nodded again.

Roach looked through the gap in the seats and out the windshield. The secluded road dog-legged to the right up ahead, but the house was on the left just before the bend. The impressive compound stood alone, looming into view from behind some trees. Tall, wrought-iron gates stood open, built into a high wall surrounding the property. The road switched from smooth tarmac to pale gravel as the cab nosed slowly inside.

The driveway wasn't too long. It was lined with neat bushes and looped around a large water feature at the end, outside the house. The cab slowed to a stop level with the front door, which was set back between two marble columns. The driver got out and hurried around the hood to open the door for Vanessa.

Roach stepped out and looked up at the house. It was a Colonial, L-shaped build, with a wing stretch back on the right. Three vehicles were parked uniformly to the left: a Mercedes sedan with blacked-out rear windows, a large pick-up truck, and Ricky Chen's Charger.

The auction business must be booming, he thought.

He heard Vanessa thank and pay the driver, then her footsteps on the gravel as she moved to his side. She managed one step toward the house before the front door was yanked open. Ricky Chen didn't make eye contact with her. He marched down the three wide steps and squared up to Roach without hesitation.

"I told you what would happen the next time we saw each other," he said.

Roach stared at him impassively, giving nothing away besides a gentle frown of bemusement. There wasn't much space between them.

Roach leaned forward, putting his face close to Chen's. "And I told you—I have no intention of leaving your girlfriend alone with her husband," he said quietly. "Not until I know she's safe."

Chen's expression changed. He took a step back and glanced at Vanessa, his wide eyes asking a million questions. She simply nodded and flashed a faint smile designed to offer apology and comfort.

He looked back at Roach and took a deep breath. "You still shouldn't be here."

Roach shrugged. "If there were any other option, I wouldn't be, believe me."

Chen sighed and turned back to the door. "Come on."

Roach gestured to Vanessa for her to go first. Chen led them both inside and closed the door behind them.

The foyer was stunning. Mahogany flooring stretched in all directions. A chandelier hung overhead. A curved staircase was built against the right wall in front of them. Rooms stood on either side, with a hallway leading past the stairs.

Chen stepped past them and headed left. "You can wait here. I'm sure Mr. Pope will be along in a moment."

He showed them inside the living room and went to leave, but not without a lingering glance at Vanessa. They exchanged an awkward smile before he disappeared.

Vanessa tossed her jacket and handbag on the oversized sofa that dominated the room, then sat down heavily on an accompanying armchair. Both faced a large fireplace with a TV screen mounted above it.

Roach turned a slow circle, admiring the décor and furnishings.

"This is a nice place," he said to her.

"Thank you," said Thomas Pope, who had appeared in the doorway.

Roach looked around as Pope entered the room.

Vanessa got to her feet and moved to the far side of the fireplace. Chen hung back by the door.

Roach turned to face him, instinctively holding his ground in front of the fireplace, making sure he stayed between Vanessa and her husband.

"I was under the impression you were leaving town," said Pope. His tone was confident.

Roach held his stare. "Actually, your wife hired me to be her personal security detail for a few days, just until she feels safe again."

Pope narrowed his gaze, then leaned to the side to stare past Roach. "Honey?"

Vanessa took a deep breath, then stepped in front of Roach, smiling lovingly at her husband. "It's only for a few days. He saved me when I was first attacked, and I'm sure he would've done it again had he been there the second time. Please... it would make me feel better."

Pope shook his head. "Absolutely out of the question. I have an exceptional security team. Any one of them could protect you better than this... *drifter* who simply wandered into the wrong town."

"Except it's been two days since your wife was attacked, and you still haven't given anyone the job," said Roach.

Pope glared at him. His cheeks colored with anger.

Roach pointed over at Chen. "What about him? He looks like he can handle himself. Give him the job, and I'll leave right now."

Chen's eyes grew wide. His jaw clenched. He stared in disbelief.

Pope didn't see the reaction. He was unable to tear his hateful gaze away from Roach. "That would be a little below Mr. Chen's paygrade," he said casually. "His duties lie with me."

Roach shrugged. "Exactly my point. The fact that your wife's safety is below anyone's paygrade says it all. But whatever. That's your business. I'm not here for the money. I'll keep her safe until you figure out why she's in danger. I'm assuming you're looking into that?"

Pope narrowed his gaze. "Of course."

Roach smiled. "Then it's settled."

"No, it isn't *settled*. Obviously, I'm grateful for what you did for my wife, but your services... such as they are... are not required. You're free to drift on to another town."

Roach paced away from the fireplace and folded his arms defiantly across his chest. "No, I'm good. I made a promise to Mrs. Pope. I don't go back on my word."

"Then make an exception," he replied through gritted teeth. "She will understand."

Vanessa stepped into her husband's eye line. "Goddamn it, Thomas. Don't talk like I'm not standing right here. This is my decision, and I want—"

"This is *not* your decision!" he yelled.

Roach tensed as Vanessa shrunk away. Pope stepped forward, pointing an arrogant, aggressive finger in Roach's direction.

"You know what? I don't care what you've done for my wife. You're leaving. Right now. I can look after her just fine."

"Clearly not," said Roach flatly.

The two men stared at each other, silently posturing. Roach didn't blink. He focused on Pope's brow until his vision blurred. His gaze became soulless. After a tense silence, it was Pope who looked away first. He smiled humorlessly and shook his head.

"I don't have time for your poor attempts at diplomacy," he said. "Diplomacy is for the weak. I don't trust you to take care of my wife, and I don't want you in my town."

"Your town?"

"Waters Point is what it is because of *me*. Because of *my* business. *My* money. So, yes... this is my goddamn town! And you're no longer welcome in it. We're done here."

He grabbed Vanessa by the wrist and dragged her toward the door. Chen watched helplessly, trying to hide his concern.

Roach took a step to follow them, but he stopped when he saw two men enter the room. The same two men who had flanked Pope in the hospital earlier that day. Their suit jackets were open, and the weapons holstered beneath their armpits were visible.

"Gentlemen, see that Mr. Roach finds the door," said Pope. "I need to have a chat with my wife. In private."

Roach was standing behind the large sofa. The living room was spacious, offering plenty of room to move. He saw Pope ushering Vanessa toward the door and knew he had to stop them leaving. They weren't done. But the men standing between them weren't about to let him through without a fight.

"You want to know your biggest mistake?" asked Roach.

Pope stopped and rolled his eyes impatiently. "Enlighten me."

"You think diplomacy is a sign of weakness. It isn't."

"Really? So, what is it a sign of?"

Roach's expression fell into a cold, emotionless stare. "Mercy."

Pope frowned, confused. Vanessa looked over, mirroring the sentiment.

Roach didn't hesitate. He took two steps forward and whipped his back leg out, kicking the guy in front of him on the left as hard as he could in the groin. He felt his foot strike bone through the thick leather of his boots. The man crumpled to his knees and vomited on the plush, navy carpet.

His colleague looked down at him, bewildered. He looked up in time to see Roach's forearm swinging toward his temple. He had no chance to block it. The thick bone of the elbow connected with the side of his head. He fell to the floor, unconscious before he landed.

The first man groaned as he tried to stand. Roach stamped the sole of his boot down on the guy's face, knocking him out.

Roach stood still, breathing hard to control the adrenaline flooding his system. He looked over at Pope, who was watching uneasily.

"Mercy, Mr. Pope," said Roach, ignoring the expression of shock on Vanessa's face. "I try to be diplomatic because *that's* what happens when I'm not. I've made peace with what I'm capable of, but I don't assume other people will be as accepting. So, I always start with diplomacy. If that fails, it's usually someone else's fault, and I have no sympathy for them."

"I see," said Pope, nodding slowly. He released his grip on Vanessa's arm and took a step toward Roach. He began to relax, his confidence returning. "Well, that was certainly impressive. I'll tell you what, Mr. Roach. My wife wants you around so much, I'm going to hire you myself. You're clearly better qualified than my current security."

Roach shook his head. "No. I'm not looking for a permanent job. Besides, you can't afford me."

Pope glared at him before swallowing his anger and his pride. He glanced at Vanessa before heading for the door.

"Come on," he barked at Chen as he passed him. "We have work to do."

Chen watched Mr. Pope leave, then looked over at Roach. He held his gaze for a moment, then disappeared out into the hallway.

Vanessa looked down at the two bodies. "That was… subtle."

Roach shrugged. "It worked, didn't it?"

"So, what now?"

"Now… you relax and try to get a good night's sleep. Do you have plans tomorrow?"

She shook her head. "Not really. But I don't want to be stuck inside the house all day. Maybe I'll make an appointment at the salon."

Roach nodded. "Okay. I'll be here at nine a.m. tomorrow to pick you up. From now on, unless you're coming here to eat or sleep, I won't leave your side. I promise."

She smiled. "Thank you."

He stepped over the bodies and headed for the front door.

"What about them?" Vanessa called after him. He looked back and saw her pointing at the men sprawled on the floor. "You just going to leave them there?"

Roach shrugged. "Yeah. Cleaning up the place is below my paygrade."

They exchanged a brief smile, then he left. It was a long walk back to town, and all that diplomacy had left him with an appetite.

Chapter Fifteen

Roach was enjoying a nice walk in the cool evening, beneath the tapestry of stars in the clear night sky. Crickets sounded in the patches of grass that sporadically filled the spaces between buildings; their chirping was the only sound. The streets were empty.

Roach was content with the silence. It had been another long day in Waters Point, and after some food and a drink, he was looking forward to getting some sleep. The peaceful stroll through town was helping him clear his mind. He had to remember his primary concern was Vanessa's safety. Nothing else.

He turned the last corner before his bed and breakfast and stopped. A squad car was parked outside. Sheriff Bushell was leaning casually against it, staring absently at the ground. He looked up as Roach was crossing the street, then ambled into the middle of the road, cutting him off from the hotel entrance.

Roach stopped a few feet away. His relaxation was replaced by a familiar frustration.

"What?" he asked bluntly.

The sheriff cocked his head, glaring at him. "Mind your tone."

"No. I was having a nice evening, and now you're here, presumably to ruin it."

"Where have you been?"

"Eating. Drinking. Not talking to anyone. It was great."

Bushell let out a weary breath. "Earlier today, we found five dead bodies in a creek about a mile south of town."

Roach stared blankly in silence.

Bushell continued. "Based on descriptions from eyewitnesses over the last couple of days, you've tangled with all five of them since you got here."

"You mean the guys who attacked Vanessa Pope."

"We don't have proof of that. But we do know you got into fights with all of them at some point since you got here."

Roach scoffed. A small, ironic smile crept across his face.

"What?" Bushell's tone was sharp with impatience.

Roach shook his head. "Nothing. I'm just surprised you actually went back to speak to witnesses. So, why are you here? Going to arrest me for something else I didn't do?"

It was the sheriff's turn to flash a wry, humorless smile. "Oh, I would like nothing more, Mr. Roachford. But no, I'm not. See, the coroner put the time of death around the early hours of this morning. Given I had personally locked you in a cell, I'd say your alibi is pretty solid."

"And yet… here you are anyway."

"Those men were killed with subsonic rounds. Single shots to the back of the head. No shell casings at the scene."

Roach nodded. "Suppressed weapon. Clean kills. No clutter. Sounds like a professional hit."

"Not quite. The executions might have been carried out skillfully, but the bodies were left for the world to see. Only an amateur would forget to hide the victims, right?"

"Not necessarily."

"Meaning?"

"Whoever pulled the trigger was sending a message, either from themselves, or on behalf of someone else. *This is what happens when you mess up.*" Roach thought for a moment, then narrowed his gaze. "Why are you telling me?"

Bushell sighed again. "Because that background check we ran on you yielded some pretty interesting reading. I know who you are, Mr. Roachford. *Roach.* I know what you did for this country, and what you went through to do it. I figured you've seen a lot of shit, so you might have a take on things."

"I need to make my history harder to find," muttered Roach under his breath.

"Excuse me?"

"Nothing. Look, if you've read my files, you'll know I'm not a detective. I don't see why you would ask for my help."

"I'm asking because, with your background, and with you having worked alongside GlobaTech in the past, you might be able to offer some insight. Think of it as me looking for some… professional consultation."

Roach ran his hand over his face and throat, scratching absently at the coarse gristle. "I really don't know what you want me to say, Sheriff," he said after a moment.

"I just want to know what the hell is going on in my town," replied Bushell. "First, with all the public disturbances, and now five dead bodies. The mayor's out of town for another couple of days, but when he gets back, he'll want answers… and right now, I don't have any. Only thing

I know for sure is that it all started going to shit around here when you arrived."

Roach shrugged. "An unpleasant coincidence, I assure you."

"Whatever it is, you know more than you're letting on. You might not be the bad guy here, but you're sure as hell involved. I just want to do my job."

Roach eyed the sheriff cautiously. He still didn't trust him. Valentine's theory still lingered in his mind. But Bushell had come to him alone, off the clock, and asked for help. Whatever the motivation might be, it felt right to extend an olive branch.

"I'll be sticking around for a few more days," he said.

Bushell frowned. "Thought you couldn't wait to leave?"

"Circumstances change."

"Mind if I ask how, exactly?"

Roach thought for a moment. "Vanessa Pope has hired me as her personal security."

Bushell chuckled incredulously. "Bet her old man loved that."

"He was ecstatic. But I'll tell you what I told him: my only concern is keeping Vanessa safe. The second I'm convinced she'll be fine without me, I'm gone. Until then, I'll do whatever it takes to protect her."

"Protect her from what? Those men are unlikely to hassle her again."

Roach didn't say anything.

"Did someone send those men after her specifically?" asked Bushell. "Do you think more people will come?"

"I honestly don't know," he replied. "But you have my word I won't do anything to jeopardize the safety of this town or the people who live here."

"Right. And I'm supposed to just accept your word, am I?"

"Yes."

"Why's that?"

Roach shrugged. "You read my files, right?"

"I did…"

"Circumstances might change, Sheriff, but I don't. That's why."

Silence hung over them like a cloud in the night sky. Both men regarded each other respectfully. Finally, Bushell nodded and walked back to his squad car. He paused beside the door and looked back.

"I'll see you around, Roach," he called out.

Roach didn't say anything. He strolled over to the sidewalk and watched until the sheriff drove away. He wasn't sure if Bushell had really been asking for himself, or for someone else, but it was late, and he didn't care to start figuring that out now.

He headed inside the bed and breakfast and nodded a courteous greeting to the man sitting behind the front desk, who peered over his newspaper as he walked by. He climbed the flight of stairs and turned left, making the short walk down the increasingly familiar hallway. He took the room key from his pocket and unlocked his door. As he was about to open it, the burner phone in his pocket began to ring.

He sighed and reached for it. The screen said Hank was calling.

The man works fast, he thought as he hit answer and held it to his ear.

"You find anything out?" he asked.

"Your friend can't talk right now," came the reply. "But to answer your question… no, he didn't."

Roach frowned. The voice was female.

"Who is this?" he asked.

"I'm someone you should really try not to piss off, Roach."

He took a breath. "Okay."

"And yet, five of my people wound up dead in that shit-hick town, and I hear you're responsible."

"And who told you that?"

"That isn't important."

"Okay."

"I think you and I should have a little talk, don't you?"

"Not really."

"Well, let me put it to you another way. If you want to see your friend again in one piece, you'll meet me on the Norwich bridge in one hour."

Roach's jaw clenched. His grip on the phone tightened. "And if I don't?"

The female voice chuckled. "Then you and Mrs. Pope can put the pieces of your friend back together before I kill you both."

The line clicked dead before Roach could reply.

He stared at the screen for a moment, his mind racing. Then he pocketed the phone, checked his door was locked, and headed back outside.

His night was apparently far from over.

Chapter Sixteen

A wide, metal bridge stretched across the river separating Waters Point from Norwich, the city to its north. It stood approximately thirty feet over the water on old, stained brick legs. Metal girders formed skeletal walls on both sides of the road, towering another forty feet.

The highway leading out of town split after a mile. Heading right led to a neighboring town on the other side of the cove; left went over the bridge.

Roach had walked, using almost all of the hour he had been given by the mystery caller. The streetlights were few and far between the farther from town he got. Trees grew taller away from the confines of civilization, blocking the moon from view.

With his hands dug into his pockets, Roach had kept a steady pace. His mind was a whirlwind of uncertainty. He found himself more concerned for Valentine's wellbeing than he thought he would be. He didn't understand what was going on, or what he had stumbled into the middle of. He wasn't sure if he was walking to his death.

He rounded a bend in the road and saw the bridge ahead of him. The gentle lapping of the water below him was the only sound. The light from the crescent moon overhead provided enough light to see the black car parked horizontally across the middle. No lights. No engine running. Roach instinctively slowed as he walked onto the bridge; the hollow, metallic thudding of his footsteps sounded ominous in the still night.

As he neared, three doors opened. Two men got out of the front and stood next to the car, facing him. A third stepped out of the rear door on the opposite side, moved swiftly around the trunk, then opened the final door, stepping to the side as he did. A woman climbed out, elegant and graceful. She wore a light-colored dress suit beneath a long, open coat. Her heels added a few inches to her height. She walked purposefully toward him, hands in her pockets, full of confidence. She stopped a few feet from him and smiled.

"So... you're the one who's been causing trouble around that sad, little town," she said.

Her voice was smooth, like velvet. Roach looked her up and down. She was an attractive woman, likely older than him, although she looked younger. Even in the heels, she was still slightly shorter than he was.

Roach glanced past her at the three men. They hadn't moved, but they were watching him. He figured they were armed.

He looked back at the woman and shook his head casually. "I wasn't causing trouble. I was ending it."

The woman's dark, thin lips formed a curious grin. "Interesting perspective."

Roach shrugged. "Not really. First, your people tried to attack an innocent woman in a diner. I stopped them, as anyone would. Then more of your people came after me. I defended myself. If any of that has inconvenienced you, that's a whole lot of your problem."

Her smile faded. "You're not very good at negotiating, are you?"

"Is that what this is? A negotiation?"

"You want to see your friend again, don't you?"

"Who, Hank?" He shrugged again. "I've known the guy two days. I don't care what happens to him. I just want to make sure Vanessa Pope is safe, then I'll leave, and no one will ever see me again."

The woman watched him for a moment. The water lapped and rolled beneath them, the only break in the silence. Then she relaxed. Her shoulders dropped slightly. Her stance changed as she rested her weight on one leg. She smiled again.

"Well, aren't you a delight," she said. "I like you."

"I don't care."

"Do you know who I am?"

Roach shook his head. "No idea. I didn't even know this place existed until a few days ago, let alone know anyone who lives here."

She frowned. "Then why are you here?"

"I'm on vacation."

"Here? Seriously?" She chuckled. "You need a better travel agent. Y'know, Maine is lovely this time of year."

"So I've heard…"

"Why not go there?"

"Believe me, I'm trying."

They fell silent again. She walked a slow circle around him. Roach held her gaze as much as he could without turning his head. When she stopped in front of him again, she was smiling almost flirtatiously.

"It's… Roach, right?" she asked.

He didn't say anything.

She held out a hand. "I'm Miss Decker. You can call me Jasmine."

He looked at her hand for a moment, then shook it gently, cautiously. He remained silent.

Jasmine nodded. "Roach, I'm going to ask you some questions, and I want you to answer them honestly. And please understand that if I think you're lying to me, you will not leave this bridge. Am I clear?"

Roach once more glanced behind her at the men waiting by the car. He didn't have many options. He couldn't run—not that he would. He was too far away to rush them. He would be shot down before he made it halfway there. He could maybe grab Jasmine and use her as a human shield, but there wasn't any long-term benefit to that. He couldn't exactly walk backward all the way back to town, and the moment he turned around, they would shoot him anyway.

He sighed, then looked back at her and nodded once. "Fine. But make it quick."

She smiled, bemused. "Why? Do you have somewhere to be?"

"Yes."

"And where's that?"

"Anywhere except here."

Jasmine laughed to herself. "Cute. Okay, question one: did you kill the five men I sent to Waters Point?"

He made a show of looking her dead in the eyes. "No."

She nodded. "Okay. But you did assault them?"

"Yes."

"Do you know who *did* kill them?"

He shook his head. "Don't know. Don't care."

"Fair enough." She paused and took a patient breath. "What does Vanessa Pope know about her husband?"

Roach shrugged. "I imagine quite a bit. They're married."

Jasmine narrowed her gaze, tilting her head slightly to one side. "Hmm, not so cute. I'll let that slide because you don't know me, but let me give you a free lesson: I don't bluff. I will have you killed where you stand if you screw me around. So, I'll ask again. What does she know about her husband that she wanted to tell me specifically?"

Roach assessed his situation again. He looked at Jasmine. He looked at her men. He glanced around the bridge. He still had no options. Except maybe negotiation.

"You say you don't bluff," he said to her. "Does that also mean you're true to your word?"

Jasmine smiled. "It does. I'm many things, Roach, but a liar isn't one of them. I keep my promises."

"In that case, I want you to promise me one thing before I say anything else."

She frowned, curious. "Interesting. Okay, I'll play along. What?"

"I want you to promise me you won't hurt Vanessa."

She grinned. "Why? Are you soft on her?"

"No."

"I mean, she's an attractive woman. I quite like the Chinese American look. If I were a little younger, maybe I would try to steal her myself…"

Roach rolled his eyes. "It isn't like that. I don't like to see innocent people punished for the crimes of the guilty. She doesn't deserve to suffer for the shit her husband does."

"How noble." Jasmine paused, searching his eyes in the darkness for a hint of anything she didn't like. Then she nodded. "Okay. You be straight with me, and I'll leave Vanessa alone."

"Thank you."

"But that *isn't* a promise that you or your P.I. friend are walking away from this. Not yet."

Roach took a deep breath. He believed Jasmine. He didn't want to play his hand too soon, but he saw an opportunity to gain an ally against Thomas Pope, and he wasn't about to let it pass him by. It might prove useful.

"Fair enough. Vanessa discovered her husband is hiding auction house profits from you."

Jasmine's posture tensed. She recoiled slightly and furrowed her brow. "Is he now? How much?"

"I don't know. She found numerous high-value transactions between off-shore accounts. I couldn't tell you how much, or for how long it's been happening."

"Interesting. And... you have proof, presumably? I mean, besides the word of an unhappy spouse."

"What makes you think she's unhappy?"

Jasmine shrugged. "Why else would she want to betray him?"

Roach didn't reply. It was a valid point.

She took a step toward him and lowered her voice. "Thomas and I have been partners for a long time. Do I like the man? Not especially. He's a medium-sized fish in a small puddle. But his auction house is a big business, and I wanted a piece of it. If he's screwing me over, I want to know, but I won't take the word of someone who backs out of a deal at the first sign of trouble. So, here's what's going to happen. You're going to get me proof of Thomas Pope's financial transgressions, or you and your friend won't live to see another sunset. Am I clear?"

Roach nodded. "But Vanessa is kept out of it?"

Jasmine took a step back. "I gave you my word I wouldn't come after her again, and I meant it. But... I can't speak for Thomas. I might not like him, but I do respect him. He's a ruthless bastard when he needs to be. If he finds out she intended to talk to me... well, I can handle myself, Roach. But his pretty little trophy wife? Oh, she'll be in a *lot* of trouble."

"I won't let that happen."

She smiled. "How admirable. But bear this in mind..." Her smile faded again. Her eyes went cold. "Thomas is my business partner. If anything happens to him or his auction house that affects *my* money, I will come for my pound of flesh. If that means burning that piss-ant town and everyone in it to the fucking ground... I will."

"Fair enough."

"Now, if you need me, you can reach me on your friend's cell phone." She reached out and straightened the collar of his jacket, then patted her hand against his chest. "Don't forget... you have twenty-four hours to get me proof, or I'll kill you all for wasting my goddamn time."

Jasmine flashed a final, flirtatious smile, then turned and walked away with a confident stride.

Roach watched her go, conflicted. He was angry at being threatened, frustrated by not being in a position of strength or control, and confused by how impressed he was.

He reached inside his pocket for Vanessa's watch and checked the time. It was late. He was tired, and it was a long walk back to town. He watched Jasmine's car drive away, then took a moment to be alone on the bridge. He moved to the side and looked out at the river below him. He couldn't see much, but the sound of the water was relaxing.

He let out a heavy breath. "Now what?"

Chapter Seventeen

He began to feel comfortable in the familiar darkness. The anonymous specters that fought to drag him deeper had become his friends. He no longer felt helpless.

He simply wondered how far the darkness beneath him went.

The more he sank into the depths of the shapeless void, the more faces materialized around him. But their screams no longer chilled him to his core. They were communicating. He might have been wrong, but the idea that these ghoulish gatekeepers weren't trying to hurt him helped him accept the inevitability of what was happening to him. They were telling him this darkness… this abyss was where he was supposed to be.

They still groped in the dark, clawing desperately toward him to rest their corroded hands on his face and body, but they were starting to feel more like an embrace than a threat.

He relaxed, rested back into the weightlessness, and let the fall take him. Almost every specter that came to him had the face of someone he had seen before. He stared at each one, no longer afraid to look into their eyes. He was conflicted. He felt pangs of guilt and regret, blaming himself for them having to be in this darkness with him.

The darkness wasn't their prison. It was his. He belonged in here. Not them.

It wasn't fair.

Suddenly, column of brilliant white light erupted, cutting through the darkness like a knife. The nameless banshees wailed with pain, scattering like minnow at the sight of a whale. He screwed his eyes shut, so tight that his face ached.

What was this? Where was it coming from?

It wasn't right.

He should be in the darkness. The light had no place here.

The white brought with it a gentle warmth, melting away the icy desolation of his black solitude. Slowly, he opened his eyes. His world was still shapeless. He still fell through the vast emptiness. He looked around at the light that inexplicably engulfed him and realized he was alone again.

There was no one but him.

Apprehensively, he turned his head and glanced over his shoulder, down into the pit to see the source of the light. It was little more than a pinprick. A solitary star in the curtain of space. But it was getting bigger.

No, wait. Not bigger...

Closer.

He felt a rising fear inside him. His comfort began to fade. The unknown had become familiar, and now it was becoming unknown again. He didn't know what awaited him in the white. All he knew was that he felt secure in the black, and he didn't want that feeling to go away again.

His fear was easier to live with in the dark.

Roach walked the half-hour from his hotel to the Pope mansion on the edge of town. He hadn't slept well. Too much on his mind. Too many things to deal with. There was no time to waste resting.

The walk helped clear his head. The air was mild and refreshing and carried with it the smell of the country. Distinctive aromas of damp earth and flourishing vegetation that appealed to him on a primal level. The trees swayed as he walked by. Their leaves rustled, breaking up the silence of the world as he wandered through it.

The road ahead began to bend right. The large gates came into view on his left. He took a deep breath as he approached them. He had no idea what the day had in store for him, but given his track record in Waters Point so far, he wasn't filled with confidence. All he knew for sure was that being at the home of an enemy wasn't the best start to the day.

The gates were closed. There was a security buzzer on the concrete pillar to the right. Roach pressed the call button and waited. After a few moments, there was a buzz, followed by a mechanical click. The gates began to swing inward, inviting him through.

His boots crunched the gravel underfoot. Halfway up the scenic driveway, he saw Ricky Chen approaching. He walked with purpose and stopped in front of him, a short distance from the large fountain outside the house.

"I don't like you being here," said Chen firmly.

Roach shrugged. "I don't like being here either. But it is what it is."

"Mr. Pope has been pissed since the moment you left yesterday."

"Okay."

"He told me not to let you inside the house."

"Good luck stopping me. I have a job to do."

Chen gritted his teeth and raised a threatening finger. "I should kill you where you stand."

Roach held his ground. "If you do that, who's going to protect Vanessa? You?"

Chen was enraged but kept his voice low.

"You know I…" He huffed with frustration. "You know I can't."

"Exactly. Under the circumstances, I would think your prerogative would be making me your best friend."

Chen pointed again. "If you say *anything*… if Mr. Pope even suspects… he'll take it out on her."

Roach looked him up and down, then raised his eyebrow. "You look pretty strong. I'm sure you could stop him if you wanted to."

To his surprise, Chen took a breath and stepped back. He swallowed hard, shrinking before him.

"No, man, you don't understand," he began, shaking his head. "Mr. Pope is…"

Roach frowned. "He's what?"

Chen sighed. "He's a powerful man. You don't want him as an enemy. If you and Vanessa have convinced him to let you stick around, fine, but don't for one second think he's happy about it."

Roach smiled. "Oh, I *know* he isn't happy about it. He isn't exactly shy about his feelings. But Vanessa's afraid, and she can't ask you to look out for her. I'm her best chance of staying safe. I know her husband is pissed. I don't care about that. I only care about doing my job without looking over my shoulder the whole time, wondering if you're coming for me. So, tell me, Ricky… are we going to have a problem?"

Chen held eye contact for a silent, tense moment, then shook his head. "No, we're good. For now. But I work for

Mr. Pope. I don't do what he says, I'm dead. So, I'm asking you… don't give him a reason to send me after you, okay? That won't help Vanessa."

Roach nodded back. "Fair enough. I'll wait outside for her."

"Thank you."

The two men walked to the house together in silence. Roach hung back at the foot of the steps, looking around aimlessly at the impressive grounds while Chen headed inside.

A few moments later, Vanessa appeared in the doorway, followed by her husband. She walked down the steps and greeted Roach with a warm smile.

"Morning," she said.

She wore makeup that almost completely hid the bruising on her face. It was heavy but tastefully applied. Her smile looked genuine.

He flashed a barely-there smile in return. "You ready to go?"

"I am." She paused, frowning at his tone and expression. "Is everything okay?"

He nodded. "Yeah. I'll tell you later."

Pope wandered out to the top of the steps. He was wearing a fresh suit, minus the jacket. His burgundy and purple tie was fastened neatly at his collar.

"Tell me again," he said. "What are you doing today?"

The question was for his wife. He didn't make eye contact with Roach at all.

She rolled her eyes and looked up at him. "I told you. I have a nail appointment at the salon this morning, remember?"

He pointed at Roach without looking at him. "And you need *him* for that?"

Roach moved to Vanessa's side, making it impossible for Pope not to acknowledge his presence.

"She needed me when she went for a coffee," he said casually. "Who's to say a salon is any safer? All kinds of sharp objects there…"

Pope narrowed his gaze and finally looked at him, staring a hole through him. "Are you trying to be funny?"

Roach shook his head. "No. I take the safety of your wife seriously. Don't you?"

Pope's jaw pulsed with restrained rage. Finally, he looked at Vanessa and forced a smile. "Have a nice day, honey."

He glared at Roach, then turned and headed back inside, slamming the door closed behind him.

Vanessa looked at Roach. "You shouldn't antagonize him like that."

He shrugged. "What's he going to do?"

"You don't want to know," she replied with a sigh. "Now, come on. I'm driving."

Roach frowned. "You have a car?"

She laughed. "Of course, I do. You think I walk everywhere?"

"I do…"

"Yes, but you don't wear five-inch heels."

Roach looked down at her feet. Her olive skin and painted nails were displayed through strapped heels. Her ankles tensed as she wrestled for balance on the uneven gravel.

"Fair point," he conceded. "Those things look deadly."

She laughed again. "You get used to them."

Vanessa walked gracefully toward the small pool of parked cars to the left of the driveway, making a beeline for a bright blue convertible Porsche. Roach followed. He let out a low whistle when she opened the driver's door of the car.

"Nice ride," he said. "The auction business must be booming…"

She glanced back at him. "Isn't that the problem?"

She flashed a wry smile before ducking inside behind the wheel.

"I guess it is," Roach muttered to himself, then reached for the passenger door.

As he gripped the handle, he looked back toward the house. Chen was standing in the doorway, leaning against the frame with his arms folded across his chest. Roach held his gaze across the driveway for a moment, then climbed inside the Porsche as Vanessa gunned the engine.

Chapter Eighteen

They sat across from one another at a small table by the window in the only chain café in Waters Point. Everything looked new and recently cleaned. The smell of freshly ground coffee wafted throughout, and there was music playing low in the background.

It was busier than anywhere else Roach had seen so far. Most tables were taken, and there was a small but consistent line of people by the counter, ordering drinks and snacks to take out.

Vanessa sat with her legs crossed, sipping a coffee that contained nuts and chocolate. Roach leant forward on his crossed arms, nursing his regular, black coffee. He had insisted he sat facing the door.

"People are going to talk, seeing me out with another man," said Vanessa, smiling.

Roach flashed a smile back in return, but there was no humor in it. He glanced out through the window, at the Porsche parked out front. It drew glances from whoever passed by.

"People already are," he replied flatly. "We should be careful."

Vanessa frowned at his tone. "What's wrong?"

He sighed. "I got a call last night from Hank's cell phone."

"What has he found out? Anything?"

He shook his head. "It wasn't Hank. It was Decker. *Jasmine* Decker."

Her eyes bulged in their sockets. She placed a hand over her mouth, gasping quietly. "Oh my God…"

"She has Hank. Told me to go and meet her."

"Did you?"

He nodded.

"What did she want?"

"She wanted to know what you were going to tell her."

Vanessa swallowed hard and looked away for a moment. "What did you say to her?"

"The truth. That you suspect your husband is hiding profits from her."

"Is she… is she going to confront him?"

Roach shook his head. "No. In her words, she doesn't trust the word of an unhappy spouse. She gave me a day to get her proof, or she's going to kill Hank, then come after me."

She glanced at the table. "And me…"

"No, she's not. I made her promise she would leave you out of this from now on. She said she would, and I believe her."

"Thank you. But that doesn't make this any better. What are you going to do?"

"There isn't much I *can* do, Vanessa. I need to get proof."

"But I don't have any," she said. "And I doubt I'll be

able to access Thomas's files again. It was a password-protected spreadsheet on his private laptop. There's no way he'll trust me to look at that now. Not with you around."

Roach held her gaze, trying not to let his frustration show. He knew she was right. Even if Pope had zero suspicion about the attacks on his wife being linked to his business, he would be more cautious now. He felt threatened by Roach's continued presence and was unhappy that Vanessa wanted him around. She wasn't getting anywhere near her husband's business.

He thought on it for a couple of minutes, occasionally sipping his coffee. Vanessa watched the cogs turning behind his eyes.

"There's another option," said Roach finally. "Perhaps our *only* other option."

Vanessa frowned. "What is it?"

He sighed. "Ricky."

"What? No! No way!" She shook her head animatedly. "I am *not* asking him to get involved."

Roach sat back and held his hands up apologetically. "If you have a better idea, you're welcome to share it. You said yourself, he won't let you help him out with me around. It's not as if I can waltz into his office and look. Ricky is the only one who can get close enough."

"He would never betray Thomas," she said quietly.

Roach raised an eyebrow. "I think we both know he already has."

She went to protest but instead let out a resigned sigh. "Yes, but not like that. He's worked for Thomas for years. He's helped that business grow too. He wouldn't. Besides, I can't ask him to put himself in danger for me."

"Then I'll ask him."

Vanessa reached out but stopped herself from actually

placing her hand on his arm, fighting with indecision. "Roach, don't. Please. He'll…"

He narrowed his gaze. "He'll… what?"

She didn't reply. She glanced away, taking a sip of her drink. Her leg bounced anxiously over her knee. When Roach leaned forward to attract her attention, she purposely avoided making eye contact.

He watched her for a full minute before he realized the truth.

"He knows, doesn't he?" he said. "Ricky knows exactly what your husband is doing with the money. That's how you knew to look for the transactions in the first place. He told you."

Vanessa finally looked up at him. Her eyes glistened with tears waiting to fall. She nodded.

Roach rubbed his eyes with one hand. "Christ."

"Look, I know this is my fault, okay? I'm the one who decided against telling Jasmine Decker. I was scared Thomas would find out and hurt Ricky. I couldn't bear the thought of…" She looked away for a moment, composing herself. "He wanted to go ahead, but I talked him out of it. And now look at everything that's happened. I want to fix this, but I don't know how."

Roach hesitated. She was right. But he felt sorry for her. Nothing she had done so far was malicious. She was in trouble that wasn't completely her own doing, and she didn't deserve that. He understood there was a time for compassion and a time for tough love. This walked the line between the two, and he needed to handle it carefully.

He finished his coffee with a long gulp. "There's no sense in trying to place blame now. It's too late for that. The sheriff came to me last night."

"What for?" she asked, confused.

"All those guys that came after you... and me... they were found dead just outside of town yesterday morning. They were executed."

Vanessa gasped again, horrified. This time, it drew stares from the people sitting around them.

"Oh, God," she whispered. Then she frowned. "Wait, did you..."

He shook his head. "No, it wasn't me. Bushell had me in a cell overnight at the time, so he knows I couldn't have done it. He's still not thrilled about me staying in town, though." Roach leaned forward, knowing he had to press. "What exactly is your husband's business, Vanessa? Why would someone like Jasmine Decker want a piece of his auction house? Has Ricky told you?"

Vanessa glanced around conspicuously, then lowered her voice. "He hasn't said anything to me. He knew about the hidden profits, but I don't think he knows exactly where the money is coming from or what it's for. Either that, or he isn't telling me to protect me."

"Okay. But what do *you* think?"

"When I saw the money trail, my first thought was that he's selling stolen goods through the auction house."

"Or *fake* ones..."

"You mean the watches? Yes, maybe. It has to be something shady, right?"

"That would be my guess, although I don't know if that's enough to attract the attention of someone like Jasmine Decker. She operates in a big city. I've met her. She's the real deal. There must be something more to it, surely?"

Vanessa thought for a moment. "Well, Thomas has a lot of connections with powerful and influential people. He would have people over to the house all the time. Businessmen, socialites, politicians. His auctions attract a prominent crowd that brings their wealth with them. Then they drink in our bars, eat in our restaurants, stay in our hotels. That's a huge boost to the economy. Without the auction house, no one would know this town even existed. That's the value Thomas adds here."

Roach nodded. "And it's that value that allows him to keep the mayor in his pocket too, right?" When she stared at him, he shrugged. "Hank's good at his job. He said your husband funds business grants that keep taxes low. Not only does he make it cheap for people to live here, but he seems content to let the mayor take the credit for it, which keeps *him* elected."

"Yeah, I guess so."

"All this definitely puts him in a position to do some real shady shit, but it also adds to his risk. He has much more to lose if he gets caught. That makes men like him dangerous. People who have money and power will do anything to keep it."

Vanessa eyed him warily. "You sound like you're speaking from experience."

"I am. I've dealt with people like your husband before. People who were much bigger and better at this sort of thing. I know how they think."

She took a sip of her drink and sat back in her chair. She tilted her head slightly as she stared at him. "Who are you, Roach? Really. You seem to know so much about how bad people operate. I mean, after everything you've done for me, I *do* trust you. It's just... I don't actually know all that much about you."

Roach sighed and stared absently at a stain on the table for a moment. He recalled the conversations he had had with Valentine and Bushell. They had discovered much of his past. Vanessa didn't really know anything.

He looked up at her. His mouth formed a taut line. "What did you do during Orion's occupation?"

She shrugged. "We had already moved here when they took over. Business essentially came to a stand-still, obviously. It didn't really affect us here. We got a few refugees who passed through. The occasional Tristar patrol. But mostly, Thomas and I rode it out at home. Why? What did you do?"

Roach ignored the question. "Did you follow the progress of GlobaTech's rebellion at all?"

Vanessa nodded. "As much as I could, yes. It was incredible, what those people did. I even found that blog the reporter wrote. You know the one? It was disguised as a cooking blog."

"Yeah, I know it." He took a deep breath, then looked her in the eyes. "My sister wrote it."

Her gaze widened with shock. Her mouth hung open. Finally, she leaned forward. "Holy shit!" she whispered. "You're the brother! Of course. It honestly didn't click until you just told me. Oh, my God. This is… *wild!*"

He smiled awkwardly. "That's me. If you read the blog, you know exactly what I did during Orion's occupation of this country. What you might not know is, before all that happened, I used to work for Tristar."

She frowned. "Wait, seriously?"

Roach nodded. "I was a low-level criminal, fresh out of jail. I did some mercenary work when someone told me about them. They trained me well. But they eventually betrayed me and left me for dead. I was in a coma for over a month. I woke up with no memory, somewhere in the forests of Thailand. When they found out I was still alive, they sent people after me."

"Oh, my God..."

"When *that* didn't work, they kidnapped my sister, Becky. I tore their New York office apart to get her back. That was right before Orion took over. I was there when Santa Clarita fell, and I was there when Moses Buchanan was murdered. In between, my sister and I walked almost the full width of this country. I fought, I killed... she would say I inspired. A lot of people suffered and died during that time. But I saw a side of what happened that few others did. It changed me."

A tear crawled down her cheek. "Roach, I'm sorry..."

He shrugged. "I walked away from GlobaTech's final battle. They lost a lot of good people that day in Nevada. I don't know how different it would've played out had I been there. I just... didn't want to fight anymore. When it was all over, Becky said I owed it to the people who died to keep fighting. To help track down the remains of Tristar. I disagreed."

Vanessa held her coffee in both hands, entranced by the story. "Why?"

"Because I didn't think the world was worth saving. I was sick and tired of seeing everyone turn on each other. Sick and tired of powerful people taking advantage of those who couldn't defend themselves, and sick and tired of them getting away with it. I was done with the world, and I wanted the world to be done with me."

She nodded slowly. "Hence your sabbatical..."

"Becky and I, we... we fell out when I left. We haven't spoken since, which I feel bad about. I'm dealing with it. Sort of. But being here, seeing you in the situation you're in... it just reminds me of how I fought to save her. Makes me think she was right. I walked away from a fight once. I don't think I can do it again."

"Jesus." Vanessa stared at her drink, shaking her head with disbelief. "I'm sorry you went through all that, Roach, I really am. You didn't deserve any of it. I mean, you're a—"

"Please… don't say it."

Vanessa leaned forward, searching for his gaze. "You're a goddamn hero, Roach. To millions." She chuckled to herself. "And now here you are, in the middle of nowhere, dealing with *my* problems."

He flicked his eyebrows. "How the mighty have fallen, huh?"

"All this must seem so trivial to you."

He shook his head. "Not at all. This is the world that's left. This is the shit that happens now. Lives are in danger. *This* is the fight. We're going to figure this out, Vanessa. I promise."

She smiled admiringly. "Thank you."

They sat in silence for a few minutes, letting the conversation settle and the mood return to normal while they finished their drinks.

"So, what do we do?" asked Vanessa finally.

Roach took a deep breath. "Like I said, there's only one real option here. If you and Ricky want to be together, and if I want Hank back in one piece, we have to get Jasmine Decker the proof she asked for. It's the only way she would consider taking down your husband for you."

"I know, but…"

Her words trailed off. She had no real argument. She knew that.

She nodded with resignation.

"Call Ricky," said Roach. "Have him meet me in thirty

minutes in the parking lot behind the grocery store across town. I'll talk with him. Ask him to help."

"No, let me. He'll listen to me…"

Roach shook his head. "You need to stay out of this from now on. I'll go alone. But I'll need to borrow your car."

Vanessa reached into her bag for her keys, then slid them across the table toward him. "What should I do?"

He picked up the keys. "Do what you told your husband you were going to do. Spend a few hours at the salon. Somewhere busy and public. You should be safe there until I get back."

"What if someone comes looking for me? Like before."

Roach shook his head. "Jasmine Decker won't be sending anyone after you. Whoever killed her people did so to send a message to her. It's unlikely you're still a target now."

"Well, I'm still glad I have you around."

He smiled briefly. "Just sit tight, get your nails done, and don't leave until I get back. Under any circumstances."

Vanessa nodded meekly and reached for her phone.

Roach stared out the window, his gaze blurring over as he looked at the Porsche sitting outside, trying to decide if meeting Chen really was the best idea.

Chapter Nineteen

Roach rested gently against the hood of Vanessa's Porsche, his arms folded across his chest. He stared blankly at the ground, trying simply to take a beat and relax.

Light clouds formed above, dulling the sunshine for the first time since he had arrived in Waters Point. The breeze picked up, still warm for the season but stronger than it had been in a while. He tilted his head back and closed his eyes as the gust washed over him like a refreshing shower.

When it died down, he sat straight again and looked around. The parking lot was much bigger than the grocery store needed it to be. He bet he could park every car in town in this one lot and still have spaces available. The store was located on one of the main strips, about a quarter-mile from the intersection statue. It seemed to act as a hub for everyone. Roach noted that half the people who had parked there weren't customers of the store. They simply left their cars and trucks while they ran their errands all over town.

He had parked alone in a corner of the lot away from

everything else. It was close to a low fence that backed onto a patch of empty land, overgrown with weeds.

He waited ten minutes before he heard the distant roar of Chen's Charger. The spluttering growl was unmistakable, especially in a town like this. Roach glanced back over his shoulder as the car eased into the lot and drove directly toward him, ignoring the markings for spaces and navigation. It circled to a stop, nose to nose with the Porsche, with only a few feet between them. Chen climbed out with gusto and marched toward him, his face narrowed with a hard frown and a tense jaw.

"Who the hell do you think you are, summoning me like this?" barked Chen as he stopped in front of Roach.

Roach stared calmly into his dark eyes, matching his restrained aggression. "I'm here to help. You want to hear me out, or do you want to mouth off until I punch you?"

"You're welcome to try." He sighed as the moment defused. "Look, just because you and I have come to an understanding, that doesn't mean Mr. Pope is okay with you still being here. I can't be seen tolerating your bullshit."

"He might not like it, but after seeing me destroy two of his security guards in his living room, even *he* can't deny I'm effective. However, this isn't about what he likes or doesn't like. This is about keeping Vanessa safe. And seeing as it's just me and you right now, you can drop the act because we both know that's all you're really concerned about. So, are you going to listen to what I have to say, or not?"

Chen held his gaze for a heartbeat, then stepped back. He mimicked Roach's body language by resting against his own car's hood.

"Fine," he said begrudgingly. "What do you want?"

Roach nodded his appreciation. "Vanessa's told me

everything. I know what the two of you were planning, and I know why she's in this situation."

"Okay."

"Jasmine Decker contacted me. I told her what Vanessa was going to give her. She wants proof, and she's going to kill my friend by the end of the day if she doesn't get it."

Chen shrugged. "Not my problem."

Roach glanced around, checking no one was in earshot and searching for a hidden reserve of patience. "Actually, it is. Once this woman has killed him, she'll come for me. If she manages to take me out, what do you think she's going to do next? Hmm? She's going to tear this town apart looking for answers, which puts Vanessa, you, and your boss in her path. If it comes to that, the fact you were going to betray Thomas Pope won't count for shit. By not telling her what you know, both you and Vanessa are just as guilty in her eyes. She'll come for you all, and she isn't someone you want as an enemy. Even I know that."

Chen shrugged again. "So, what? What am I supposed to do about it?"

"I want proof of the hidden auction house profits, and you're the only one who can get it."

Chen shook his head, laughing incredulously. "No way! I knew you were going to ask me something like this. I just *knew* it. There isn't a goddamn chance in hell Mr. Pope would let me anywhere near his private files. The only time I'm in the house is by his side. It would be impossible without him finding out."

Roach went to reply but caught his words with a sigh. Any argument he had was pointless, and he knew it. He stared at Chen, silent, begrudging. He knew he was right, and he wasn't about to waste what time he had on a lost cause.

"Okay," he said finally. "But I still need information, even if Jasmine can't have her evidence. You might not be able to access the files, but you sure as hell know what's going on, and you're going to tell me."

Chen shook his head slowly. "I… I don't know anything, okay? Only what Vanessa saw in those files."

"Bullshit. You just said you're never away from his side. You must see what's really going on. Plus, Vanessa told me it was you who first alerted her to the money and suggested using it as a way out for you both. If you're keeping things from her to protect her, I respect that. But don't keep things from me. Not now. Start talking."

Chen looked around the quiet lot, suddenly feeling conspicuous.

"Officially, I know nothing more than I need to know to be able to do my job for Mr. Pope," he said reluctantly. "But yeah… I've seen things."

Roach nodded. "You can start by telling me exactly what Thomas and Jasmine's scam is."

Chen let out a long, taut breath. "Most of what goes up for auction is genuine. Artwork, vinyl records, antiques, you name it. But some things aren't."

"The watches."

Chen nodded. "That's the scam. Every watch he sells is fake."

"Why them? Surely, fake artwork would sell for much more."

"That's the thing. These watches shift for huge amounts. All the important people Mr. Pope invites snap them up."

"And Jasmine caught wind of the scam and muscled her way in for a slice?"

"Yeah. Except she doesn't know the half of it. She

153

thinks she's in on the scam, right? But she isn't. Not really. Mr. Pope's scamming her along with everyone else."

Roach frowned. "How?"

"The official deal is this: he gets the watches made for next to nothing. Wholesale discount kinda thing, right? Jasmine Decker thinks he gets a watch made for a couple of hundred bucks, then sells it at auction for forty to fifty grand, to someone too stupid to know the difference and too rich to care."

Roach let out a low whistle. "That's a nice profit margin."

"It is. And that's what she gets her take from."

"Okay. So, how is Thomas scamming her?"

"That sale isn't a sale. It's a deposit. What he *actually* sells them for is ten times that."

"That doesn't make any sense. Even real watches aren't worth that much, let alone fake ones... no matter how good they look."

Chen shrugged. "That's all I know, I swear to you."

Roach thought about it for a moment, then shook his head. "I'm not buying it. There's got to be something more to this. Why watches, specifically? Surely, no one believes it's real? You want to fleece millions from people, you sell artwork or antiques."

"He's made it work for a long time. He's a smart man."

"Where does he get them made?"

"The watches? I—"

Chen broke off as his attention was pulled to something across the parking lot. Roach followed his concerned gaze and saw a pick-up truck heading toward them. He could make out four guys inside it.

"Shit," hissed Chen.

Roach raised an eyebrow. "Friends of yours?"

"Oliver Sutton. He works for Mr. Pope."

"So, I'm guessing this meeting's over?"

Chen pointed a threatening finger close to Roach's face. "Bet your ass it is."

Roach nodded, seeing it was to keep up appearances. "You do what you gotta do. I promise I'll keep Vanessa safe no matter what. But tell me where Thomas gets the watches from."

Before he could answer, the truck slid to a halt beside them, and the four men clambered out. They formed a line along next to them. The man standing second from the left took a step forward and stared at Chen challengingly. He was in his early thirties. He was tall and lean, wearing a sleeveless, insulated jacket over a plaid shirt. The men who accompanied him varied in height and build, but all looked similar.

Chen looked at him. "What are you doing here, Sutton? I didn't send for you."

Sutton sneered. "I'm here because one of my guys saw you come here and meet with *this* sonofabitch. Naturally, I told Mr. Pope. He wasn't happy about it, so we came to see what's going on."

Roach rested back against the Porsche's hood, quietly watching the exchange.

Chen rolled his eyes. "I'm here *for* Mr. Pope, asshole."

Sutton took another step forward, squaring up to him. "Well, he didn't seem aware of that when I spoke with him…"

Chen didn't back down. He exuded confidence, secure in both his position and his abilities. "Do you know why I'm head of Mr. Pope's security and you're not? It's because I fix problems *before* they happen. Most of the time, I tell the boss *after* the fact that he has nothing to worry about. I think ahead, whereas you just go where he tells you like a dumb, blunt instrument. You're in construction... I'm a surgeon. Understand?"

The men behind Sutton all tensed. Chen and Sutton stared each other down. Finally, Sutton took a step back, falling in line with the rest of his crew.

"You need any help with this prick?" he asked.

Chen shook his head. "No. I was just reminding our friend here that I don't care how much Mrs. Pope vouches for him. She doesn't run this organization... her husband does." He turned to Roach. "So, like I was saying, you find a way to tell Mrs. Pope you no longer want to work for her, then you get your ass out of our town. I don't care where you go, just do it by the end of the day, or you're dead. I hear Churchville is a nice little town. Why don't you go and irritate them instead, hmm?"

Roach didn't say anything. His left eye twitched slightly. A barely perceptible gesture of silent thanks.

Then he nodded. "Okay. You've made your point. I'll return her car to her, make my excuses, and leave this backwater hellhole. Frankly, after all the shit that's happened since I got here, I'll be glad to see the back of the place."

Sutton moved to Chen's side, turned to face Roach, and sat back against the hood of the Charger. "You want me to stick around, make sure he actually goes?"

Chen didn't take his eyes off Roach. He shrugged and smiled. "Do whatever you want. Just make sure he can still walk out of here unaided when you're finished." He took a step toward Roach. "Nice knowing you, asshole."

He walked away toward the driver's door. As he passed Sutton, he glanced at him. "Get your ass off my car, dickhead."

Sutton stood and moved to the side as Chen climbed

inside and gunned the engine. The wheels spun as he reversed away. He performed an unnecessarily fast J-turn, then accelerated out of the lot, leaving smoke and tire marks behind him.

All five men watched him leave, then Sutton and his crew turned back to stare at Roach.

"So, Churchville, huh?" said Roach. "I don't suppose you want to tell me where it is and let me leave peacefully?"

Sutton smiled. "Not even a little bit."

"I figured."

Roach quickly looked at each man in turn, expertly assessing them and prioritizing their threat level. Sutton, he already knew was a mouthpiece. He seemed to dislike Chen. Perhaps wanted his spot. He didn't look like much, but he was eager to impress the boss. Men like that shouldn't be underestimated.

The first of his crew wore a backwards baseball cap and sported a thin, black handlebar mustache. He wore a constant sneer on his face. Roach figured he was there making up the numbers. He was no one on the food chain but thought he was a big shot because he rolled with the people who were. No threat there.

The second guy was the one Roach was most concerned with. Broad shoulders and visible gang tattoos from a stint in prison. He had seen similar ink before. The person sporting them usually wasn't someone to be taken lightly.

The final guy was tall. Roach gave up a solid three inches in height. He had to assume a level of physical competency. The reach advantage the guy had could cause a problem.

Satisfied, Roach took a deep breath and pushed away from the hood of the Porsche. As he did, he launched a stiff right punch from the hip, aimed at Sutton's head. The blow struck clean with no warning, and Sutton fell away to the ground.

Roach immediately turned to his right, dropped his shoulder, and charged the tall guy like he was sacking a quarterback. He buried himself in the guy's gut and pushed him back against the pick-up. He bolted his torso upright, bringing with it a left uppercut the guy didn't see until it was too late. It connected with the underside of his jaw. He followed it with two hard rights to the side of the head in quick succession. The guy's legs crumbled beneath his unconscious weight.

Anticipating a reaction from Mustache and Tattoo, Roach spun around, arms raised. The movement naturally blocked the haymaker from Tattoo that was swinging from the right, surprising both men. Roach reacted first, shoving him away to create some distance before following up with a stiff kick aimed at the groin. Tattoo saw it coming and turned his body, deflecting it and sending Roach off-balance. As he stumbled away, Mustache drove his fist deep into his side, just below the ribs. The shot knocked the wind out of him, and he fell back against the Porsche's hood.

Tattoo and Mustache swarmed him, raining down hard blows to his face and body. Roach did his best to protect himself, bringing both arms up and rolling side to side, trying to avoid being hit.

More connected than didn't.

Roach tried to stay calm. He flung a leg out, grateful that it caught Mustache in the side of his knee. He buckled and fell away, leaving Tattoo momentarily alone. Roach reached up for him and grabbed two handfuls of collar. He yanked him down as he sat up, thrusting his forehead into Tattoo's nose. The thick part of his skull impacted with the bridge, shattering it across Tattoo's face. With blood in his eyes, his vision became obscured, granting Roach valuable seconds to gain more of an upper hand. He pushed himself up off the hood and squared up to Tattoo, measuring his next shot.

But he never got to throw it.

Sutton charged him, slamming him back against the Porsche. Before he could react, Mustache and Tattoo recovered and moved to either side of their colleague. Each man grabbed an arm and held Roach in place, spreadeagled and exposed across the hood. Sutton was standing too close to effectively kick him.

Roach was pinned and vulnerable.

Sutton produced a knife from his pocket and flicked it in his hand to expose the blade. The mirrored surface and sharp edge glistened in the daylight. Sutton held it a couple of inches from Roach's face.

"You think you're so tough," he seethed, sucking in desperate breaths. "Let's see you walk out of here after I gut you like a fucking fish!"

Roach stared up into the dark, venomous eyes looming over him. Sutton's figure blocked out the natural light from around him. He fought against the grips on his arms, but it was futile. He had no leverage to power out of it.

He glared with primal fury at the blade as it danced in front of his face, teasing him with impending agony.

Then the siren sounded.

All four men looked over as a police cruiser raced into the parking lot, the whoop and wail accompanied by flashing lights.

Roach looked back at Sutton. He felt an initial wave of relief, but he was uncertain if the sheriff's arrival was enough to save him. Pope had a lot of pull in the town. He could realistically talk his way out of a sanctioned murder in broad daylight.

Sutton looked down at him, his eyes wide with frustration. "Today's your lucky day. Just pray you don't see me again, bitch."

The three men hurried to scoop up their fallen comrade from beside the pick-up truck, then hustled inside and sped away.

Roach slid down the hood and sat on the ground, breathing hard. He was angry at himself for letting that situation get away from him, but also felt gratitude for the sheriff's impeccable timing. His life had been a dark journey, filled with violence and suffering, but even he believed he deserved better than to die in a parking lot in the middle of nowhere.

He got to his feet as Sheriff Bushell and Deputy Henderson walked over to him.

"You okay?" asked the sheriff.

Roach leaned forward, resting his hands on his knees as he caught his breath. "Never... better."

"Those men work for Thomas Pope. What did you do to piss him off enough to send *them* after you?"

"Visit this town, apparently," he replied, standing slowly upright again.

"Uh-huh." Bushell took a deep breath. "Then maybe you should think about moving on. Next time, I might not be around."

"Next time, I'll be better prepared. Besides, I can't leave. I promised to protect Vanessa Pope, remember?"

"Oh, I remember. I also recall you weren't exactly forthcoming with more details." Bushell looked him up and down. "I just want to keep my town safe. What do you know that I don't?"

He had no issue with Bushell, but he also had no patience for small talk after what had just happened. Roach fixed him with a hard stare. "I probably know lots of things you don't, Sheriff, but I'm not in a sharing mood right now."

Bushell sighed and rolled his eyes. "Right. Well, you should watch yourself."

"I'll be fine. Hopefully, I'll be out of your little town soon."

"How soon, exactly? I don't like trouble, Roach, and neither do the fine folks who live here."

"Neither do I, believe me. But when it finds me, I don't walk away from it." He moved around the Porsche and lingered with a hand on the driver's door. "Now, I got somewhere to be."

Roach yanked open the door, ducked hurriedly inside, and slammed it closed again behind him. He revved the engine and drove away, past a small crowd who had apparently gathered nearby to watch the drama unfold. He turned left out of the parking lot and glanced in his rearview, watching the sheriff and his deputy shrink away.

Chapter Twenty

Churchville was situated only ten miles west of Waters Point, just across the river, yet it felt like a new world. Over twenty thousand people lived and worked there. Compared to Waters Point, it was a metropolis. Streets and sidewalks bustled with seemingly constant activity. The average height of buildings in the commercial districts was only six or seven stories, but they towered over anything seen ten miles back east.

The air still felt clean, with a freshness to it only found in more rural areas. But the hue of the world was a little darker. Maybe it was the higher skyline. Maybe it was pollution. Maybe it was the swarms of people and vehicles, all moving at a faster pace, burdened by responsibilities not found in smaller towns.

Roach hated it. He felt disoriented and lost.

He was no stranger to big cities. A lifetime ago, he acquainted himself intimately with a New York City skyscraper, with nothing but a shotgun and a smile. But his time in Waters Point had shrunk his concept of the world.

The small town had consumed his every waking moment for the last few days, as well as some of his non-waking ones.

He had blissfully forgotten how big and busy the world could be.

After leaving Sheriff Bushell standing in the parking lot, he had swung by the salon, driving by slowly to make sure he could still see Vanessa in the window. She was sitting in a chair, being fussed over by two women who were talking animatedly to her.

She was fine.

The short drive to Churchville took less than twenty minutes, even with the increased flow of traffic the closer he got. The picturesque, serene roads lined with tall trees soon fell away to make room for congested highways and gray buildings.

Roach wasn't sure what to expect when he got there, but he was altogether unprepared for how out of his depth he felt. His plan had been to take a leaf out of Valentine's book —talk to people, get to know the lay of the land, and try to find someone who was apparently a master counterfeiter. He had walked the streets for just over an hour and felt like he was drowning. This wasn't Waters Point. He couldn't go to a bar and find half the population sitting there drinking.

He wandered aimlessly along a busy street, shoulders hunched as he weaved his way through the crowds, desperately trying to figure out his next move. Up ahead, a homeless man sat in the doorway of a closed building. People swerved to avoid being too close as they walked by.

He subconsciously glanced left and right as he passed by an alley between two buildings. Then he stopped, double-taking as he stared along it. At the end, where a left turn was formed naturally by surrounding buildings, he saw two men. He couldn't make out specific features, but given their casual clothing and over-styled hair, he figured they were young. Perhaps early twenties. They stood huddled together, their hands close.

Roach narrowed his gaze and stared, focusing on their body language.

He knew a drug deal when he saw one.

In that moment, he realized he had been going about this all wrong. Valentine's logic was sound, but he had forgotten who he was looking for. He was searching for a criminal. Best person to ask about that was another criminal, and Roach had just found two of them.

He looked around once more, then headed inside the alley. Even from a distance, the two young men heard his footsteps. They both looked over at him, then back at each other, scrambling to put their hands in their pockets. The taller of the two disappeared around the corner, out of sight. The other dropped his head and walked quickly toward Roach.

As he got closer, Roach inspected him. He was right about him being early twenties. His smooth jawline had likely never seen facial hair. A spattering of blemishes lined his forehead. He wore a hoodie emblazoned with two large letters, which he figured were either for a sports franchise or a local college.

The kid probably weighs a buck-fifty soaking wet, he thought.

The young man was almost level with Roach. His head was down, avoiding eye contact. Without warning, Roach shot his arm out, wrapped his hand firmly around the young man's throat, and spun him around, slamming him into the nearby wall.

"Hey! What the hell?" he yelled.

Roach leaned close, so his mouth was an inch from the

guy's ear. "Don't make another sound, or I'll tear out your voice box and hand it to you. Understand?"

The man's eyes bulged with fear. He nodded urgently, silently.

"Good." Roach released his grip and took a step back. "Now… what's your name?"

"K-Kevin," he stammered. The blood had rushed from his cheeks, leaving him pale.

"Okay, Kevin. I need your help."

He frowned. "Are you a cop?"

Roach tilted his head and glared at him with disbelief. "Do I look like a cop to you?"

Kevin looked him up and down. Some mild bruising had formed around Roach's eye socket from the unprotected shots he had taken not two hours ago. His dark, sunken eyes betrayed no emotion. His defined, unshaven jaw was set with impatience.

"N-not really," he said.

"Right. So, let's make that the last dumb thing you say."

Kevin nodded again.

"Who was that guy you were with just now?" asked Roach, nodding toward the end of the alley.

Kevin glanced sheepishly at the ground. "No one."

"Uh-huh. So, *no one* was just selling you drugs?"

He looked up and frowned. "How did you…"

Roach raised his eyebrow. "This isn't my first rodeo, kid."

"Are you… are you looking to get high or something?"

"No. I'm looking for someone. The kind of someone people who buy and sell drugs might know."

Kevin smiled uneasily. "Look, man, I just buy a little weed off that guy. I'm not some big-time criminal or nothing, okay?"

Roach made a point of looking him up and down. "No shit. But if you know people who sell drugs, you might know people who sell other things."

"Like what?"

"Like fake watches."

Kevin frowned. "Why would you want to buy a watch you know is fake?"

"I don't. I want to speak to the guy who makes them."

"W-what for?"

"That's between me and him. You know anyone or not?"

"Hey, I ain't no rat, man. I can't—"

"You're not ratting on anyone. I told you, I'm not a cop. I'm just looking for someone. You help me out, I'll make it worth your while."

Kevin relaxed a little. His eyes lit up as fear gave way to opportunity. "Yeah?"

Roach smiled. "Yeah. You tell me what you know, I'll leave here without breaking both your arms."

The fear returned to Kevin's face. He held his hands up. "Hey, hey, come on, man. Most people offer money for shit like this."

Roach leaned forward. "Do I look like most people to you?"

Kevin stared back into his soulless eyes. "Nah, man... you look like you really hate most people."

"Exactly. So, imagine how little patience I have for worthless stains like you. Do you know someone or not?"

"Okay, okay, chill." Kevin took some deep breaths. "I ain't never bought anything like that, man. But there is one guy. I don't know if he makes them or just sells them or what, but he owns the convenience store on Looker."

"Looker? Where's that?"

Kevin looked back toward the street and pointed. "Looker Street. It's… two blocks down, one block over from here. Word is, he has a stash he sells out back. Watches, jewelry, that kinda thing."

"Sounds promising. What's his name?"

"I don't know, man, I swear. He's the owner, that's all I know. Like I say, all that ain't my thing."

"Okay. Please understand, Kevin, if you're lying to me, I will make it my mission in life to find you and dissect you with a spoon."

Kevin nodded eagerly. "I get it, man. I get it. You're a scary bastard. I don't know if this is the guy you want, but I know he's probably the best person to ask."

Roach took a step back. "I appreciate that, thank you. Now, turn out your pockets."

"W-what?"

"Did I speak Mandarin? Empty your fucking pockets."

Kevin's hoodie had a front pouch. He rummaged inside it, pulling out a wallet, a cell phone, and a small plastic baggy with a couple of ounces of weed inside it.

Roach grabbed the wallet, looked inside, and took the fifty dollars he found there. He then dropped the wallet and held the money up to Kevin's face. "Consider this an anonymous donation to a cause that will spend it more wisely than you." He nodded at the bag of weed. "Make better life choices. Now, get out of here before I decide I need a new phone too."

Kevin crouched to scoop up his wallet, then ran away back along the alley and disappeared around the same corner his dealer had minutes earlier. Roach watched him go, then smiled to himself.

"Kids."

He headed back to the street and turned right, walking

with renewed purpose. As he drew level with the homeless man, he ducked low and dropped the fifty dollars in the man's lap.

"Get yourself something to eat, friend," he said quietly.

The man looked up at him. His face was black with dirt, and his beard was long and unkempt. "God bless you. Thank you."

"Don't mention it."

He continued walking, ignoring the looks of disgust from people around him. That reaction was exactly why he turned his back on the world.

The directions Kevin had given him led to a run-down corner store. Iron bars were bolted over the windows on the left and right sides. The door was stood open in the corner between them. Above it was a broken sign; the red fiberglass was shattered in places, revealing the wiring of the lights behind it.

Roach headed inside. The rattle of an air conditioner on its last legs hummed in the background. The faint aroma of stale coffee drifted over from the self-service machine halfway along the right wall. Three aisles stretched from front to back, lined with alcohol, magazines, snacks, and toiletries.

He walked over to the counter on the left. Its surface strewn with stands displaying candy bars and soda. Standing behind it was a man who looked much older than him, hunched over a newspaper laid open on the counter. Loose, weathered skin hung from his face. His eyes were sunken behind a pair of glasses resting low on his nose.

"Afternoon," said Roach politely.

The man nodded courteously. "Afternoon."

"Are you the owner here?"

The man straightened and removed his glasses. "I am. Can I help you?"

"I hope so." He looked around casually, making sure there was no one else nearby. "I'm looking to buy a watch. A nice one. But I don't want to spend a fortune, and I was told this was the place to come."

The owner eyed him warily. "This ain't a jewelry store, pal. Only watches I got are plastic with pictures of SpongeBob on them."

Roach nodded. "Well, the way I hear it, there are some things you don't keep out on display."

"Is that right? And where did you hear that?"

"A guy I know from around here, Kevin. Honestly... he's where I get my weed from."

"Weed's legal in this state."

Roach smiled. "Not the amounts I use."

The owner stared at him for a moment, then shook his head and smiled. "I think I might have what you're looking for. Just give me a second." He walked out from behind the counter and looked back toward the storeroom in the far corner. "Donny!" he shouted.

A young man appeared in the doorway, wearing a stained apron and holding a box. "Yeah?" he called back.

"Come watch the store for a few minutes, would ya?"

Donny placed the box down and wandered over without complaint. The owner watched him take the spot behind the counter, then set off toward the storeroom.

"Follow me," he said over his shoulder.

Roach walked a couple of steps behind him as he led him through the store and into the back room.

"I'm Carl, by the way. People around here call me Ticker."

Roach suppressed an eyeroll. "Because of the watch thing... got it."

Carl chuckled. "You catch on fast. So, what are you in the market for?"

"Something... I don't know. Shiny?"

Carl glanced back at him. "First time buying a high-end timepiece?"

"First time buying one, period."

"Well, you came to the right place."

The storeroom was a large square with racks of metal shelving in the middle for storage. They were half-full of boxes and packs of various items sold in the store. There were also three doors. Two were on the left. One was open, leading to a small kitchenette. The other was closed, with a sign stuck unevenly to it, declaring it was the fire exit. The third was opposite, in the right corner. It had a chain and padlock around the handle.

Carl headed for it, taking a key out of his pocket. He wrestled with the lock and slid the chain free. He opened it and reached around, fumbling for a light switch. He clicked it to reveal a small space with metal stairs descending to a basement. Without a word, he headed down them into the gloom. Roach looked around skeptically, then followed.

At the bottom, Carl flicked another switch. There was a buzz and a click, and pale fluorescent flooded the basement, forcing Roach to squint. Once his eyes adjusted, he failed to hide genuine surprise.

Before him was a large workshop. Every inch of the walls was covered by shallow display cases, showing off dozens, if not hundreds of watches. Various workstations were placed throughout, each housing different tools that Roach assumed were used to make watches.

"Holy shit..." he muttered.

Carl ignored his shock. "Feel free to look around. Anything you see in the cases is for sale. Something catches your eye, I'm sure I can do you a good price."

"Yeah, thanks," said Roach absently as he walked slowly through the clandestine workshop.

He was genuinely surprised by the scale of the operation. His gamble with Kevin had paid off in a big way. This Carl *had* to be the man he was looking for. But he needed to know for sure.

"So, Carl," he began. "This place is… impressive. Do you actually make some of these yourself, or…"

Carl laughed. He leaned against one of the benches nearby, puffed his chest out, and folded his arms across it. "I make *all* of them."

Roach looked at him and frowned. "On your own? Damn. How do you find the time?" He smiled. "No pun intended."

Carl laughed again. "I like that one! Might use that myself. But the truth is, since business upstairs picked up a little, I don't make many new ones myself anymore." He gestured to the walls. "Everything here, that's all me. But new stock, I usually outsource. I have suppliers I trust. I just do the odd one here and there, when the price justifies it."

Roach wandered slowly, aimlessly around until he was close to Carl.

"So, decided what you want?" he asked.

"Yeah," said Roach. "Answers."

He lunged for Carl, pinning him backward over the workbench he was leaning against, clasping a hand over his mouth. His arms flailed with shock, but Roach simply moved closer to his side, inside his reach. He grabbed a nearby screwdriver and pressed the sharp head against the soft flesh of Carl's throat.

"I want to know everything about the deal you have with Thomas Pope," he said, glaring into Carl's wide, fearful eyes. "If you lie to me, I'll kill you. If you leave anything out, I'll kill you. You make any noise besides speaking words to me, I'll kill you. All things considered, from here on out, you're going to need to work *really* hard to stay alive. Was anything I just said unclear to you?"

Beneath his grip, Carl shook his head.

"Good." Roach lifted his hand from over his mouth, then stepped away. "Start talking."

Carl leaned on his side, catching his breath. "What the hell is this? Are you a cop?"

Roach rolled his eyes. "Jesus. Why does everyone think that? No, I'm not a cop."

"Then how do you know Thomas Pope?"

"Oh, he and I go way back."

"How do you know about my deal with him?"

"Okay… you seem to have forgotten how this works. *You* answer *my* questions, not the other way around. Do you make fake watches for Thomas Pope to sell at auction?"

Carl hesitated, swallowing hard. "If I say anything to you, he'll kill me."

Roach shrugged. "Weren't you paying attention a minute ago?"

"Yes, but he—"

"Isn't here. I am. You should be more concerned about your immediate future."

Carl sighed. "All right, all right. Fine. Yes, I make watches for him."

"How does it work?"

"I make them to order. Usually, four or five per week. I tell him when they're ready. He sends someone over to pick them up and drop off payment."

Roach nodded. "Why you?"

"Take a look around, pal. My work is flawless. Indistinguishable from the real thing."

Roach stared at him. He had heard that phrase before, a few days ago. The guy in the pawn shop.

"They would be," said Roach, "if it weren't for the serial number. Right?"

Carl frowned. "What?"

"You know, the engraving on the back. The small one that should be the manufacturer I.D. That's what gives yours away." He saw the look of disbelief on Carl's face. "I got one appraised. The person who gave it to me didn't know it was fake."

"Look, I don't know, okay? I engrave what Mr. Pope tells me to. Made to order, whatever he wants. He pays good money. I don't care what it says."

"But you know it's effectively gibberish, right? As a professional."

He shrugged. "I mean, yeah, I know it's not a legit manufacturing signature or nothing."

"And you don't care?"

He shook his head. "Why would I?"

Roach stared at him. He was confident he had been told the truth. It might not make much sense to him right now, but he had more information than he had before. He had Pope's supply chain. He had the details of the scam from Chen, so he knew how Pope was playing Jasmine Decker. What he didn't have was proof. He also didn't know what the endgame was. He didn't understand how Pope was able to sell the watches Carl made for him for such ludicrous prices. But his gut told him the key to it was the engraving. It had to be. Why else would he order Carl to customize it?

He checked the watch Vanessa had given him, which he still had in his pocket.

He should get back.

"Okay, Carl," he said. "If anyone asks, I was never here, and we never had this conversation."

Carl held his hands up with resignation. "Hey, suits me. If Mr. Pope found out I said anything to anyone, I'd be dead within the hour."

"Are you really that scared of him?"

Carl huffed. "Are you kidding me? The man's a goddamn lunatic. You're damn right I'm scared, and if you're poking around his business, you should be too."

"Well, I don't scare that easy. Don't leave town. I might need you again."

Carl scoffed. "Couldn't if I wanted to. There's an auction tonight. Mr. Pope's guy will be here to collect the delivery in a couple of hours."

Roach held his gaze for a moment, briefly considering waiting around, but decided against it. He needed to get back to Vanessa.

He turned and headed for the stairs. As he set foot on them, he looked back over and smiled. "Thanks for your time, Carl."

Chapter Twenty-One

Roach kept the needle at sixty after he left Churchville's limits. He figured the only person who would pull him over for speeding was Sheriff Bushell, and right now, seeing him might not be a bad thing.

The trip to see the watchmaker took longer than he intended, but it proved useful. He now knew how Pope sourced the watches. He also all-but confirmed the significance of the serial number, although he still didn't understand its meaning.

Pope was running two scams: selling fake watches to rich idiots and hiding the unbelievable profits from his business partner. The problem was, Valentine would be dead in less than six hours if Roach didn't get proof of the second one, and to do that, he needed to fully understand the first one.

His frustration and concern made him press his foot a little harder on the gas, suddenly worried about Vanessa. His hand gripped the top of the wheel tightly, draining the color from his knuckles.

He was angry. This all started because he wanted break-fast. Now he was involved in something he didn't under-stand, with local criminals threatening his life. He should have left when he had the chance. The moment Bushell asked him to stay, he should have left the hospital, kept walking, and never looked back. This wasn't his problem.

Except now it was.

Vanessa might be safe from Jasmine Decker, but he didn't trust her husband. Thomas Pope was hiding some-thing, and Roach believed he would do anything to protect it, including jeopardize the safety of his wife.

Or worse.

He was out of options. He knew the moment he left Churchville, he only had one real move to make, and he didn't like it. It was risky, and if it backfired, it could expe-dite Valentine's pending execution.

But what choice did he have?

He took out the burner phone and hit speed dial to call Valentine's number. He put it on speaker and rested it in his lap, so he could focus on driving.

"Do you have what I asked for?" Jasmine Decker asked as she answered.

Roach winced begrudgingly. "Not yet."

"Then why are you calling me?"

"Because getting you proof isn't easy. I'm close, but..."

"But what?"

He sighed. "But I need your help."

Jasmine's laugh distorted over the poor-quality speaker of the cheap phone. "Are you kidding me? I expected more from you, Roach. This is... disappointing."

"Just... hear me out. Vanessa can't get the proof because it would draw too much suspicion from her husband, and I can't exactly walk into his house and go searching through his computer. But… I think I'm onto something, and I need help bringing it home."

There was a moment's pause.

"While that all sounds incredibly exciting," said Jasmine firmly, "it also sounds a lot like your problem. You know what I want, and you know what will happen if I don't get it. I don't have time for this."

"Believe me, if there was another way, I'd be taking it. I know the deal you have with Pope is a cut from the sale of the fake Churchville watches."

"Well, aren't you sharper than a tack? What do you want, a medal?"

"No, Jasmine, I want answers. I wish to God I didn't, but I'm invested in this thing now, and I need to see it through. I know exactly how he's scamming you. I just don't have the proof you want. Not yet."

"And how did you come by this information?"

Roach chose his words carefully. "I was given the inside track by a reliable source. Someone I trust."

She sighed. "I already told you. I'm not taking the word of his wife."

"The source isn't his wife. It's someone else."

Jasmine fell silent.

Roach shot past the hospital, approaching the center of town.

"And what did this… *source* tell you?" she asked finally.

Roach quickly debated with himself how much to reveal. He never liked revealing his hand. It left him vulnerable. It diminished his value. But he saw no harm in telling her what Chen had told him.

"The profits you get a piece of aren't from the sale of

the watches. Those payments are a deposit. The real sale happens after, for ten times that. That's what Pope's keeping for himself."

"Really…"

"Yes. It makes no sense to me why a rich asshole would buy a fake watch for half a million dollars. But to get you your proof, I need to figure it out."

"Fine. I'll play along," she said. "How can I help you, exactly?"

"There's an auction tonight. I intend to go and see for myself how all this works."

"Okay…"

"I need Hank with me."

Jasmine began laughing. It was exaggerated and without humor. "You expect me to surrender my only leverage over you and take your word you'll still deliver what I asked for?"

"I don't expect it. But you should."

"Why?"

"Because I'm many things, Jasmine, but I'm not a liar. I gave my word I would protect Vanessa and get you proof of Pope's transgressions. Right now, I need Hank's help to do both."

Jasmine sighed. "Uh-huh. That's admirable, Roach, but what's stopping me from just killing you and your friend right now, and forgetting about all of this?"

He thought for a moment, knowing the wrong answer could be deadly. He slowed to a sensible speed as he hit the center of Waters Point and took a left, bringing him back to the salon where Vanessa was waiting. He parked across the street and took the phone off speaker, holding it to his ear.

"Because you'll never know if you can really trust your business partner after this," he said finally. "I don't take you for the kind of woman who would be comfortable with that. You're smart, and you place a lot of stock in trust and respect. I knew that the moment I met you. Pope will never tell you the truth if you ask him outright. I'm your only real shot at finding out what's really going on here."

A tense silence hung over him. His jaw muscles pulsed with anxiety.

"Fine," said Jasmine eventually, sighing her reluctance. "You have until morning, and you can have your friend's help."

Roach relaxed his shoulders, breathing a silent sigh of relief. "Thank you."

"I don't like to be disappointed, Roach. Make sure I'm not."

"You won't be."

"Oh, and understand this…" Her tone darkened. "If you try to screw me, I will hunt you to the ends of the earth and kill you slowly in front of everyone you care about."

"Jasmine, if I were going to screw you, I'd have the decency to buy you a drink first."

She laughed. "There's the cutie I met last night. Your friend will be on *our* bridge in one hour."

The line clicked dead as Vanessa opened the door and slid gracefully inside. She was sporting a freshly styled hair and new nails.

"Are you okay?" she asked. "You were gone for ages. I was beginning to worry."

Roach looked over at her and forced a smile. "I'm fine. Sorry. You look great."

"Thank you," she replied, blushing slightly. "So, where were you?"

He started the engine, checked around, then spun the

car around the quiet street, heading north. "I'll tell you on the way."

Vanessa frowned. "On the way where?"

Roach didn't answer. He simply let out a long sigh, relieved that his negotiating skills were better than he thought.

Chapter Twenty-Two

The sun was beginning its descent as they approached the bridge. Pale yellow had morphed into deep orange, turning the sky into an oil painting. The tall trees were losing their definition, becoming silhouettes that loomed over the quiet roads.

They cruised along the road just above the speed limit. Inside the car, Roach had turned the air conditioning off, comfortable enough with the evening temperature. The silence was palpable. Vanessa hadn't spoken since Roach had told her what he had learned in Churchville.

Roach glanced at her, growing uneasy with the quiet. "You okay?"

Vanessa shook her head and bit her bottom lip to keep her tears at bay.

"Yeah… silly question, I guess."

"Sorry. I'm fine. It's just… *God*…" She let out a long, tired sigh. "I knew there had to be something about Thomas's business he wasn't telling me, but this… I just can't believe it. How can he be involved in something of this scale?"

"I know it's a lot to take in," said Roach, trying to offer some comfort. "Believe me, I know. But right now we need to accept the fact this is happening and focus on figuring it all out so we can get Jasmine her proof."

The bridge was just ahead, around a slight bend.

"Look, Vanessa, I think it's best if you—"

"Oh my God!"

She pointed animatedly at the road ahead. Roach looked and saw a dark shape lying in the middle of the bridge. It quickly took the form of a body. A heartbeat later and he recognized Valentine's discolored coat. He slammed on the brakes the moment he crossed the riveted metal of the bridge's edge, sliding to a halt with only a few feet to spare.

"Jesus!" he gasped, gripping the wheel tightly with both hands. "Are you okay?"

Vanessa nodded but said nothing.

Roach clambered out of the car and rushed to Valentine's side. He knelt beside him and rested a hand on his shoulder. There was an audible groan. He threaded his other hand beneath the arm and guided Valentine up on one knee. From there, he pushed himself upright of his own accord. Roach stood and stepped back, holding his arm out should Valentine need it for balance.

"Shit, are you okay?" asked Roach.

Valentine turned to him. His face was bruised and bloody. His long coat was more stained with dirt than ever. His left knuckles were split, and his hand was shaking slightly, seemingly beyond his control. He smiled weakly. "Heh. You should… see the other guys."

Roach shook his head. "You manage to take a few of them out?"

Valentine furrowed his brow. "Huh? No. They kicked the crap outta me. I'm saying… you should've seen them. It was impressive."

Roach rolled his eyes. "Come on, we need to get you cleaned up."

Valentine stubbornly brushed him aside as he staggered toward the Porsche. "Ah, fuck that. I just need a drink and I'll be… I'll be fine."

He stumbled toward the car as Roach followed close behind. As he passed by the front of the vehicle, his legs buckled. He raised his hands to protect himself, slapping both palms down on the hood, leaving bloody handprints behind. Valentine looked up and saw Vanessa standing beside the open passenger door, watching him. He looked down at the hood, then back up at her.

"Heh. Sorry about that," he said drowsily. "I'll get it… cleaned."

Vanessa smiled sympathetically and moved to his side. "Don't be silly. Just… try not to get any blood on the upholstery, okay?"

Valentine chuckled, then looked back over at Roach, who had moved to the driver's door. "I like her."

Roach and Vanessa exchanged a brief smile, then she stepped aside, gesturing to the rear seat. "Come on, let's get you freshened up. You're no use to anyone like this."

Valentine shuffled to the side. "Ah. You sound like… my mother."

Before he could duck inside, Roach clapped a hand on the roof to get his attention. As he looked over, Roach pointed at him.

"Hey, don't be a hero, you stubborn asshole. Jasmine

Decker only let you go because I told her I needed your help, and I wasn't lying. We have work to do tonight, and I want to be sure you're not going to collapse on me."

Valentine waved him away. "I've been through worse. Bunch of goddamn city boys. Punch like Girl Scouts. I told you, I just need a drink."

"Yeah, yeah… you said. Now, get in the car. Time's a-wasting."

He went to duck inside again, but was distracted by a single loud whoop, accompanied by blue and red flashing lights. The three of them looked back along the road to see the sheriff's cruiser prowl into view. It stopped at an angle across both lanes of the road leading onto the bridge. Sheriff Bushell and Deputy Henderson climbed out, their hands hovering over their weapons.

"Mind telling me what the hell's going on here?" asked the sheriff. His tone was relaxed but authoritative.

Roach threw his head back, sighed exasperatedly at the sky, and muttered, "Are you fucking kidding me?"

"What are you doing here, Sheriff?" asked Vanessa.

Bushell nodded courteously toward her. "Mrs. Pope. I'm glad to see you up and about." He pointed at Roach. "After I bumped into our mutual friend here earlier, I knew something was off. So, I decided to follow him. And here, I find you loading a barely conscious body into the back seat of your car. Someone care to explain?"

Roach walked slowly around the car, putting himself between the new arrivals and his friends. "Sheriff, look. Now isn't the time. My friend is hurt and needs medical attention. Unless you're going to escort us to the hospital, I need you to get out of my way."

Bushell shook his head. "Not until you tell me what's going on. I know you're involved."

"Involved?" spluttered Valentine impatiently. He wrestled himself upright using the roof of the car for leverage. "He's trying to help stop what's going on here, you blind idiot. We all are."

Bushell looked at him. "Uh-huh. And how's that going for *you* so far, eh?"

"Ah, a minor setback."

"Right. Tell me, sir, what are you today? A lawyer or a doctor?"

Roach sighed again. "Sheriff, we're wasting time. I want to figure out what's going on around here just as much as you do. Hopefully, by tonight, I'll have some answers for you."

Bushell relaxed his posture and frowned. "What do you mean?"

"There's an auction tonight. I suspect the reason you have five dead bodies and keep finding me in fights is because of something shady going on there. I intend to find out what."

The sheriff shook his head. "No way you'll get in there. Aside from the fact that Mr. Pope clearly dislikes you, you're dressed like shit. No offense. Those things are really fancy. Black tie, suits, the whole nine. Town's already filling up with folks visiting for it."

Vanessa stepped to Roach's side. "He'll be escorting me. He *is* my personal bodyguard, after all. You think my husband is going to turn me away?"

Bushell took a symbolic step back and his hands up in apology. "Of course not, Mrs. Pope. I meant nothing by it. I'm just trying to figure all this out and keep this town safe." He turned to Roach. "You just said something about answers. Care to elaborate? You think the auction is rigged or something?"

Roach glanced back at Valentine. "We really can't—"

The gunshot came from nowhere, amplified by the silence around them. Vanessa screamed. Roach jolted with shock, stepping back into an instinctive yet futile fighting stance. Valentine didn't react. He was too tired and sore.

Bushell dropped to his knees, then fell forward. A pool of blood expanded out from beneath him. The warm light of the setting sun reflected in it.

Deputy Henderson took a step forward. His gun was trained on Roach. Whispers of smoke danced from the barrel.

"This has gone on long enough," he said. "Mrs. Pope… get in the squad car. Your husband would like a word with you."

Roach stared, dumbstruck. The timid, uncertain deputy that had cuffed him a couple of days ago was gone. The man in front of him was calm, calculated, and confident.

He was a killer.

"Now, Mrs. Pope," urged Henderson.

When she didn't move, the deputy began walking toward them. Roach stepped in front of her, ensuring his body shielded hers completely.

"Touch her and I'll break your neck," he stated.

Henderson stopped and smiled. "Is that so?"

He put a hand to his mouth and unleashed a loud whistle, then waved a hand at something behind them. Roach frowned and turned to see lights approaching them from the other side of the bridge. As they got closer, the shape of Sutton's pick-up became clear.

Roach's shoulders dropped with defeat. He looked back at Henderson. "You're working for Pope. This whole time."

"I help him stay informed on the movements of the sheriff's department."

"The whole bumbling idiot routine… all just an act?"

Henderson smiled. "No one thinks twice about a nervous rookie."

Roach glanced down at the sheriff. He was still alive, but his movements were restricted to an uncomfortable squirm.

"Bushell didn't know?"

Henderson scoffed. "Please. Bushell's never set foot outside this town. He's so filled with the pride of home. He has no idea how the world works. Walks around this place like he's Clint fucking Eastwood. It's insufferable."

Roach narrowed his eyes, boring a hole into his skull with his cold gaze. "Before all this is said and done, I'm going to kill you. I want you to know that."

Henderson grinned. "Sure thing, Buttercup."

He nodded with a flick of his head. Roach turned around to see Sutton standing right behind him, flanked by the two guys he didn't manage to knock out earlier.

"Nighty-night, asshole," said Sutton. His sickening sneer revealed his yellowed teeth.

Roach saw the swing. It came fast, out of his blind spot. He didn't see what Sutton was holding in his hand. He didn't have time to react. He felt the impact on the side of his head, but he was unconscious before he hit the ground.

Chapter Twenty-Three

The journey through the darkness had felt infinite. An endless nightmare that had evolved into a twisted blanket. The demons that swirled around him had become friends. The fall had become almost meditative.

But he sensed it was almost over.

The specters of his sins no longer fell with him. They circled together, watching him from above. The white light beneath him was getting warmer. Its source grew closer with each heartbeat.

He was afraid. Always afraid. Of his life. Of his surroundings. Of himself.

At first, he was scared of the darkness. But then he embraced it and learned to enjoy it. Now that he was leaving it again, he was scared of what the light would bring.

He stared up at the ghosts of his past, who had dragged him into this abyssal prison in the first place. He pleaded with them to let him stay. But he made no sound. They simply stared back at his silent screams, watching patiently.

He had been scared of them too. When they first yanked him free of his resting place, he had been frightened by them. They clawed at his flesh and tugged at his clothes. They screamed at him. They were desperate to get him here, into their darkness. But as they took form… as they revealed themselves to be faces from his past, his fear subsided. He saw them for what they were.

Friends.

So, why would friends allow him to feel afraid? Why would they take him here and help him feel comfortable and safe, only to stand by and do nothing as he was pulled away again?

The light got warmer. The darkness had all but melted away from around him. He lay back, suspended in nothing between the black and the white.

Maybe that was it.

His ethereal companions stopped on the precipice, where darkness became light. They didn't follow him. Perhaps they couldn't. Maybe this whole time, they were never trying to drag him further into a punishing solitude…

Maybe they were trying to free him from it.

The realization hit him like a freight train. It frustrated him that he didn't see it sooner.

This was his journey. He began trapped, buried beneath guilt and hatred. These spirits broke him out and guided him through the darkness, leading him to where he needed to be. Where he should've been all along.

To the light.

He stopped trying to scream. He took a calming breath and reached out, holding an arm up to the dark sky, filled with untold numbers of past demons. In unison, each one extended a thin, bony arm back.

They were saying goodbye.

He took another deep breath. He closed his eyes, held both arms out to side, and turned, rolling over so that he was no longer looking up at the darkness he had come from. He was now facing the light that awaited him.

He took another deep breath. Slow. Calm. Accepting.

He opened his eyes.

Roach was sitting on a cold, damp, wooden floor. It was dark. It took a moment for his eyes to adjust to the gloom. It took another for him to process his surroundings.

In front of him, he could see the cove. The water lapped beneath the last remnants of daylight. A speedboat bounced lazily on the flow, moored alongside a jetty, partially enclosed with them. To his right, a wooden frame jutted out from the wall, with steps on both sides leading up to a small mezzanine and the door leading out of the boathouse.

His head hurt. His hands were bound behind him. He was disoriented.

A sudden thought of Vanessa overwhelmed him, and he looked around desperately to find her. She wasn't there.

"He's awake," said a voice.

Valentine.

Roach searched to find him. He found his friend sitting a few feet away, against a wooden wall. He was slumped slightly to the side. His hands were behind him, presumably bound. But he was conscious.

"Where… where are we?" Roach asked drowsily. "What happened? Where's Vanessa?"

A deep, muffled moan from his right dragged his attention away. He looked around to see Sheriff Bushell sitting upright against a small stack of wooden boxes. He looked in pain. His face was contorted with discomfort, and he winced with each breath. The sheriff's hands were pressed against his gut. Blood seeped through his fingers.

"Shit…" he muttered.

Bushell looked at him. "To answer your… questions, given there's a speedboat in front of us, I'm guessing we're in the... old boathouse on the cove, at the foot of the... of the hill the auction house is built on. We... we got jumped by Thomas Pope's men shortly after my... my goddamn deputy betrayed me. As for Mrs. Pope... she ain't here. I don't know if she's... if she's safe."

Roach nodded. "Okay. Sheriff, you need to get to the hospital. That gunshot wound isn't getting any better."

"I'd love to, but I'm... ah... kinda busy right now."

"Yeah." He turned to look at Valentine. "How are you doing?"

The bruised and battered P.I. raised his head slowly. "I'm peachy."

Roach rolled his eyes, impatient with the sarcasm and annoyed at himself for asking such a futile question. He looked back at the sheriff. He studied the wound as much as he could in the growing gloom.

He had to keep Bushell conscious somehow.

"Sheriff, I... I owe you an apology," he said.

Bushell frowned. "Why?"

"Because I figured you were in on this thing. Whatever it is. That's why I was so guarded around you. But you're clearly not."

The sheriff looked at him with tired eyes. "Clearly. So, you finally gonna tell me what... the hell is going on around here?"

Roach glanced over at Valentine. "Hank, you care to explain? You'll likely be more concise than me."

Valentine scoffed. "I doubt it. I haven't had a drink in a few hours. But here goes. Sheriff, I'm working a missing person's case. A couple hired me to find their kid. Local cops were nowhere. My own investigation led me to Waters Point. A vehicle from the scene of the abduction was registered to a company owned by Thomas Pope. Things went cold the moment I arrived. I hung around because I hoped to catch a break.. Two days later…" He nodded to Roach. "This guy showed up and saved Mrs. Pope from an unnecessary ass-kicking. Things have been going to shit ever since."

Bushell sighed. "Okay. Now, get to the part where I'm tied up with a hole in my gut…"

Valentine flashed a small smile of admiration. "The men who attacked her… and then tried attacking Roach… work for Jasmine Decker."

"Never heard of her."

"She's Thomas Pope's business partner. He's running a scam through the auction house, selling fake watches to all the rich assholes who descend on this place each week. She's taking a cut."

"Huh. So, the patron saint of Waters Point is crooked? Honestly, I'm not surprised."

"You suspected something?" asked Roach.

Bushell shrugged. "Yes and no. Stranger moves in and starts flashing money around, buying popularity… to me, that always feels off. But there was never anything to suggest he… he was doing anything wrong. I was just glad to see this place thriving again."

Valentine coughed up a little blood, which he spat unceremoniously on the floor beside him. "Well, I ain't got to the best part yet. Turns out ol' Thomas is actually scamming his partner too. His wife found evidence of large profits he wasn't exactly rushing to declare on his monthly P and L reports. She reached out to Decker but changed her mind before giving her the proof. Decker wanted the information, so sent people after her."

Bushell frowned. "So, the fellas who came after her… they were Decker's boys?"

"Yup."

"So, who killed *them*?"

Roach shook his head. "No idea. But she knows someone did, and she's pissed. I don't get her the proof to back up Vanessa's claims by tomorrow, she's going to wage war on this town."

Bushell rolled his eyes. "Wonderful. Does Thomas know?"

"I don't know for sure, but he definitely suspects something. Especially after Vanessa asked to hire me to protect her."

"Huh." He stared at Roach. "I guess that explains why you've been going all over town kicking people's asses."

Roach smiled. "I was just protecting myself and Vanessa when I needed to. But... I get that it looked bad. Sorry."

Bushell tried to smile. The result more closely resembled a crooked grimace. "Your unwillingness to talk to me didn't help."

"I didn't know if I could trust you."

"Do you trust me now?"

"Yes."

Bushell chuckled, resulting in another wince of discomfort. "Well, how about that. Only took me... getting shot."

Suddenly, the door clicked and creaked open above them. They fell silent and waited. Three men filed inside and headed down the left set of steps. Chen was first, with Sutton behind him and Mustache at the back.

Chen stopped and turned to face them, putting his back to the water and the boat. He nodded to Sutton, who looked at Mustache and pointed toward Valentine. Between them, they hustled around the small pier and rough-housed Roach and Valentine over to where the sheriff was slumped, positioning all three of them in a row against the stack of crates.

Roach seethed quietly, glaring daggers at the new arrivals.

"Is Vanessa okay?" he asked through clenched teeth. "Where is she?"

"None of your goddamn business, asshole." said Sutton before stepping forward and slapping Roach across the face.

He started laughing as he stepped back.

Roach looked up at him, staring through his brow, his eyes losing any glint of humanity.

Sutton saw his expression and laughed harder, wiggling his fingers at him like he was a child on Halloween. "Ooo, scary! Prick."

He fell back in line beside Chen, who watched impassively for a moment, then took a deep breath and looked along the line at each of them in turn.

"Mr. Pope wants the three of you gone," he said. He drew a gun from the back of his waistband and held it low, by his side. "So, any last words?"

Bushell grimaced and groaned as he tried to shuffle more upright. He pressed hard against the hole in his side, trying to ignore the pain. "You can't just kill me, asshole. I'm the sheriff. You'll have state troopers crawling all over this town by morning."

Sutton scoffed. "You think that's an issue for Mr. Pope? Please! Besides, who's gonna tell them? Your deputy?"

He threw his head back and belly laughed. On the other side of Chen, Mustache joined in.

Chen remained calm and emotionless. He hadn't taken his eyes off Roach. He paced idly away to the side, moving closer to Valentine. He stopped and turned, looking at the three men, all beaten and bloody and bruised, huddled together on the floor.

"You should've left town when I gave you the chance," he said directly to Roach. "What happens next is on you."

Roach shook his head slightly, not breaking eye contact. "You have no idea the whirlwind of shit that's about to hit this place. Kinda glad I won't be here to deal with it."

The corner of Chen's mouth curled slightly. Then he snapped his arm up and fired twice.

Roach flinched. The sudden noise surprised him. Neither Valentine nor Bushell reacted. They just stared blankly ahead and watched as Sutton and Mustache fell backward into the water, dead.

Chen held his arm out for a moment, temporarily mesmerized by the whisps of smoke dancing from the barrel. Then he took it back behind him and retrieved a flick knife from his pocket. He walked over to Valentine, then Roach, and cut the ties that held their hands behind them.

Roach was first to his feet. He rotated each wrist in turn, loosening the joints. He nodded his gratitude toward Chen.

"Thanks," he said.

"You need to get out of here," he said with urgency. "Vanessa's safe for now. But Mr. Pope won't let her leave his side. He suspects something, and I don't think we have much time before he figures out what she intended to do."

"No, we don't. Jasmine Decker has given me until morning to get proof of what Pope's doing. If I don't deliver, she's coming here looking for blood."

Chen didn't look concerned. "Honestly, she wouldn't stand a chance."

Roach frowned. "Are you serious? She's a much bigger deal than your boss ever will be."

Chen smiled, but it wasn't out of humor. It was pity. "Mr. Pope isn't the man you think he is."

"An asshole?" scoffed Valentine.

Chen rolled his eyes. "Not what I meant."

"I'm not afraid of Thomas Pope," said Roach. "But I have no wish to be standing in the middle of a turf war when Jasmine Decker comes knocking at your door."

Chen sighed. "Then maybe this will help."

He handed him his gun, then a set of keys and a small flash drive from his pocket.

"What's this?" asked Roach, holding the drive between his finger and thumb.

"The proof you wanted."

"Seriously? How did you—"

"It doesn't matter. You have it. Do whatever you have to do. I need to go before someone starts asking questions." He stood upright, pushing his shoulders back. "Make it look good."

Roach nodded back, then dropped him with a stiff punch to the jaw. Chen was out, but he wouldn't be for long. He didn't want to injure him too badly. Just enough to be believable.

He turned to Valentine. "Get the sheriff in the boat. We don't have a lot of time."

Valentine simply nodded, then shuffled over to Bushell, who was already trying to get to his feet.

"Does somebody want to tell me what in the blue hell is going on?" he said.

"I will once I figure out how to drive this boat," said Roach, who had already climbed inside it.

A few moments later, the engine spluttered into life. Valentine and Bushell were slumped side by side in the back. Roach guided them out of the boathouse berth, then opened it up and sped away across the cove, heading south toward the road that led him into town a few days ago.

Chapter Twenty-Four

The moon had risen by the time they reached Waters Point. They had moored the speedboat beside the southern bridge and quickly discussed their next move. Their priority had been getting to the hospital. Sheriff Bushell was on borrowed time, and Valentine could barely stand up. Roach was sore, but the overwhelming waves of fury crashing over him like a tsunami helped him power through.

Walking to the hospital wasn't an option. Bushell's suggestion to call his remaining deputy, Mills, and have him pick them up was initially met with skepticism. Henderson had been bought and paid for by Thomas Pope, so who was to say he was the only one? But Bushell had vouched for Mills. He was family—his brother-in-law's youngest cousin. He said he would bet his life Mills wasn't corrupt. Valentine had pointed out that was essentially what he was doing by calling him. But call him they did. Deputy Mills arrived within twenty minutes and drove like the devil, straight to the hospital.

An hour later, Roach was pacing back and forth inside

the room like a caged animal. Valentine was sitting shirtless on the bed, and a doctor was standing over him, stitching one of the deeper cuts on his shoulder.

"Jesus Christ, would you sit down?" said Valentine coarsely. "You're giving me a headache."

Roach ignored him. He was trying to work through his anger, so he could think clearly.

The doctor straightened and took a step back. He took a deep breath and rested his hands on his hips. He was a young man, not long removed from his internship. His eyes weren't yet permanently darkened by years of sleep deprivation.

"There," he said. "That should heal fine in a week or so. Just try not to aggravate the stitches in the meantime. Everything else… well… you're gonna be sore for a few days. I can give you something for the pain if you'd like?"

Valentine looked up at him as he shrugged his shirt on. "If I take your meds, can I drink?"

The doctor shook his head. "It's not recommended, no."

"Then you can shove them up your ass."

The doctor didn't reply. He headed for the door, nodding courteously to Roach as he passed.

Valentine got slowly to his feet and reached for his coat, which lay on the bed. He held it up and fumbled inside the pocket for his hip flask. He took a deep swig from it, grimacing at the taste, then sucked in a breath through gritted teeth as he felt the comfort of the afterburn.

He held the flask out to Roach, who declined with a shake of his head. Valentine shrugged and took another sip.

"How's the sheriff?" he asked.

Roach shrugged. "They took him into surgery almost

immediately. It's going to be a few hours before we know anything. That gut shot, though… it didn't look good."

Valentine sat back down on the bed. "Try not to think about it. There's nothing more we can do for him now. We need to figure out what we do next." He checked his watch. "We've lost a couple of hours. The auction has already started, and by now, Pope is sure to know we escaped. No way we're getting within a mile of that place now."

Roach stopped pacing. He leaned back against the strip of wall between the doorway and the window of the room. He started at the floor. He was angry, but he felt in control of it. It felt… useful.

"What do we know?" he asked.

Valentine took a deep breath. "We know Pope's fake watches are selling for ten times what the real thing would be worth. There's more to them than we know."

Roach nodded. "We know Jasmine Decker gets a cut from the initial sale, but not from the secondary sale, where the real money is. That's all Pope."

"We also know she's prepared to come after him if we get her proof, which we definitely don't want to be here for."

"Agreed. I don't know what Chen gave me on that flash drive. We should find out. If it's enough to satisfy her, we need to get Vanessa to safety before she tears this place apart."

"That might be easier said than done. Even if Decker gives us the time, Chen said Vanessa wasn't allowed to leave her husband's side. If he's at the auction, she will be too. She won't be easy to get to."

"Here's what I don't understand," said Roach, pushing himself away from the wall. "Everyone who works for Pope seems scared of him, like he's some dangerous psychopath.

Even Chen, who can handle himself. You seem to know this town inside and out. What am I missing?"

Valentine shook his head. "I don't know. People in town are grateful for what he's done for the place. I think some of them suspect he isn't exactly on the level. Bushell certainly did. But lack of evidence means nobody says anything. They're happy to ride the wave of increased business and low taxes. Pope is a ruthless sonofabitch, but I just can't see him being a physical threat."

"Me neither. I've met people who are. They don't hire this much security. Hurts their ego."

"So, there's something else. Something more to him. If he doesn't have strength, he has power. He certainly has the financial means to acquire it."

Roach nodded. "And the influence. Vanessa said the auctions attract a lot of rich and powerful people from all over the country. She mentioned CEOs and politicians. Pope's phonebook must be overflowing with people he can call on for favors. Maybe that's it?"

"Maybe. Which *does* kinda make you think…"

Roach frowned. "About?"

"About whether it's smart to pick a fight with someone with so much power and influence."

Roach held his gaze. "I've done it before, with people much more powerful and influential than Thomas Pope will ever be."

Valentine stood gingerly. "Yeah. I've been meaning to ask you about that."

"What?"

"Well, for the last few days, you've been wandering around this place playing detective for a woman you barely know, despite having negotiated her safety with the person who was threatening it. Yes, her husband's a piece of shit.

And yes, I know I encouraged you to help her. But why are you still here, risking your life?"

Roach raised an eyebrow. "You can't talk."

Valentine shrugged. "Yeah, but I *am* a detective. And all this bullshit is an extension of the case that brought me here. But you... I know what you've done in the past. The good and the bad. A few years ago, you helped save this country from a dictatorship, for Christ's sake. You traveled the length and breadth of this country, inspiring millions of refugees. Giving people hope when there was none. You're a... fucking *hero*, Roach."

Roach grimaced at Valentine's use of the word, then shook his head and smiled weakly. "You know, Vanessa said the same thing to me earlier today."

"You told her?"

He nodded. "Didn't feel right, her not knowing who I was when everyone else seems to."

"Well, she was right. But the point I'm trying to make here, Roach, is that after a couple of years in exile, you resurfaced *here*, in the middle of nowhere, and landed yourself between two criminals who, as far as we know, don't even officially know they're on the brink of war with each other. We have conspiracy, corrupt cops, unexplained deaths, *and* a damsel in distress... and we're doing what? Standing here clueless with our thumbs up our asses when we have a goddamn nuclear warhead in our arsenal! Isn't it about time you just put an end to all this?"

Roach took a deep breath. He thought about what Valentine said. He thought about his conversation with Vanessa earlier. He thought about the sheriff, currently undergoing surgery that may well save his life. He thought about the dreams he had been having lately, about coming out of the darkness.

"You're right, Hank," he said quietly.

"Excuse me?"

Roach sighed. "I said, you're right. Whatever's going on here pales in comparison to the shit I've seen and done. But I... I can't explain it..." He began pacing again in front of Valentine, who watched patiently. "I've been having these dreams. I think they're symbolic of how I've been at war with myself. For a long time. Since before all this... before what happened with Orion, and Tristar... before my coma. See, I've always known I'm capable of violence. I've always tried to do the right thing, but I know I often didn't. I decided it was better for me and safer for everyone else to just walk away and leave the world behind. But maybe I wasn't the danger. Maybe I just wasn't ready to accept the way things are now."

Valentine smiled. "Roach, my friend, I could've told you that the first time I spoke to you."

Roach rolled his eyes. "My sister really would like you."

The two men shared a moment of silence.

"So, what are you saying?" asked Valentine finally.

Roach sighed. "I'm saying, my priority has always been protecting Vanessa, not stopping a war between Jasmine Decker and Thomas Pope. But maybe I've been looking at this all wrong. She has the numbers. He has the money. But I have *time*. I've got all the time in the world to put a stop to whatever the hell is going on around here. Not just because it will save Vanessa, but because it's the right thing to do."

Valentine shook his head, smiling begrudgingly. "Not sure many people in this town would agree with you."

"Not my problem. They're all living a better life on dirty money. If they know or suspect something but choose to do nothing and reap the benefits, they don't get a say in what happens."

"Huh. That's fair, I suppose."

Roach checked his watch. Vanessa's watch. The fake watch.

"You said the auction has started, right?" he said.

Valentine nodded. "Yeah, maybe an hour ago."

"And people who come to town for it tend to stick around afterward, right? Spend the night."

"Usually. What are you thinking?"

"I'm thinking there might be another way to get the answers we need without antagonizing our enemies." He smiled. "Let's go for a drink."

Valentine let out a huge sigh, throwing his head back exaggeratedly. "*Finally*, a plan I can get behind!"

Chapter Twenty-Five

The bar was busy. George and his staff were working hard, supplying drinks to the well-dressed patrons, fresh from the auction with money to spend.

Roach and Valentine sat quietly together at a small, round table in the back corner, in the shadow between a staircase and a jukebox. They watched as the place continued to fill with people, all dressed like they didn't belong. A sea of tuxedos and expensive dresses surrounded them. The air filled with laughter and conversation. Everyone talked loudly, as if volume was a sign of wealth and people were desperate to show off to their peers.

Roach stared at the crowd, lost in a trance, watching the movement without really seeing the people.

Forget my twisted dreams, he thought. *This is my nightmare.*

Valentine took a grateful sip of the expensive whiskey in his hand, admiring the glass like a connoisseur as he relished the warm taste. Then he tapped Roach's arm to get his attention and leaned forward slightly.

"So, while I appreciate the… finer points of your plan,"

he said, shaking his half-empty glass. "You wanna tell me why we're really here? I know it ain't because you're feeling sociable…"

Roach smiled briefly. "Everyone keeps saying how the auction is big business for the town. It attracts rich assholes from all over, right?"

Valentine glanced over his shoulder at the bar, then shrugged. "Yeah. Just a little."

"Well, Waters Point is in the middle of fucking nowhere, which means all those rich assholes are likely to stay the night. If you're staying the night, you're going to look for something to do."

Valentine nodded along. "You're going to come and drink and celebrate spending all that *rich asshole* money."

"Exactly. You keep telling me the best way to get to know a place is to talk to the people who live there. Idle conversation, right? Well, who talks more than a rich asshole looking to show off?"

Valentine smiled. "A *drunk* rich asshole."

"Ten points to you."

Valentine shuffled his chair around, putting his back to the wall so he could sit and face the room. Roach did the same. Both men scanned the crowd with expert eyes. Bodies swayed in the tide of humanity, constantly adjusting to make room for each other without spilling the drinks they were holding.

"It's busy," observed Valentine. "Lots of groups. Not gonna be easy to interrupt anyone and make it look casual. Even for me."

Roach nodded thoughtfully.

Then he saw it.

A momentary parting of the sea gave him line of sight to the bar. He saw two men standing side by side talking, away from the crowd, talking animatedly. Occasionally, they looked at each other and laughed, offering their side profiles. Neither was old, but they weren't young. Neither was overweight, but they weren't athletes. Neither was unattractive, but they weren't fighting off the ladies. They were two rich assholes enjoying their rich asshole lifestyle together, away from everyone else.

The perfect marks.

"There," said Roach. "By the bar."

Valentine leaned forward slightly to see them. He nodded. "Agreed. How do you want to play it?"

Roach thought for a moment. "Follow my lead."

He moved to stand, but Valentine shot his arm out to stop him. When Roach looked questioningly at him, he winced. "Are you sure that's the best way to go? I mean, you're… you know…"

Roach frowned. "What?"

"You."

"Meaning?"

"Meaning *that*. Right there. That look you're giving me now."

"What look?"

"The one that says you're trying to pull my spleen out through my ear with your mind."

"That's just how I look."

"I know. That's why you going over there and sparking a conversation with two douchebags in tuxedos is possibly the worst idea you've had since I've known you. We need to—"

Roach held his hand up. "Hank, look. We need answers. You might be better at this, but we don't have time to play the long game here."

"I completely agree. But that doesn't mean you can

threaten people into talking to you. This needs some finesse."

"It'll be fine. Come on."

Roach stood and set off toward the bar. Valentine hurriedly finished his drink and followed.

"Oh, this is a bad fucking idea..." he muttered.

He caught up to Roach just as he rested against the bar, beside the two men in tuxedos. He ordered two drinks, then turned to face them, smiling.

"Evening, fellas," he said. "You been to the auction tonight?"

The men looked around, eyeing him warily.

"No," one scoffed. "We're dressed like this because we live here."

He turned to his friend, and they shared an exaggerated laugh between them.

Valentine stared at Roach, expecting him to put the guy's head through the bar. But he didn't. In fact, he didn't acknowledge the comment at all.

"Yeah, my friend and I, we were late getting into town," he continued, seemingly oblivious. "Hoping to catch the next one, though."

The man looked back at him and scoffed. "You?"

Roach frowned. "Yeah. Why? Is something wrong?"

The man turned to face him. He laughed. "There's no way someone like *you* would get into a Pope auction. I bet you couldn't afford to open the door, let alone buy anything."

"What makes you think that?"

He laughed again. "Well, I mean, look at you. Scruffy jeans. A ten-dollar shirt. The cheapest item on offer tonight was thirty-seven thousand dollars."

Roach looked shocked. "Damn. What was it?"

"It was a watch," said the man's friend, leaning slightly to see past him. "A real beautiful piece."

"Does it do anything besides tell the time?"

The man frowned. "No…"

Roach chuckled. "Man, for that price, I'd expect a reach-around whenever I put it on!"

Neither man looked amused.

"Thomas Pope only finds the finest items to auction off. I bet that watch was worth more than you make in a year."

Roach nodded. "Huh. That's a little judgmental, don't you think? I'm just trying to be friendly. For all I know, you might not be able to afford anything either."

"Are you… are you kidding me? I'm Lyle Johnson. Of Perkins, Johnson, and Yates."

Roach stared blankly. "Okay…"

Johnson shook his head incredulously. "We're one of the biggest law firms in New York City."

Slowly, Roach began to nod. "Oh, right. Of course. Sorry. I didn't recognize you. You know, you look like a Johnson."

Valentine glanced away to hide his smile.

The comment was either misheard or misunderstood, as Johnson's beratement was unrelenting. "Not that you could afford a firm like mine anyway."

George appeared and placed two beers in front of Roach. As he reached for his wallet, Johnson held out his hand.

"You know what, allow me. It's the least I can do."

He produced a hundred-dollar bill and slapped it on the bar.

"Keep the change," he said to George. Then he looked at Roach. "Anything to help the less fortunate."

Roach took the drinks without hesitation and passed one

to Valentine. They locked eyes for a brief moment. Valentine flicked an eyebrow when he saw Roach's jaw pulsing.

Roach shook his head, then looked back at Johnson and his friend. "That's real kind of you. Thanks."

Johnson smiled. It was disingenuous and smarmy. "Any time. Now, if you'll excuse me, I want to get back to enjoying my night."

Roach held up a hand. "No problem. Sorry to interrupt." He looked at Valentine. "Come on, Hank. We should go."

"Yeah, you should," called Johnson as they walked away. "The dive bar is a few streets over."

The laughter faded behind them, swallowed by the noise of the bar as they headed for the door.

"How hard was it for you to not break that guy's jaw?" Valentine asked as he pushed the door open, allowing the night breeze to hit them.

He stepped outside. Roach chugged his bottle empty, placed it on a table, and followed him. They stood together at the side of the entrance.

Roach shrugged. "I would've felt bad for getting blood on such a nice suit. Besides, I got what I wanted."

"The free drink?"

"No. First, I got confirmation the watches are as big of a deal as we think they are. That prick could've mentioned anything that was listed for auction tonight. But he chose a watch. A rich lawyer like that, he's only interested in having the best. That means the watches are important. It also means he doesn't know what he's talking about because he clearly didn't know the watch was fake."

Valentine nodded. "Okay. I'll buy that. What was the second thing you got?"

Roach looked at him. "A target."

Chapter Twenty-Six

"We're up," said Roach quietly.

He and Valentine had stood in the shadows of a doorway across the street from the bar for the last hour, waiting. They had filled the time with idle conversation, but the temperature was dropping, and patience was beginning to wear thin for both men. Then Roach saw Johnson and his friend stumble out of the bar, laughing to each other.

They turned right. Had they gone left, Roach and Valentine would have tailed them back to their hotel, then stormed the room once they were settled. But they went right. That meant they needed to rush them as they drew level with the alley next to the bar, force them down it until the streetlights had no effect, and interrogate them there, as quickly and quietly as possible.

Their plan worked exactly as intended.

They were standing between the bar entrance and the alley. As Johnson and his friend walked past them, Roach and Valentine ran across the street, low and quiet. Johnson saw them as they stood in the jaws of the darkness between the bar and store next to it. Roach clasped a hand over his mouth and muscled him inside. Valentine did the same with his friend. Their footsteps crunched on the dust and grit and broken glass. Once they were away from the lights, the silence set in. It was palpable, as if the world was miles away. They held the men firmly against the wall, shielded by a large dumpster containing the bar's accumulation of trash.

"I have questions," said Roach. "You're going to answer them, or I'm going to leave you shitting in a bag for the rest of your life."

He stared into Johnson's eyes. They were wide, full of fear, and glistening with tears.

"I'm going to move my hand," continued Roach. "Are you going to behave, or are you going to be an idiot?"

Johnson shook his head urgently. Roach nodded. He removed his hand. Valentine did the same, expecting the message was understood by both men.

"W-what do you want?" said Johnson. "An apology, is that it? Because I'm sorry, man. I was a dick to you. Or money? Do you want money? I can give you whatever you want, just don't hurt us."

Roach rolled his eyes. "It's always the same with you people. You think you can buy your way out of anything. I have money… despite what you think of me. I told you, I want answers."

"O-okay."

"Thomas Pope's auction. Tell me about it."

The two men exchanged a look. Fear and worry and confusion.

"I don't understand," said Johnson. "It's… it's an auction. People bid for things."

"I know how auctions work. But most auctions don't sell fake items for ten times what the real thing is worth. Help me understand."

The man Valentine was holding began to struggle against his grip. Valentine slammed him against the wall, rammed his forearm into his chest, then held it over his throat.

"Easy there, asshole," he snarled. "What were you there to buy tonight?"

Again, the two men exchanged a worried glance.

"Answer the question," said Roach.

Johnson winced. "We were looking for... for a watch."

"Lyle, shut up!" hissed his friend.

Roach grabbed a handful of Johnson's jacket and pinned him against the wall. "I'm short on time and need you to get to the point. Earlier, in the bar, you told me the cheapest item that sold tonight was a watch for... thirty-seven grand, right?"

Johnson nodded.

"And now you said *you* were there to buy a watch. What's so special about them?"

"Th-th-they're good watches." Johnson shrugged.

"No, they're fake watches. But... you knew that already, didn't you?"

"No."

Johnson looked to the ground. Roach narrowed his gaze, then looked over at his friend.

"What's your name?" he asked him.

"Pike. Daniel Pike."

"Okay, Daniel, let's try a different approach, seeing as Lyle here seems content with bullshitting me."

Johnson looked up. "I'm not lying!"

Roach whipped his fist forward, jabbing him on the

nose. Heavy enough to make his eyes water. Light enough to not break it.

"Be quiet." He looked back at Pike. "Let's see if you're smart enough to learn from his mistakes. I'll even give you an incentive. If I think you're lying to me, I'll hurt your friend. Understand?"

Pike nodded animatedly under Valentine's grip.

"Good. Let's try again. Did you know the watches were fake?"

Pike swallowed hard. "No."

Roach rolled his eyes and punched Johnson again, this time beneath the ribcage on the left side. Johnson huffed and wheezed and whelped with discomfort.

"Try again, asshole," he said, glaring.

Pike's eyes popped wide. "Okay, okay! Yes, we... we know they're fake."

Valentine frowned. "So, why buy them?"

Pike hesitated. He cast a glance at Roach, silently begging for mercy.

Roach raised an eyebrow and punched Johnson in the face.

"Stop, please!" begged Pike. "I... I don't know, okay? I don't know, I swear. That's just... what we were told to do."

"Told by whom?" pressed Valentine.

Pike looked at him. "Come on, man, please. I can't..."

Valentine looked over at Roach. "This isn't working. These two idiots are scared to death. And not just of us. They'll say anything at this point."

Roach sighed heavily. He looked around, searching for answers and patience but finding neither.

"Fuck this," he said eventually.

He drove his knee into Johnson's gut, then hammered three blows into the side of his head, knocking him out cold.

He stepped to the side, shoving Valentine out of the way, and grabbed Pike's throat.

"Listen to me, you little prick—I don't have the time for this. Back in the bar, you knew I was full of shit when I said I was going to the auction. I could tell. How?"

Pike struggled to look away from his unconscious friend lying on the ground next to him. When he finally looked at Roach, the color drained from his face.

"They're invite only," he said. "Real select clientele. If you really intended to go to one, you would've known that."

"How do you get an invite?"

"There's an app... on my phone. Costs ten thousand dollars to download and install it. You get the invite on there. It's a QR code. Scanned on the door."

Roach nodded. "Okay. Then what?"

"Once inside, the brochure for the evening's lots is sent to the app thirty minutes before it starts. Then you take your seats."

Valentine shook his head. "Uh-uh, that's bullshit. Auction houses publish their brochures weeks in advance to promote them. No one shows up to one without already knowing what's on offer." He turned to Roach. "Even if the watches are fake, everything else is supposed to be legit, right? Why hide it?"

Roach frowned. He stared at Pike, but he wasn't really looking at him. He was thinking. Nothing about this made any sense, yet deep inside his brain, it was beginning to. Like he knew he had all the information he needed, but it was swirling around like water circling the drain. He couldn't see what was right in front of him.

He refocused, tightening his grip on Pike. "The app. Show me."

Pike fumbled blindly in his pocket and took out his

phone. Valentine snatched it from him. The screen lit up, requesting a thumbprint to unlock it. He held it up for Pike to see.

"Open it," he said.

Pike did. His hand shook as he lifted it.

Valentine searched the phone, quickly finding the app. He clicked it. The loading screen asked for a passcode.

"Jesus…" he muttered. He held the phone up again. "What's the code?"

Pike took a deep breath that quivered past his lips. He glanced at Roach. His cold, dark eyes stared back. He then sighed and looked away.

"Four, three, five, seven," he said.

Valentine keyed it in. The app unlocked. It was a simple layout with minimal content. It had two buttons. One was to display the QR code invitation. The other was to view the brochure. He hit it and moved so Roach could see. He scrolled through it.

"Every third lot is a watch," he said.

"Coincidence?" asked Roach.

"I doubt it, given what we know. But all it shows is a picture and the serial number…"

"…which we know is the one thing that proves it isn't real. Why omit any actual information about it? It's like they're not even trying to hide the fact it's fake."

Valentine frowned, then looked at Pike. "Wait. You said you knew the watches were fake, and you were told to bid on them, right? Does *everyone* at the auction know they're fake?"

Pike looked away and didn't answer.

Valentine turned to Roach. "That's a yes."

"Why go to an auction knowing one of the items isn't real, and still bid for it? What are we missing?"

Valentine shook his head. "I don't know."

Roach slapped Pike in the side of the head, making him whimper and shake with fear. "Start talking. You must know."

Before he could say anything, the phone began beeping. Valentine looked at the screen. A red border had appeared and started flashing in time to the sound. Like an alarm.

"What the hell?" he said.

Roach pulled Pike toward him, holding him inches from his face. "What's happening?"

For the first time since confronting them, Roach saw a glimmer of confidence in Pike's eyes.

He smiled. "Security, asshole. The app has two pass-codes. The one you choose yourself, and four, three, five, seven. If your phone is ever compromised, we're told to use the second code. It means help. It turns on the phone's GPS and sends your location to a security team." He began laughing. "You have no fucking idea what you're involved in, do you? You made the biggest mistake of your life by attacking us."

Roach narrowed his gaze. "You think so?"

As he spoke, two black pick-ups slid to a halt on the street in front of the alley. Valentine saw them first.

"Um, Roach... we might have a problem," he said.

Roach looked at the vehicles, then turned back to Pike. "Thanks for your help. I'll be sure to let Thomas Pope know *you* talked to us when I see him."

He stepped back and smashed his fist into the side of Pike's jaw, knocking him out instantly. He released his grip and let him drop to the ground beside Johnson.

"Jesus Christ," said Valentine quietly. He locked the phone, shutting off the alarm, and slid it inside his pocket. "Now what do we do?"

Roach stared out at the street. "We go and see how good this security is."

Chapter Twenty-Seven

Roach and Valentine stepped out of the alley and stood side by side in front of the two pick-ups. They had parked across the middle of the street at an angle, their hoods forming an arrow that pointed almost accusingly at the mouth of the alley.

Six men climbed out of them and moved to form a line in front of the vehicles. Ricky Chen stood third from the left. Roach didn't recognize any of the others. He saw no visible weapons, although he had no doubt each man was armed. They all wore dark, tailored suits. He figured they were working the auction before they got called out.

He had never understood why people fought in a suit. It restricted movement and cost a fortune to dry-clean the blood out.

Valentine cast a sideways glance at Roach. "Gotta be honest, I'm not sure I'm gonna be much help here."

"Don't worry about it," replied Roach. "Just stay close enough to one of them that no one will risk shooting at you."

He took a step forward. There were maybe fifteen feet between him and the new arrivals. He ignored the others. He just looked at Chen. He knew he wasn't there by choice. But he also knew he had to keep up appearances, so no one suspected his involvement. If they did, it was only a matter of time before Pope found out about him and Vanessa, which wouldn't end well for her. Consequently, they both understood that everything that had happened before this moment no longer counted for anything. One of them wasn't walking away from this.

"Where's your second-in-command?" said Roach. "Sutton, was it?"

Chen visibly tensed. "You know damn well where he is, you sonofabitch. Mr. Pope wants your head for killing his men. And now, you're harassing his clients? You're about to have a real bad night."

Roach's expression betrayed nothing. "Not as bad as the one your boss is about to have."

Chen shook his head and laughed with disbelief. "I don't get how one man can be so fucking stupid. We gave you chance after chance to leave. Even when Mrs. Pope insisted on hiring you, we offered you a peaceful way out."

"There's nothing peaceful about sending people to kill me."

Chen stepped forward and jabbed the air with his finger. "Because you can't take the fucking hint! So, it's come to this. We got the call from Mr. Pike… I didn't need to hope it was you. I just *knew* it. Is our client even still alive?"

Roach nodded. "Yeah. He's back there feeling sorry for himself." He paused, then smiled. "He was extremely helpful."

Chen's eyes narrowed. The men behind him shifted restlessly.

"Well, that is unfortunate," he said.

Roach shrugged. "You gonna tell me to leave town again?"

"No."

"You gonna try and make me? Because, if you are…" He made a show of looking past Chen at the line of security. "You should've brought more men."

Valentine frowned. "Are you kidding me?"

Roach ignored him.

Chen shook his head. "This is plenty. Mr. Pope is good at maintaining the privacy of his business interests. You aren't the first person to threaten everything he's built."

"Bet I'll be the last."

Away to the left, a sudden burst of noise flooded the street as the door to the bar opened, releasing the atmosphere within. A man and a woman stumbled out, laughing. They were dressed smart and holding hands. They stopped when they saw the scene before them.

Roach pointed at the bar. "Go back inside. Now."

The couple stared at him, then quickly hustled back through the doors.

Chen took a deep breath.

"Take them," he called over his shoulder. "Kill the old man. Try to leave Roach alive, if possible. But his wellbeing isn't a priority."

Valentine glared, genuinely offended. "Old man? I know you didn't mean me, you little piss-ant."

Roach turned to him. "I think he did. What are you gonna do about it?"

Valentine stepped forward. The man standing to the far right of the line moved to meet him, marching with confidence. As they met, Valentine dropped his left shoulder and slammed the heel of his right palm upward, smashing it into the man's face. His nose shattered across his face. Valentine followed up by jamming the crook of his left hand into the guy's throat. He stumbled back, unsure which injury to prioritize, too concerned by the fact that he couldn't breathe. Finally, Valentine reached out, grabbed the back of the man's head, then yanked it forward into his rising knee. The man's jaw unhinged from the impact, and he fell backward, landing stiff and awkward on the road.

No one moved. Silence and shock filled the air.

Roach and Chen looked at each other, stunned. Then Roach shrugged. "I guess he doesn't like being called old."

Chen's expression hardened with frustration. "Don't just fucking stand there. Get them!"

The remaining four men rushed forward, splitting into teams of two. The two on the left charged at Roach. He was ready. He stepped back as the first man threw the first punch, slipping out of the way. The blow glanced across him. He countered with one of his own, sending the guy off-balance as he connected with the side of his face.

He stumbled away, clearing the path for the second guy, who dropped his shoulder and buried it into Roach's gut, like he was sacking a quarterback. The impact forced the wind from him, but Roach managed to stay upright. He pushed his legs back to steady himself, then dropped the point of his elbow between the guy's shoulder blades. As he released his grip of Roach's waist, Roach dropped another elbow, this time on the back of his head. The guy fell like a stone at Roach's feet.

The first guy recovered and attacked again. He managed to get a strike in before Roach could focus on him; a well-placed kick buried itself into his thigh, on the outside of his leg, just above the knee. The dull pain was instant and spread around his leg like wildfire, knotting his quad. He staggered back, giving the guy a window to follow up. He delivered a hard combination of three punches to Roach's face, which he ate unprotected. They sent him crashing to the ground, just inside the alley, leaving him in the dirt next to the wall of the bar, half-shrouded in darkness.

Roach blinked hard. He was light-headed, dazed by the shots. He lifted his head and saw the man stalking forward. Beyond him, he could see Valentine struggling against his two adversaries. He took a breath and tried to block out the pain in his leg and head. He had come too far to be taken down now.

The man loomed over him. Roach reacted on pure, violent instinct. Primal programming buried deep inside his brain told him it was kill or be killed. He felt the darkness within him start to rise, like a tide coming in for the night.

He reached up and grabbed the guy's belt and yanked him forward. It caught him by surprise, and he smashed head-first into the wall. Roach quickly got to his feet, spun around, and pressed his hand flat against the side of the guy's face, pressing him against the brickwork. Without a second's pause, he swung his arm like a scythe, bent so the solid part where the elbow met the forearm smashed into the man's temple. The contact was so fierce, it numbed his fingers. But he didn't relent. He unleashed three more in rapid succession; the man's head was pinned between the wall and shots. The third one fractured the skull. Roach felt the bone give way. He stepped back and let the man fall. There was a dent the size of a cereal bowl on the back left side of his head. His eyes were open, locked lifelessly.

Roach didn't linger. He released his grip, turned, beelined for the second guy, who was recovering and slowly getting back to his feet. Before he could fully stand, Roach arched a haymaker with his left hand, crashing his fist into the man's face. He stayed on one knee. Roach moved behind him, stalking his prey. He reached down and wrapped his arm around the man's neck and throat. He wrenched back, forcing him up onto his feet. His hands clawed at Roach's forearm but with little effect. Roach took a deep breath and held it, forcing his chest to swell. As he did, he squeezed harder with his arm, increasing the pressure on the man's carotid artery. He held it there until he felt him go limp. As he let go, he caught the man's head in his hands, one cupped around his chin, the other around the base of the skull. He looked around, searching for Chen, who was watching from beside one of the pick-ups. He fixed him with a hard stare, then twisted his body violently, reversing the position of his arms. He broke the man's neck like he was unscrewing a bottle cap.

Roach stood and looked behind him. Valentine was trading body blow for body blow with one of the security guards. The other was out cold on the ground. Trusting he had his situation handled, Roach turned back to Chen.

"I don't have a choice," Chen said, walking toward him. "Mr. Pope knows Vanessa was going to betray him to Jasmine Decker."

Roach stood in front of him in the middle of the road, breathing hard. Partly from the exertion and fatigue. Partly from the adrenaline. In his periphery, he could see the windows of the bar crowded with faces, watching with grim fascination. They didn't concern him. They couldn't exactly call the sheriff. He was having surgery. Of his deputies, one was barely old enough to drink, and the other was a crooked piece of shit who was unlikely to come to anyone's aid.

He focused on Chen. "How did he find out?"

"He pressured her. Threatened her. She had no choice."

"So, you're out here saving your own ass? That's true love for you."

"It ain't like that!" snapped Chen. "The only thing keeping her alive right now is the fact that Mr. Pope doesn't know the extent of her betrayal. He doesn't know how much Decker knows, and he has no idea how involved *you* are. But if he finds out Vanessa and I were... he would kill her. I have to do what he says. It's the only way I can protect her."

"Well, then. We have ourselves a predicament, don't we?"

"I can't go back empty-handed. He wanted you either dead or brought to him alive, so he could torture you himself. You killed more of his men. He'll never believe I let you get away with that."

"I don't want to do this, Ricky. But I promised Vanessa I would protect her, and the only way I can do that now is to stop whatever Pope's doing in this town."

"I don't have a choice, Roach."

"Yes, you do. There's more to what's going on here than just the watches. All this..." He gestured to the bodies scattered across the road. "It's too much for a scam that could be run by two college students from a street corner. Even if you don't know what it is, you must see that. You never leave his side. You have to know something? Help *me* help *her*."

"I can't. I... I don't know. I swear I don't. Yes, I'm with him all the time. Well, except when he meets the mayor, but still... he doesn't tell me more than I need to know."

Valentine appeared at Roach's side. He was still trying to catch his breath after having successfully taken out the last remaining security guard. "Why aren't you there when the mayor meets him? Does he not trust you?"

Chen shook his head. "The mayor sends his own security to pick Mr. Pope up and drive him to and from the meetings. I'm simply not needed. Honestly, you should be thankful. He was with the mayor earlier. I used the window to get you that flash drive."

Roach sighed. "Whatever. Help us, Ricky. Last chance."

He stared at Roach, then shook his head regretfully. "I can't. I appreciate what you've done for Vanessa, but... I can't. If I don't go back... if I don't stop you... Mr. Pope will know."

"You're more afraid of him than you are of us..." observed Valentine.

Chen nodded. "You don't know what he's capable of."

Roach took a deep breath. "No, but I think I want to find out. You should walk away, Ricky. I have no issue going through you to get to him."

"I can't let you do that..."

Chen walked toward them. Roach moved to meet him.

"So, this is how it's gonna be?" asked Roach.

"I guess so."

"Okay, then. But know this: I'll save Vanessa. You have my word."

Chen shook his head. "Don't make promises you can't keep, Roach. I'll lose respect for you."

Roach didn't say anything else. He lunged forward without warning, launching into a flurry of punches aimed at Chen's face and body. Almost every one of them was blocked or deflected. As exhaustion slowed his attack, Chen snapped his right hand out into Roach's sternum, sending him shuffling backward.

Then it was Chen's turn. He leapt four feet forward from a standstill, thrusting a kick forward, aimed at Roach's gut. He managed to avoid it, but Chen followed it up with his own combination of punches, each one thrown with deadly speed and accuracy. Roach dipped and shimmied and blocked as many as he could, but enough got through to do damage. He fell away but rolled with his momentum back onto his feet. He remained bent over, catching his breath.

Valentine took the initiative and moved in on Chen. The first punch he threw was blocked, but Chen made a circular motion with his arm, trapping Valentine's under it, locking him in place and leaving him exposed. He then delivered a stiff shot to the chest. Valentine's eyes bulged as he gasped, trying to reclaim the oxygen that had just been forcibly expelled from his lungs. Chen released him, then buried a side kick into Valentine's stomach, sending him crashing to the ground, incapacitated, struggling to breathe.

Roach got back to his feet and stormed toward Chen. He knew he couldn't match him for speed or technique. But he could hit harder. He needed to pick his spots; otherwise, Chen would dissect him.

As he approached, Chen yelled with a primal fury, unleashing another tirade of wild, swinging haymakers, thrown from the hip, yet still technically sound and seemingly too fast to block effectively. Roach did his best to roll with them, avoiding as many as he could, trying to remain patient, waiting for the window he needed.

He grunted as one punch made it through and connected stiffly with the lower left side of his ribcage. He didn't think it broke anything, but taking a breath instantly became more challenging. Again, he staggered away, desperately sucking in as much air as he could.

"Fuck..." he muttered.

Chen planted a strong right on Roach's cheek, sending him spinning away.

"You should've left when you had the chance," he growled.

Roach winced. "I don't… walk away from a fight."

"You damn sure won't walk away from this one."

Chen jumped and spun clockwise, bringing his leg around and whipping his heel into Roach's jaw. He landed gracefully in time to see Roach fly backward and land hard on the ground just inside the alley entrance.

Roach lay still, staring up at the night sky, willing the fog in his head to clear. The bitter taste of blood and adrenaline filled his mouth. His breathing became a contradiction. It hurt to do it, yet gulping in as much air as he could seemed to lessen the pain he felt.

Since the day he met him, he had suspected Chen was a competent fighter. He had the physique and body language to suggest it would come naturally, despite likely having had years of training. He always seemed a heartbeat faster, and Roach knew he wouldn't win this standing toe-to-toe with him. But he had to figure something out. He was too far into this mess not to see it through, and there was too much at stake for him to lose now. They both wanted to keep Vanessa safe, but Roach was the only one of them who could realistically do it.

He rolled over on his front, scraping his hands across the ground to push himself up. He was slow to get to his feet, and he struggled to stand upright when he did. But he breathed through the discomfort to do so. One arm hung at his side, loose and sore. The other formed a fighting guard.

Chen kept his distance, watching him patiently. The cockiness had gone, but the confidence remained.

Roach beckoned him with a lazy gesture of his hand. "Is that all you got?"

Chen took a long, reluctant breath. "I guess you really do want to die, huh? So be it."

He rushed toward him, arms raised, preparing for another assault. Roach side-stepped and lashed his loose arm out. Chen shouted in pain, sliding to a halt and resting against the wall. He clutched at his stomach. When he looked down, dark blood was seeping from beneath his shirt. He frowned, then looked over at Roach. He was smiling, holding a shard of glass in his right hand that he had scraped up moments earlier.

"You bastard!" shouted Chen.

He ran forward again. Roach watched his movement, trying to time his steps and anticipate them. As Chen stepped through and unleashed a leg kick, Roach slid to the side and dropped to a knee, slicing down with the glass. It tore through the outside of Chen's thigh effortlessly.

Once more, Chen cried out with pain. He limped to a stop and turned to stare at Roach.

Roach beckoned him forward again, taunting him.

When Chen obliged, his pace was notably slower. His movements weren't as fluid. Roach smiled with menace and satisfaction. He met Chen in the middle, easily avoiding the punches he threw. Each time he ducked to the side, he jabbed him with the glass, piercing the flesh on both sides, just above the waist. Chen grunted and staggered away. His posture began to shrink, hunching more and more with each breath to relieve the pressure on his wounds.

"Fuck... you..." he seethed.

Roach sucked in breath through gritted teeth. "You wanted this. Not me."

"If I die... he's going to kill her."

"No, he won't. I told you that. Walk away from this, right now. Let me bring her to you."

He shook his head. "I... I can't."

"You're beat, Ricky. You're losing too much blood. Don't attack me again."

Chen's breathing was visibly labored. He shook his head, barely able to keep his eyes open. "No... no... you don't understand. You don't know what he's capable of."

Roach dropped the glass. The fight was over. He took a deep breath, forcing himself upright once more. "Then tell me."

"It doesn't matter. Not anymore. You have to die. Then Mr. Pope will... he will... forgive her. It's the only way."

"It's too late for that, Ricky. He doesn't know it, but right now, I'm the only thing stopping Decker from tearing this town apart. And even if I manage to get proof of whatever he's doing with all the money he's hiding from her, that's only going to save the town. Not him. He has a war coming, and I don't care how dangerous you think he is. He isn't going to win."

"You're wrong..." Chen looked up at him. His eyes burned with renewed vigor and rage. "You're wrong!"

He arched his back, stretching through the pain, then set off running toward Roach. He made it halfway before a gunshot consumed the silence. Chen's body was punched away as if hit by a speeding car. A thin cloud of dark mist exploded from the side of his head as he flew to the ground.

Roach caught his breath in his throat. He looked over at Valentine, who was only just beginning to stir on the road. Shock gave way to confusion. He looked along the street, wondering where the shot had come from. He got his answer almost immediately.

Standing beside the pick-up truck on the left was Jasmine Decker. A small group of her men were huddled behind her. She wore a brilliant white coat that came down to just above her knee. Beneath it was a thin sweater and scarf. Her arm was outstretched, holding a gun. Roach saw the smoke dancing from the barrel.

He stared at her blankly.

She smiled at him. "Hi, Handsome."

He walked out into the middle of the street. "You didn't need to do that."

"He looked pretty pissed at you."

"Most people are. But he was… he didn't deserve to die."

Jasmine frowned. "Were you, or were you not about to kill him?"

Roach sighed. "Not if I didn't have to."

"Well, what's done is done. Now…" She trained her gun on him. "Do you have my proof?"

Roach let out a long sigh. "Depends. I don't suppose you have a laptop, do you?"

She frowned. "Why?"

"I was given a flash drive and told the proof you wanted was on it. I just… haven't looked myself."

"Roach… this is disappointing. What if this flash drive proves useless, hmm? You didn't even make time to check?"

He glanced over his shoulder at the sea of bodies and blood strewn across the street.

"I've been a little busy," he said.

She looked past him. "So I see."

Valentine shuffled once more to Roach's side, interrupting them.

Jasmine smiled at him. "You look worse than when you left."

He stared at her, tired and impatient. "No offense, lady, but fuck off."

She smiled wider. "You two are just peas in a pod, aren't

you?" She focused on Roach. "Yes, I have a laptop with me. I always work when I'm traveling. But I'm warning you, if this is useless…"

"You'll kill us both and burn the town to the ground." Roach waved his hand dismissively. "Yeah, yeah. I know. Look, I'm confident this is the proof Vanessa was originally going to give you. Additionally, I'll tell you everything we know about Thomas Pope. If you're still not happy after all that, by all means, shoot us both. Frankly, at this point, I could use the rest."

Jasmine stared at each of them in turn. Both men were tired and barely able to stand. Both were bleeding. She took a breath, then lowered her gun. She held it out behind her, and one of her group took it. Then she glanced at the bar and pointed to it. "Clear that place out."

Immediately, the men stormed inside. Moments later, the doors burst open. Everyone flooded out, hurried and panicking.

Jasmine smiled at Roach. "You look like you could use a drink. How about you and I sit down like civilized people, and you can tell me all about it?"

Roach took a heavy breath, then gestured toward the bar. "After you."

"Such a gentleman…"

She walked confidently inside. Roach set off after her. Valentine was beside him.

"You sure this is a good move?" he asked.

Roach looked at him and shrugged. "You got another one?"

"Huh. Fair point."

They headed inside and each took a seat opposite Jasmine at a table in the middle of the now-deserted bar. Her men stood in a semicircle behind her.

Then they told her everything.

Chapter Twenty-Eight

It was after one a.m. The adrenaline had long since worn off, and the pain from the skirmish was setting in for both Roach and Valentine.

Between them, they had told Jasmine everything they knew. Roach didn't hesitate. He would usually keep as much to himself as he could get away with. Strategically, it was unwise to tell an enemy everything and risk negating any power or control over a situation. But these were desperate times. He wasn't sure Jasmine even *was* an enemy. If he was wrong, then at least she wasn't as big an enemy as Pope. But the one thing he could be sure of was that he had almost no power or control over the current situation, so he was sacrificing nothing by telling her what he knew.

Jasmine had sat in silence, listening, sipping a neat vodka on the rocks that one of her men had made her. When they finished, she leaned forward on the table, tapping her fingers idly as she processed the information.

"So, let me get this straight," she said finally. "Thomas's

head of security was screwing his wife. He told her about the money. She saw it for herself, and between them, they decided to come to *me* in the hope that I would be mad and take out her husband, his boss, so they could run away together."

Roach nodded. "Basically."

"However, she changed her mind because she's scared of Thomas. Then *you* happened to get involved when some of my men came after her."

"Yup."

"Men you assaulted... but didn't kill."

"That's right."

"And then, because of some archaic sense of chivalry, you took it upon yourself to stick around and keep Mrs. Pope safe. In doing so, you not only figured out the scam Thomas and I had going at the auction, but you discovered that the profits he's apparently hiding from me are somehow linked to the fake watches... and the made-up serial numbers, although you don't understand what they have to do with anything. That's just a hunch."

"More like an educated guess, but yeah."

"Whatever. Then... you attacked two guests of the auction, who ultimately called in Thomas's security to kill you both. You know his wife is with him and likely in danger. He knows she was going to betray him to me, but he doesn't know she was screwing his security guard, and he doesn't know you know anything. Is that about right?"

Roach and Valentine glanced at each other and shrugged.

"Yeah, that's about it," he said.

"Well..." Jasmine sat back in her chair and finished her drink. "Assuming you aren't lying to me—which I'm inclined to think you're not—you have to be about the unluckiest sonofabitch I think I've ever met."

Roach flicked his brow up, smiling briefly. "Tell me about it."

She looked back at one of her men. "Fetch my computer."

The guy disappeared outside and returned a moment later with a laptop, which he placed on the table in front of her and opened. Jasmine looked over the screen at Roach and held out a hand.

"Well, let's see this proof of yours."

He took the flash drive from his pocket and handed it to her. It was scratched and dented, but it remained intact. She plugged it in and accessed the drive. Roach and Valentine watched curiously as she studied the information, occasionally exchanging a worried glance.

"Sonofabitch," Jasmine said finally.

She spun the laptop around for them to see. Both men leaned forward to look at the screen. It displayed a spreadsheet. The sea of numbers and gridlines all blurred together. Roach blinked hard. He looked over at Valentine.

"What am I looking at?" he asked. "I've been hit in the head too many times today for this to make sense."

Valentine rolled his eyes. "Oh, and I haven't? Look." He pointed to the screen. "A lot of this is meaningless. It's *these* figures we're interested in. Projected auction revenue from tonight's lot."

He took Daniel Pike's phone out of his pocket. He put it on silent and opened the auction app using the security code from earlier. The screen began flashing again, but he ignored it. Pope was unlikely to send anyone else, given Chen and his crew never returned. He clicked on the brochure and held it up next to the laptop screen.

"See here," he explained. "Each amount in these cells relates to an item in the brochure. Must be the starting bids."

Roach nodded. "Okay. Every third lot was a watch, right?"

Valentine traced the list with his finger, tapping the screen on every third cell in the column.

"Prices match," he said. He moved his finger along one of the rows. "This empty cell will have the actual sale price entered into it. Then it would calculate Miss Decker's twenty percent in the cell next to it. However... *this* figure is what the secondary sale is worth. Must be a pre-agreed price."

Roach let out a low whistle. "So, that watch actually sold for half a million dollars?"

"Apparently."

Roach looked across at the table at Jasmine. "Satisfied?"

Jasmine raised an eyebrow. Her lips pursed together with frustration. "Not in the slightest. But do I accept what that backstabbing fucker's wife claimed? Yes, I do. Thank you."

"So, what are you going to do?"

She shrugged. "Exactly what I said I would do. I'm going to destroy Thomas Pope and take everything he has."

"Well, I'm not sure it's as easy as that," said Valentine.

"And why's that?"

"Because whatever he's really doing up there is likely bigger than any of us realize. If he's dealing with that kind of money, it means he's involved with serious people. The kind of people who might not appreciate a disruption to their regularly scheduled programming... if you catch my drift."

Jasmine leaned forward. "I don't give a shit. If I have to burn this town to the ground to do it, I will."

"Hank's right," said Roach. "Almost everyone I've dealt with in this town is terrified of Pope. His people act like he's someone to fear."

She scoffed. "Thomas Pope likes to think he's a big deal. He always carries himself with a self-importance far beyond his station. I ignore it because, a prick though he may be, our partnership was always good for business, and money trumps stupidity every time. But he's always been and will only ever be small-time compared to me."

Roach took a deep breath. "I think you might be underestimating him."

Jasmine smiled at him. Her lips curled, but the rest of her face didn't move. There was no humor in it. "I appreciate your thoughts. But this is no longer your concern. I will deal with Thomas Pope now. You and your friend are free to go."

She moved to stand, but Roach moved an arm to catch her attention and keep her seated.

She stared impatiently. "What?"

"I'm sorry, Jasmine, but you're wrong. This *is* my concern."

She held his gaze. Her demeanor changed. She relaxed back into her seat and tilted her head at him, smiling again, warmer this time.

"Of course. The wife."

"I made her a promise."

"And as admirable as that may be, I don't care. This is business. If I don't deal with this, I look weak. I can't have that."

Roach thought for a moment. He understood her position. She was angry and out for blood, and she wasn't going to listen to reason. But he needed her to hold off starting a war until he could get Vanessa to safety. He needed another approach.

"Okay, look," he said. "Pope's screwed you out of a *lot* of money and you want what he owes you. I get that. But you need to be smart about this. Think about it. We've been right about everything else so far. What if we're right about this whole thing being bigger than we realize? If there are powerful people involved, there will be powerful protection there too. You have everything to gain and nothing to lose by letting me go in first."

Jasmine narrowed her gaze thoughtfully. "How so?"

"If I go in there and get myself killed, you haven't lost anything. You can still march your own men up there, wage your war, and no one will think you're weak for doing it. But if I save Vanessa and put an end to whatever Pope's doing... you can simply walk in and pick up the pieces, along with whatever you feel you're owed. No risk at all to you or your people."

"Well, when you put it like that..." She fell silent, biting her lip absently, lost in thought. Then she nodded. "Okay. You have until sunrise. I guess you've earned that."

"Thank you."

"Besides, I admire your dedication to the promise you made her."

Roach got to his feet. He didn't say anything.

"Just to be clear, I'm not sending any of my people with you," she said flatly. "This has nothing to do with me."

He stared down at her. "I wasn't going to ask."

Another small smile flickered across her lips. She glanced to the side and nodded. The same man as before stepped forward. He drew his weapon and placed it on the table in front of Roach, then fell back in line.

Roach picked it up. He checked the mag and racked the slide and made sure the safety was on, then tucked it behind him in his waistband.

"Thanks," he said.

Valentine stood, a frown etched deeply onto his face. "So, wait, Roach… what *exactly* is your plan?"

Roach looked over at him. "I'm going to go to the auction house and get Vanessa."

He narrowed his eyes with disbelief. "The auction house that's likely teeming with countless, heavily armed members of Pope's personal security?"

"Yes."

"That's fucking suicide!"

Roach shrugged. "Yeah, well… I'm going anyway. Come. Don't come. That's up to you. No judgment from me."

He turned to Jasmine, nodded a final gesture of thanks and respect, then headed for the door. Valentine smiled awkwardly at her and followed.

She leaned forward and slowly closed the lid of the laptop, then picked up her drink and smiled. "Go get 'em, tiger."

The trucks and the bodies and the blood were all still there, on display like a cruel exhibition. The town was quiet, peaceful, devoid of life or movement. Even the air seemed unwilling to move, as if fearful it would disturb the eerie calmness felt only in the aftermath of battle.

"Jesus Christ, will you stop a second!" Valentine called out.

Roach stopped.

Valentine hustled around his friend and stood blocking his path.

"Can we just... talk about this?" he pleaded.

Roach shrugged. "What's to talk about? You got something to say, you should've said it back there."

"Pretty sure I did. Look, I understand where you're coming from, Roach. I do. But I wasn't kidding when I said what you're thinking about is suicide."

"Don't underestimate me."

Valentine rolled his eyes to the sky, then shook his head, laughing. "Don't... heh... look around you, man." He stepped to the side and made a grand gesture to the carnage scattered across the street outside the bar. "It's the middle of the night, and Pope sent a hit squad to take you out within ten minutes of someone pushing a button on a goddamn phone." He stepped to the other side and pointed along the road ahead of them. "Now, you tell me, if he can do *that*... what the fuck do you think is waiting for you at ground zero? Hmm? You just told Decker you thought she was underestimating this sonofabitch, and now here *you* are doing the exact same goddamn thing." He sighed. "Believe it or not, I've come to... y'know... tolerate you being around. Given the choice, I'd rather you weren't brutally murdered because you were too stubborn to stop and take a breath."

The tension hung over them like a cloud. The silence seemed to somehow get quieter, like a vacuum. Roach stared ahead, looking without really seeing the road that stretched out before him. He knew it led directly to the auction house, which sat on its own private lot atop a small rise, surrounded by dark trees, overlooking the cove below. He didn't blink. His jaw pulsed with distant frustration.

Valentine watched him. "I know we don't have a lot of time. But that's no excuse to not think about this."

Finally, Roach blinked, pulling himself out of his trance. He looked at Valentine. "And what would you suggest?"

He shook his head. "I don't know. This isn't exactly a typical day at the office for me. But I would start by looking at the facts. I just got my ass kicked. I'm tired and sore and of little use to you from here on out. Jasmine Decker isn't sending anyone to help. She gave you a gun, but you're essentially alone in this. I'm no expert, but I would suggest a less direct approach might help your chances."

Roach shook his head. "I don't have the time. Or the patience. They must've figured by now their people aren't coming back. Pope will know I'm coming."

"All the more reason to remain unseen as long as you can."

"If you were Pope, sitting up there, surrounded by God-knows-how-many armed security guards, what do you think I would do?"

Valentine sighed, shook his head, and looked away. "I'd think you were going to sneak inside and try to take out as many of them as you could before anyone noticed."

Roach raised an eyebrow. "Right. And what do you think he would *never* expect me to do in a million years?"

"Walk in the front door, guns blazing."

Roach shrugged, silently acknowledging his own point.

Valentine rolled his eyes. "Yeah, and why do *you* think he would never expect you to do that? Because it's fucking insane! You have one play here, Roach. Just one."

"No, I don't."

"Okay. Let me rephrase. You only have one that might actually work."

Roach huffed and paced away, frustrated with the

conversation. Valentine watched him, giving him time and space to calm down.

After a few minutes, Roach walked back toward him. "Okay. What do you think?"

Valentine shrugged. "I think you really are on your own. The local authorities aren't coming. Someone from the bar might have called in the state troopers, but it's unlikely, given most of them were guests at the auction. The feds won't even know this place exists. And probably the last honorable man in Waters Point is getting surgery right now because he has a hole in his gut, which is all the more reason to play this smart."

Roach stared at him. "You know my background. My history. You know what happened in New York a few years ago."

Valentine swallowed hard, unnerved by what he saw in Roach's eyes. He nodded. "I... yeah, I do. But this isn't—"

"This is *exactly* the same. I didn't care who was in that building when I pulled up outside it, and I don't care who's sitting in that auction house right now. You said it yourself in the hospital, Hank: I'm a nuclear fucking warhead in a goddamn fistfight. I make no apologies about who I am and what I'm capable of. What I've done... what I *can do*... it ain't pretty. There have been times when my actions have been downright ugly. But you know this town. It's corrupted to its core, and the cancer that's causing it is sitting a mile up the road. Right now, we need a little ugly."

Valentine shook his head slowly. "Do you really think this will work?"

Roach took a deep breath. "All I know is... this is who I am. I know now that I've been waiting my whole life to find a fight that will define me as something other than a monster... that will give me a cause that shows me there are still things worth fighting for. This is it, Hank, and one way or the other, this ends right now."

He set off walking along the middle of the street, heading east, eyes narrowed and focused, jaw set, fists clenched. A moment later, hurried footsteps brought Valentine to his side. Roach glanced at him.

"Don't look at me like that," said Valentine. "As if I'm gonna stay back and do nothing after that speech."

Chapter Twenty-Nine

The walk toward the auction house allowed enough time to formulate a plan. Common ground had been reached. Valentine waived some of his reservations, acknowledging it was a *now or never* situation. In turn, Roach had conceded that a head-on attack was a move borne from emotion, not logic. It wasn't the time for emotion.

Emotion would get them killed.

They focused on what they knew. Neither of them had set foot inside the auction house. Neither of them knew the layout, how many men were inside, or if Pope was even there. But they did know there was a rear entrance accessible from the boathouse, due to their incarceration there earlier. They also figured it would be less guarded than the auction house itself.

As the road began to bend and rise on its final approach, they broke away and headed right, cutting between the buildings to weave a path down to the water's edge. The cove looked beautiful and serene. The light of the full moon reflected on the water. Distant lights from the town across the bay were like pinpricks. Roach briefly recalled his first time seeing it, standing alone on the hill, close to the auction house entrance. The sun had been shining. He'd felt at peace.

But now, that peace was gone.

The embankment was narrow but flat, allowing for easy navigation. They moved as quickly as they dared, careful not to disturb the surrounding undergrowth. The plateau was roughly twenty feet above them, looming over them, shrouding them in sporadic darkness.

Roach was in front. He saw the boathouse ahead of them. He moved as close as he could while remaining out of sight from anyone who might be hidden by the outer wall, then held out a hand behind him, signaling for Valentine to stop. They both crouched and listened. The only sound was the gentle lapping of the water as it ebbed and flowed around the enclosed jetty.

Roach glanced back and nodded, then set off again. It was maybe thirty feet to where the embankment joined the boathouse. As they approached, a noise began to carry across the water. A distant rumbling grew louder with each second that passed. Once more, they stopped; only, this time they stepped to the side, crouching in the untamed undergrowth. In the darkness, they were all but invisible.

They waited.

The speedboat blipped into view on the far side of the cove, getting larger as it roared toward them, bouncing on the water as if drumming along to the spluttering of the engine.

"Reinforcements?" whispered Valentine.

Roach stared. "No. The boat isn't big enough."

They watched as the boat slowed and nosed into the enclosure. Roach saw the shapes of two men, their features lost in the darkness. Slowly, quietly, he edged forward, trying to see around the boathouse wall. He saw one of the men step out onto the wooden pier. The other disappeared down inside the small cabin of the boat. Moments later, he reappeared, followed by an uneven, shapeless mound, shuffling beneath a large blanket. It was too dark to make out any detail.

Roach frowned.

The blanket climbed out of the boat like a caterpillar and was led up the steps of the mezzanine by the first man. He unlocked the door at the top and held it open, ushering the blanket through. His colleague followed, and the door closed behind them. It wasn't slammed, but no effort was made to be quiet either.

Roach waited for a full minute, then stepped back out onto the embankment.

"The hell was that?" asked Valentine.

"No idea. Right now, I'm not interested. We need to get inside the auction house."

Valentine pointed at the boat. "At least these bastards were kind enough to leave us a getaway vehicle."

Roach nodded. "First bit of luck we've had. Let's hope it's not the last."

"Not much chance of that."

They moved quickly inside the boathouse. The moon cast a pale light inside. They could see the bloodstains on the wooden floor. Some belonged to Bushell. Some were there because of Ricky Chen.

Roach glanced at them as he moved up the steps of the mezzanine toward the door. He listened for any signs of movement beyond. He heard nothing. He gripped the handle and gently turned it. The door clicked open. He cracked it an inch and looked out. The angle didn't give him much, but he was able to see a gravel path away to the right, winding up the hill, out of sight, presumably toward the rear of the auction house.

"Come on," he said quietly. "We're clear."

He pushed the door open just enough for them to fit through, then closed it gently. The plateau was away to the left and ten feet lower than before. A large tree stood next to the stone wall that bordered it, jutting out and hanging low over the edge. He had stood next to it a few days ago, admiring the view.

They headed right and followed the path as it curved around the hill. There was nothing on the outer edge of the graveled path except a short outcrop before it fell away toward the cove. It took only a few minutes to reach the summit. They crouched just before the final bend. Roach peered around the corner. Stretched out before them was the rear of the auction house, enclosed by a high fence topped with razor wire. There was a small parking lot to the right of two large loading bays. The wheeled gate was open.

"Must be how they transport the items for auction back and forth," observed Valentine quietly.

"Hidden away from prying eyes…" added Roach.

He scanned the area with an expert eye. He saw no cameras. No motion sensors linked to security lights. Only two guards walking the perimeter, dressed in tuxedos. No visible weapons, but Roach had to assume they would be armed.

"There's a disturbing lack of security in place," he said.

Valentine frowned. "Either we got this all wrong, and they have nothing to hide, or…"

"Or they're extremely confident no one's going to try breaking in."

"Fine line between confidence and arrogance."

Roach glanced back at him and smiled. "As I'm about to show them. Come on."

Keeping low, they rushed toward the gate and ducked inside, keeping close to the shadows formed by the trees that lined the fence. The auction house was a large, low, square building with a domed roof that covered much of the land on top of the hill. The two guards each patrolled a corner of the rear, meeting in the middle without crossing paths. Roach watched them. He needed to take them out quickly and quietly, and the best chance of that was when they were together.

The guard on the right was closest. Roach waited until he had turned his back, then rushed across the lot, pressing himself against the wall. It was dark, but the guard was still visible. He would have to move quickly.

Roach watched and waited. As the two guards neared each other, he sprang to his feet and charged them. Neither had their weapons drawn. Roach dropped a shoulder and plowed into the first guard's back. It sent him flying into his colleague, and both tumbled to the ground.

Roach didn't allow them time to recover. As one began to push himself upright, he unleashed a kick to the side of his head. Blood sprayed from his nose and mouth. He fell flat again, immediately still.

Roach dropped to one knee, looming over the second guard as he pinned an arm down. He then drove his fist into his face. Three heavy shots in quick succession. The third knocked him out.

He quickly frisked him and retrieved his gun, then glanced back over to the trees. Valentine emerged and ran across to him. Roach handed him the gun, then drew the one Jasmine had given him.

"Be ready," he said. "There will be more of them inside. We won't have many chances to stay quiet."

"Don't worry about me," said Valentine. "I've got your back."

Roach nodded and headed for the door set between the shutters covering the two loading bays. He pulled it open and stepped inside. A network of narrow corridors wound through the back area of the building, with doors at regular intervals leading into other rooms and areas. Warm lighting, pale colors on the walls, and a deep red carpet underfoot made everything feel luxurious and cozy. Roach felt like he had stepped through a portal to another world.

He took the lead and moved door to door, checking each one. If it was unlocked, he opened it carefully and checked inside. He found storage rooms and offices and meeting rooms. No sign of any guards. No sign of Thomas Pope. No sign of Vanessa.

They followed the corridor around to the right. Around the turn, Roach saw a man standing guard outside a room, casually holding a handgun low in front of him. From the shape of him, he was pretty sure it was one of the men who had arrived on the boat.

Roach stopped and pinned himself to the near wall. Valentine did the same. Roach looked back at him and used hand signals to explain there was one guard, armed, and that he would take him out. Valentine nodded.

Roach edged along until the bend in the corridor no longer shielded him from view. Then he stepped out, raised his gun, and fired once. The guard didn't see him. He dropped to the floor, revealing a circular blood stain splattered on the doorframe where he had stood.

Valentine caught up to him. "There goes our element of surprise."

"I'd never have reached him in time to stop him getting a shot off," he explained. "No choice."

"Let's see what he was guarding," said Valentine, nodding to the door.

Roach tried the handle. It was unlocked. He checked along the corridors for signs of movement, then eased the door open. Inside was a small, circular space with a stack of wooden crates piled up on the left side.

"Hold the door," said Roach.

Valentine did, and Roach dragged the dead guard inside by his ankles. He left him in a heap by the crates and looked around as the door closed behind him. There were no windows. The room was quiet apart from the low rattle of an air conditioning unit. And something else.

Breathing.

Both men turned and followed the right wall until their gaze rested on a shapeless mound obscured by a blanket. They exchanged a look of curiosity and concern, then walked slowly toward it, weapons ready.

Roach reached out slowly and tugged the blanket free. Four pairs of fearful eyes, sunk into dirty faces, looked up at them. Tears flowed down their cheeks.

"Holy shit," said Roach quietly. "They're… *children*."

Two boys and two girls were huddled together, wearing ragged, torn clothing, shaking with a combination of fear and fatigue.

When Valentine didn't immediately respond, Roach looked around to see him standing wide-eyed, a hand covering his mouth in silent shock. Valentine let the gun slip from his grip and stepped carefully toward the children. His eyes were locked on one of the boys.

Roach tracked his gaze and frowned. "Hank, what is it?"

Valentine simply pointed at the boy, raising his arm slowly, as if too heavy to lift.

"I don't believe it," he said. "Michael?"

Chapter Thirty

"Wait... *that's* your missing kid?"

Valentine ignored him. He walked toward the boy, his mouth hanging open with shock. "You're... you're alive. Michael, your parents sent me to find you. I just didn't think I would. I mean... not here. Not like this. But you're safe now, I promise. You... you all are. We're going to get you out of here." He looked back at Roach. "What the hell is going on?"

Roach shook his head. His eyes glazed over as he stared blankly at the threadbare carpet, trying to wrap his head around what he was seeing. Incoherent thoughts swirled around inside his mind, each one rushing in a thousand different directions all at once. The confusion, the noise... nothing made sense.

Then his eyes snapped back into focus. The pieces fell into place like a lightning strike.

"Give me that asshole's phone," he said.

Valentine stepped away from the kids and handed Daniel Pike's cell phone to him. He unlocked the app and opened the brochure. He began scrolling through it, hoping his theory was wrong.

"What is it?" asked Valentine.

Roach closed his eyes and gritted his teeth. "Shit…"

"Roach, talk to me."

"It's the serial numbers. They've been the key to this all along."

He pointed to the screen. Specifically, at the lots for the watches.

"I don't see it," said Valentine.

Roach spoke with urgency. "We know Pope wanted custom engravings on the watches, which we thought were meaningless and gave away the fact they're fake."

"Right."

"Except they're not meaningless. What was that first transaction we saw in Pope's reports? Half a million dollars?"

Valentine nodded. "Yeah…"

"It's all there in the serial number. Look at this first one. *WP Michael 9500K.*" Roach looked over at the boy. "Michael, how old are you?"

The young boy swallowed. He looked at Valentine for help. He simply nodded, offering silent reassurance it was okay to answer.

"I-I'm nine," he said quietly.

Roach stared at Valentine. "WP has to mean Waters Point, right? Michael is the name of the child. Nine—his age. Five hundred K… five hundred thousand. That must be the… the price."

Valentine took a step back. He clasped his hand to his face and shook his head, horrified. "No…"

Roach nodded. "We knew there were two transactions. *This* is why the second one was so much higher. It was never about buying a fake watch. The watch must be, like, a... a token, or a... deposit. Whoever bought one was only doing so to secure the chance to buy..." He looked over at the group of children. "To buy one of them."

"It... it can't be."

Roach took a deep breath. He wasn't sure what would be waiting for him at the auction house, but nothing in the world could've prepared him for what he had found.

"Thomas Pope is trafficking kids," he said. He almost choked on the words.

"No," said Valentine. "I don't believe it."

"I don't want to either, but... they're standing right there, Hank."

"Do you think Jasmine knows?"

Roach shook his head. "I don't think so. She was genuinely pissed to learn Pope was hiding money from her. She can't know about this. She just wants her cut from the watches. That's her deal with him."

Valentine looked at him. "Do you think Ricky Chen knew?"

Roach took a steadying breath. "I would like to think he didn't."

"Same. But maybe he did. Maybe that's why he never told Vanessa everything?"

"Well, I guess we'll never know now."

They fell silent. The only sound in the room was the chattering teeth and the scared sniffles from the children in the corner.

Valentine took the phone from Roach. "Okay. Let's test your theory."

He scanned the list for the next watch listed for auction. He scrolled across to the serial number.

WP Skylar 9750K.

He looked over at the two girls. "Is one of you called Skylar?"

The taller of the two girls raised her hand slowly. She had mousy brown hair and bloodshot eyes.

Roach felt his heart break as he stared at them, unable or perhaps unwilling to imagine what hell they all must have been through.

Valentine cursed to himself. "Skylar, are you nine years old?"

She nodded timidly.

Roach and Valentine looked at each other, eyes wide.

"I feel sick," said Valentine.

Roach frowned, then tucked his gun behind him and reached inside his pocket for Vanessa's watch. Valentine looked on as he flipped it over to read the serial number. Roach looked over at the other young girl, then dropped to one knee and smiled at her.

"Hey, sweetie. Can you tell me your name?" he asked softly.

The young girl cleared her throat. "Anna."

Roach looked at the serial number in his hand.

WP Olivia 6800K.

He knew what the number meant. He closed his eyes, desperate to keep the tears of sadness at bay. Desperate not to think about a family somewhere missing their little girl, not knowing the horrors Olivia had gone through. It was too late for her now, whoever she was.

He looked at Anna again and smiled. He reached for her hand, holding it gently in his. He fastened the watch tightly around her thin, frail wrist.

"This... ah... this belonged to another little girl," he said. "She was brave, just like you are. I haven't found her yet, but I'm going to go and look for her. Would you look after it for me, until I find her?"

Anna pursed her lips together and nodded slowly.

"Thank you, Anna."

Roach stood and paced away. He drew his gun again, clenching his fist around the butt of until his knuckles turned white. He snarled and growled, trying to control the waves of anger desperate to escape. He knew with complete certainty he had never before experienced the hatred he felt in that moment toward Pope.

Then another thought occurred to him, which instilled an even greater sense of dread in him. He cursed himself for never having thought of it before, but the more he ran it through his head, the more it made sense. The serial numbers, Jasmine Decker's involvement, everything.

He looked over at Valentine. "This isn't Pope's only auction house, is it?"

Valentine went to reply, but the words caught in his throat. He hadn't thought of that either. The two men looked at each other, silently understanding the scale of what they were faced with. It had never made sense that Jasmine would want to work with Pope when all she got was twenty percent of three watch sales once a week. It wasn't anywhere near enough money to justify her being interested. But if he owned more auction houses across the state, or the country, then her cut would be significantly higher.

Reaching the same conclusion at the same time, both men once more turned to look at the children. Their hearts broke all over again. But as Valentine's eyes misted with tears, he saw Roach's fill with venom.

"What are we going to do?" he asked, gulping back his concern.

Roach looked at him. "*We* aren't gonna do anything.

You're going to get these kids out of here. Go back the way we came. The path's clear. Get them on the boat, and get them the hell away from here."

Valentine nodded without question. "What about you?"

Roach stared at him. "I'm going to tear this fucking place apart."

258

Chapter Thirty-One

Roach marched out of the room and waited as Valentine gathered the children and set off back to the boat. Happy there was no immediate threat, Roach then followed the corridor to the right. It curved left and led him to a large art gallery. A variety of items were displayed in stands, cases, and on plinths. Old weapons, tools, pottery, items of clothes... all laid out like a museum exhibition. The floor was made of dark mahogany. Paintings were hung on the left wall. The right wall was glass. Roach stepped over and glanced out. He was overlooking the auction house main floor.

He pressed on, weaving through the aisles of items, sensing he was moving away from the inner workings of the auction house and toward the public-facing part of the building. Ahead of him, the open plan space passed through a threshold into another, smaller display area. As he neared, a security guard walked across the gap. He had a submachine gun hanging from his shoulder by a thin harness. He nursed it casually in one hand as he looked around, no doubt alerted by the gunshot minutes earlier.

Roach raised his gun and fired once. The bullet went straight through the guard's neck, killing him instantly. He hurried over and retrieved the submachine gun from the guard's dead grip. He looked around and saw two exits, in the top left and right corners of the space. He saw stairs leading down to the right and headed for them.

They led him to the back of the auction house floor, close to the entrance. The area resembled a ballroom. Rows of circular tables were decorated extravagantly with flowers, bottles of champagne, and centerpieces featuring a number etched into a brass triangular stand. Chairs surrounded each one, some of which were askew.

It was quiet.

Roach tightened his grip on the gun, holding it up and ready. His finger rested against the side of the trigger guard, ready and willing to fire if needed. He moved across the floor, looking around in all directions for any signs of movement. He made it to the front without incident. There was a small stage, raised only a couple of a feet and blanketed in thick, red carpet. In the center was a pulpit, with a full-size printout of the evening's brochure laid open across it. To its left was a large table, which Roach assumed was for displaying whatever item was being auctioned at the time.

Roach stood on the stage and looked back out at the room. He pictured it full of rich tuxedos and ballgowns, laughing and drinking, enjoying their opulence without a care in the world for the people they were hurting. His vision blurred as his mind wandered. His anger grew. Inside his head, he began screaming to everyone and no one that he was right. That his disdain for humanity was justified and this was why. Because people like *this* existed, and they were so entitled and arrogant, they thought they could get away with anything. They thought there were no consequences to their heinous acts.

His teeth ached as his jaw clenched like a vise.

He was the consequence.

An image of the kids he and Valentine found swirled around his head. He vowed in that moment to personally hunt down every single person who had ever taken part in one of Pope's auctions and put a bullet between their eyes.

Movement in his periphery yanked him from his furious trance. He looked up and saw a security guard in the gallery above, staring down at him through the glass. He saw the guard's expression change from surprise to anger. He saw him talk into a radio, then turn and head for the stairs.

"Here they come," he whispered.

The guard reappeared a moment later, sprinting out from the back left corner. Roach sprayed a burst of automatic fire in his direction. He knew he was too far away to be reliably accurate, but all he wanted was to give the guard something to think about while he closed the gap.

The guard dove for cover behind the nearest table. Roach was about to press forward, but a sudden flurry of movement all around him changed his mind. More guards appeared from behind doors that surrounded the auction floor. He counted eight. All armed.

He was suddenly aware of how exposed he was, standing on the stage.

"Shit!" he hissed.

Roach leapt to his left, upturned the table, and sat behind it a heartbeat before gunfire broke out. The stuttering cacophony of bullets and death reverberated around the large, domed space. The table chipped and splintered around him. It was thick wood, but he knew it wouldn't provide much cover for long.

He reached up and fired blind, casting three bursts of return fire until the hammer clicked on an empty chamber. He discarded the weapon and drew his handgun. He had one spare magazine. He looked around for somewhere else to find protection from this assault.

There weren't many options.

He chanced a quick peek over the slowly disintegrating table to see the positioning of the guards. There were nine in total. Most were scattered across the floor and away to the right, but he saw two approaching slowly to his left. They were close, trying to flank him.

Roach paused for a split-second, then popped up and fired three rounds into the glass of the gallery above them. The glass exploded and began raining thousands of shards down on them. The two guards hunched against the lethal downpour, raising their arms for added protection. Using the distraction to his advantage, Roach adjusted his aim and fired another four rounds. Each one found their mark, and the two guards dropped dead, staining the glass that surrounded them with their blood.

Two down, seven to go, he thought.

Bursts of submachine gun fire continued to ring out, filling the air like a deadly drum solo. Roach lay on the stage, balled into the fetal position, desperate to utilize every remaining inch of cover from the table. He glanced over to the right and saw three more guards moving around to the side of the stage. He opened fire, taking the first guard down almost immediately. The second dropped a moment later. The third was in his sights and raising his own weapon when Roach shot his final round. The guard ducked away instinctively, which bought Roach a valuable couple of seconds, but he knew it wasn't enough time to reload.

He scrambled to his feet and sprinted to his right, hoping he was running fast enough to throw off the aim of the four guards still spread across the floor. Gunfire sprayed around him as he ran. He reached the edge of the stage and jumped feet-first, driving himself down into the remaining guard's legs like an arrow. Both men landed heavy and awkward, but Roach recovered first. He stood and dragged the guard upright, holding him as a human shield. He delivered a stiff punch to his face, then grabbed the gun hanging over his shoulder. He turned it around and fired a burst at point-blank range into his body. The bullets punched through the guard's body and out the other side with ease.

Roach pushed the fresh corpse forward and ran for the nearest doorway to his right, slamming himself against the wall as he urgently reloaded his weapon. He glanced around the corner. The four remaining guards were sweeping counterclockwise across the room in a loose line. The guard on the far left was stepping onto the stage. He was seconds away from having a clear shot, and Roach had no cover.

He took a breath, set his jaw, and stepped out from the doorway. He dropped to one knee and took aim. He started firing, moving his aim left to right. He took out three of the four guards before running out of ammunition. The remaining guard charged at him. Desperate to close the gap between them, Roach lunged forward, shoulder-tackling him at the knees. The guard spun away and collided with the right wall. Roach fell flat on his stomach. He clawed his way toward the guard across the floor and wrapped his hands around his throat. There was no space for the guard to fire his gun, but using the wall for leverage, he managed to push himself up and over, rolling Roach onto his back. His arms flailed for defense as the guard tightened his own grip around his throat. Roach tucked his chin down and tensed his neck, desperate to relieve any pressure he could. The guard loomed over him, snarling and spitting as he squeezed.

Roach felt his eyes try to roll back in his head. The guard was leaning too far forward for him to bring his legs up and hook the head. His peripheral vision was beginning to fade, pulsing in and out as consciousness grew increasingly harder to maintain.

Then Roach grabbed the guard's head with his hands and placed his thumbs over his eyes. He let out a guttural, primal growl as he pressed them hard into the sockets. Blood and mucus and fluid soaked his hands as he slowly blinded the guard, who unleashed a howl of agony before releasing his grip and falling away to the floor. Roach scurried upright and retrieved his gun. He spun to face the guard and watched as he writhed on the floor, clutching his face, which was blackened by thick blood. He fired once, putting a hole between what remained of his eyes.

Roach stumbled away, using a nearby table for support as he caught his breath. An eerie silence descended on the auction house floor. He waited almost a full minute, making sure no more guards were coming for him. Then, he stood straight, checked how many shots he had left, and walked away without looking back.

Three doors were set into the right wall. The one farthest from him and closest to the main entrance had a small sign stuck to it. A thin, black rectangle with white lettering that said OFFICE. He opened it to reveal a small corridor. There was a door on the right and a door straight ahead at the end. He passed the first door. It was unlocked, and inside was a small, empty room with a desk and two chairs.

He stared at the door ahead of him.

He reached it and tried the handle. It was locked.

There was a muffled noise from inside. It was high-pitched. Feminine.

Vanessa.

Roach took a step back, then launched his leg forward. He connected just above the handle. The door swung open, torn from its hinges by the force. Roach stepped inside, gun raised.

In front of him was a long desk. A laptop, a landline, and a thin stack of papers sat on it, neatly organized and evenly spaced. Standing behind it was Thomas Pope. In front of him, with his hand around her throat and a gun held to the side of her head, was Vanessa.

To the left of the desk was Deputy Henderson. He also had a gun raised, pointing directly at Roach. He was wearing Bushell's sheriff's badge. There was a visible speck of blood on one of the tips.

To the right was a man Roach hadn't met before. He recognized him but couldn't remember where from. He was dressed in a tailored, charcoal-gray suit with a red tie. His thinning, straw-colored hair was combed into a side part. His face was clean shaven and artificially smooth.

"That's far enough," he said. "Put your gun down."

Roach was aiming at Pope. His arms were locked and steady. He looked over at the man and frowned. "What the fuck is going on here?"

The man smiled, wide and confident. "We haven't formally been introduced. I'm Calvin Rhinehouse, the mayor of Waters Point. Now, put your gun down, Mr. Roachford, before you cause any more damage to my auction house."

Chapter Thirty-Two

"*Your* auction house?" asked Roach. He nodded at Pope. "I thought it was *his*."

Rhinehouse smiled. "Yes. That's the idea."

Roach tried to hide his surprise. He was committed to the situation. There was no going back. He needed to end this. But to do so, he needed to think clearly, and in that moment, he wasn't.

The mayor was behind this. It made no sense to him. The town, the sheriff, *everyone* knew it was Pope's money. They also knew the mayor kept quiet and took the credit, leading them to quietly assume he was in Pope's pocket. But he wasn't.

Pope was in his.

Then he remembered something Chen had said right before he died. He said the mayor sent his own people to collect Pope for their meetings. He wouldn't do that if Pope was in charge. Pope's ego wouldn't allow it. He also said Pope had met with the mayor earlier that day, despite the local news reporting he was out of town for a few days.

It all started to make sense.

The entire town had been played.

Rhinehouse took a step forward. "I must say, Roach, you've caused me a *lot* of trouble since you arrived in my town."

Roach's aim didn't waver an inch. His gun remained trained on Pope. He ignored Henderson. He held Rhinehouse's gaze. "I don't care. This is over."

Rhinehouse chuckled. "Oh, it really isn't. You're out of your depth. You just… haven't realized it yet."

Roach frowned. "I guess, seeing as you've been hiding back here like a fucking coward, you haven't been paying attention. Everyone out there is dead. You have no people left. Your little *delivery* in the back… gone. You're finished."

"Well… that *is* disappointing," said Rhinehouse, "but ultimately irrelevant. Nothing more than a minor setback."

"Is that right?"

"Yes. Waters Point isn't home to my only auction house. I have *dozens* across the country. I've even expanded into Mexico. This is a global enterprise, Mr. Roach. This is money on a scale you cannot comprehend. Our clientele do not accept failure. This little interruption… you're making enemies whose wrath you will not survive."

"You think highly of yourself, don't you? The problem with people like you is your ego. You believe your own hype and assume you're a big deal. Do you think I give two shits about the sick fucks that visit your auctions? If anyone has a problem, and they can find me, they're welcome to voice their concerns… see how much good it does them. But as the saying goes, there's always a bigger fish."

Rhinehouse laughed. "Is that what you think?"

"Yes. I can even name one for you. Jasmine Decker."

Pope's expression dropped. He swallowed hard and cast a concerned glance at the mayor. Rhinehouse looked over at him and shook his head gently, reassuringly.

He turned back to Roach. "I understand she has her suspicions... thanks to Mrs. Pope. But she doesn't know anything. Her involvement was a necessary evil to help... grease the wheels with certain aspects of the business. But she knows her place. She doesn't know anything that could hurt us."

A smile crept across Roach's face. "Interesting."

Rhinehouse tilted his head. "What is?"

"How much you think you know... and how much you *actually* know."

"Meaning?"

"Jasmine Decker knows everything. That's why she's sitting in a bar back in town right now, surrounded by her own heavily armed people, waiting for me. I don't walk out of here with Vanessa before sunrise, she storms the castle and kills everyone." He looked at Pope. "You fucked with the wrong person there, asshole."

Before Pope could reply, Rhinehouse took another step forward. "She's a means to an end, nothing more. Enterprising though she may be, I'm not concerned by a former stripper who's watched *The Godfather* one too many times. You may have killed a handful of Thomas's men, but I have plenty of my own on the way. I also have people in Washington and New York waiting for my call to arrange delivery of their auction wins. Now, they *are* people you should be concerned with, Mr. Roach."

Roach shook his head. "I'm not worried about anyone. Not anymore. I don't care how far your twisted empire stretches. You're done. Vanessa and I are walking out of here. That's it. No second chances. No bargaining. No authorities. You're all going to die tonight."

Rhinehouse stepped back toward the desk. "Defiant to the end, Mr. Roach. I'm impressed. You certainly live up to the hype." He gestured to the room. "But look around you. There are three of us. You're outnumbered and outgunned. You're in a small space. There's a hostage whom we all know you care about. My men will be here soon, which will leave you no way out. I'm afraid it's you who is going to die tonight."

Roach looked around. Henderson was stood at his ten o'clock. His finger was already inside the trigger guard. Pope was straight ahead. His gun hadn't moved from Vanessa's temple. Roach couldn't tell for sure whether he was prepared to shoot his own wife. Then there was Rhinehouse. Cocky. Arrogant. Undoubtedly in charge. But unarmed and unlikely to be anything more than a power suit and a fake smile.

Roach took a deep breath. He wondered if Valentine had managed to get the children to safety. He was sure he had. He trusted him completely.

His eyes narrowed, transfixed on Pope.

Would he kill his wife?

He flicked his gaze to Vanessa. Her eyes were dark and bloodshot. Some of her makeup had worn away, revealing the old bruising on her face. She clutched onto her husband's forearm, which was wrapped loosely around her neck, but she wasn't trying to break free. She had accepted her situation.

He winked at her.

Fuck it.

He snapped his aim left and put a bullet between Henderson's eyes. The gunshot was like an explosion in the enclosed space and took everyone by surprise. He retrained his aim on Pope before the deputy hit the floor.

"Now it's two-on-one," he said casually. "And only one of you has a gun… which isn't pointing at me. You've lost, and you're too stupid to admit it. The people of this town are going to find out what you did."

Rhinehouse scoffed. "They won't care. All they will see is that *you* forced the auction house to close, which will cut off this hellhole's only source of real income. The local economy will crash and burn without me, and they're going to blame you for it. Not me. *You*."

Roach shrugged. "I don't care. I'll be gone by the morning, and no one in this town is smart enough to find me. But before I leave, you can bet your ass I'll make sure everyone knows that money they've all been so fond of was earned by selling children, you sick fuck."

Vanessa gasped. Her eyes popped wide at the revelation, shocked and confused.

Finally, Pope spoke. He tightened his grip around his wife's neck but aimed his gun at Roach. "I'll kill my wife if you don't drop your fucking gun," he spat. "One way or the other, she will pay for her betrayal."

Roach felt an uneasy relief to have Pope's gun aimed at him instead of Vanessa. That was the first step to getting her out of there. But he needed Pope to let her go.

"Why?" asked Roach. "It wasn't Vanessa who betrayed you."

"What do you mean?"

"Yes, she *was* going to tell Jasmine Decker you were hiding money from her. But she didn't. She changed her mind. It was Jasmine who sent those men after her. To get the information she had promised." Roach looked at Rhinehouse. "Speaking of which… should I assume it was you who killed those five assholes to send a message?"

He nodded slowly. "Of course."

"Okay. Just checking."

"So, how did that bitch find out?" demanded Pope. "Who else betrayed me?"

Roach smiled. "Ricky Chen."

Pope scoffed and shook his head. "No. You're lying. Ricky has worked with me for years. I took him in. Gave him a job. Gave him a purpose. He would never do that."

Roach shrugged. "I don't know what to tell you, Thomas. He gave me the information when he killed two of your men to help me escape from your boathouse earlier."

"Impossible!" he yelled. "Why would he betray me?"

The gun was shaking in his hand.

Vanessa locked eyes with Roach, who nodded to her. She grabbed her husband's forearm and tore it from around her neck.

"Because he loved me, you sick bastard!" she shouted.

He turned to her, eyes wide, stunned silent. She slapped him across the face with everything she had, then shoved him, although she moved farther than he did.

Pope was speechless. His entire world had just shattered around him, and he was lost. He looked back at Roach, his face contorting with rage.

Roach smiled. "Face it, Thomas. You're done. Your business is over. Your marriage is over. You have nothing left."

"No… no… I don't believe it." He looked at Vanessa. "How could you?"

"Easily," she said, her confidence returning. "He cared for me. He paid attention to me when you were too busy with your precious work. He looked out for me when you lost your temper. We were going to have Jasmine Decker kill you, then we were going to leave together."

Pope's expression hardened. Her words cut into him, and his anger was taking over. "You… you fucking bitch!"

He screamed and reached out to grab her, but she had given Roach all the opportunity he needed. He fired once, hitting Pope in the side of the head. Vanessa shrieked and fell backward, scurrying into the corner of the room behind the desk. She hugged her knees to her chest and began sobbing.

Roach aimed his gun at the mayor as Pope hit the floor.

"And then there was one," he said.

Rhinehouse smiled uneasily. "Okay. Let's just talk about this. I'm sure we can come to some arrangement."

Roach shook his head. "Were you not listening before? I said no bargaining, remember?"

Rhinehouse went to speak but hesitated. He looked around, suddenly aware of how alone he was. He eyed Roach up and down, looking for a weakness to exploit.

There wasn't one.

Roach stared at him with cold, dark eyes. He couldn't shake the image of seeing those children for the first time, huddled together beneath a dirty blanket, afraid. He wasn't sure he would ever forget it.

Rhinehouse saw the anger. He saw the hatred. He knew enough about him to know he would not hesitate to kill him.

He panicked.

The mayor charged at Roach, lunging for his gun, to wrestle it from his grip and use it himself. Roach saw it coming and side-stepped, cracking the side of the mayor's skull with the butt of the gun as he stumbled past him. Rhinehouse fell to the floor but rolled with the momentum and pounced back to his feet. He swung wildly at Roach, who simply watched with amusement. He stepped back, easily avoiding the punch, then countered with one of his own. He smashed his fist across the mayor's jaw, knocking him down again. This time, he didn't get back up.

Roach stepped over Rhinehouse's unconscious body, straddling him. He looked down and leveled his gun to aim right between the eyes. His finger tightened against the trigger. His hand shook as he wrestled with his own conscience and anger. His heartrate quickened. Each breath hissed through gritted teeth.

After a moment, he dropped to one knee, resting on the mayor's chest. He placed the barrel of his gun against his forehead. When he exhaled, it came out like a primal roar.

The mayor stirred. His eyes opened slowly. Then they widened as he saw what was looming over him. The color drained from his face. He was frozen with fear. All he could do was stare up at the personification of death, about to claim another soul.

Roach screamed, unleashing a howl of anguish from the pit of his stomach. Then he tossed the gun from his hand and lurched forward, driving his forearm down across Rhinehouse's face. He struck him multiple times, each one accompanied by another violent scream of inner turmoil. As he wound up the sixth shot, he felt hands wrap around his arm. He looked around, his eyes ablaze with rage, and saw Vanessa standing there. Tears still stained her face. She held his arm and stared into his eyes until the fire in them went out. His body relaxed. His breathing slowed. She let him go as he lowered his arm.

"It's over, Roach," she said quietly. "It's okay. It's over."

He turned back to look at the mayor, sprawled out beneath him. His face was a crimson mask, broken and swollen. The faint rise and fall of his chest was the only sign he was still alive.

Roach closed his eyes for a moment as he let out a long breath. Then he got to his feet. As he did, Vanessa threw her arms around his waist and hugged him tightly. Slowly, he put his arms around her shoulders and embraced her.

It truly was over.

After what felt like a lifetime, Vanessa stepped away and looked up at him.

"Ricky," she said. "Is he…"

Roach took a deep breath and shook his head. "I'm sorry, Vanessa. He… didn't make it."

She put her hands to her mouth as fresh tears began to flow.

Roach put his hands on her shoulders and held her steady. He looked at her, debating what he should say. In the end, Chen had only done what he thought he had to, and despite everything, Roach respected him for it. But he was also prepared to kill him if Jasmine hadn't. Knowing the truth wouldn't give Vanessa any peace.

"He… he died fighting for you both," he said finally. "I was with him at the end. With his last breath, he made me promise him I would protect you. He truly cared for you."

She buried her face in his chest, and he held her close as she wept.

Finally, he moved her away and looked at her. "We need to go."

"Okay," she nodded.

Roach crouched beside Henderson's body and took the cuffs from his belt. He used them to secure the mayor's wrists behind his back, then he took the laptop from the desk, retrieved his gun, and headed for the door.

He looked back at Vanessa, who was standing beside the desk, staring down at her husband's body.

"Come on," said Roach. "Let's go."

She walked uneasily over to him and took his hand. She let him lead her outside and back toward the town, where the residents would soon be waking to face a day none of them were prepared for.

Chapter Thirty-Three

Roach told Vanessa everything on the walk back to town. She didn't say much. He understood it was a lot to come to terms with anyway. Especially with her husband involved, he figured she would be numb for a long time.

The first pink streaks of dawn began to stretch across the night sky. The cool wind was dying down. The street was still deserted. They walked along the middle of the road, in no danger of any cars coming their way.

The bar was up ahead. He saw no sign of Valentine. Just the small fleet of black SUVs belonging to Jasmine Decker and her entourage. He figured she had her men clear up the bodies and the other vehicles, which he was secretly relieved about. The last thing Vanessa needed was to see Chen's body lying in the street.

He slowed his pace and looked over at Vanessa.

"Would you hold this?" he asked, handing her the laptop.

She frowned. "Sure. Is everything okay?"

"Yeah. Just… wait here a minute."

Roach marched forward toward the vehicles. As he neared them, the doors opened with a collective click. Jasmine and her men climbed out and formed a line along the road. He ignored the cautious stares from her security. He beelined straight for Jasmine. He drew his gun and stopped in front of her, resting the barrel gently against her forehead.

"Did you know?" he asked firmly.

The men around her twitched nervously. Their hands shifted to their weapons.

Jasmine frowned. "Excuse me?"

"Did you fucking know?"

"Know what?"

"Your watch scam. It was a double front for child trafficking."

Jasmine's eyes grew wide. Her mouth hung open. She said nothing.

"That was where Pope's excessive profits came from," he continued. "The watches he sold, that you got your cut from, they were… tickets that allowed the buyers to purchase children. Fucking *children!* I found four of them who had been delivered to the auction house tonight. One of them was the missing kid Hank was looking for this whole time. I swear to God, Jasmine, if you were in *any* way involved…"

She raised her hands slowly and stared at him. She could see him shaking with rage. She saw the fatigue in his dark, bloodshot eyes. She saw his jaw pulsing. She saw the tapestry of cuts and bruises. She saw a man balancing on a knife edge.

"Roach, I give you my word, I had no idea," she said calmly. "If I had known, I would never…" She sighed. "I'm a mother. I would never have gotten involved if I had known."

Roach held her gaze. The tension was palpable, suffocating the air around them. Then he let out a heavy sigh and lowered his gun. He ejected the magazine and the chambered round, then tossed everything away to the ground.

"That's all I needed to know," he said.

The mood relaxed. She nodded to her men to stand down.

"Are they safe?" she asked. "The children… what happened?"

"Hank got them out of there," he said. "I'll check in with him soon, but I assume they're all safe. Thomas Pope is dead. All of his men are dead. He wasn't even in charge. Mayor Rhinehouse was the brains behind it all. He's got auction houses exactly like this one all over the country."

"Jesus. Is he dead?"

"No. He's tied up and unconscious. He said he had more people on the way…"

"I'll send my men up there to clean up."

Roach smiled weakly. "You might want to leave town. No way Hank didn't call the state police or the FBI. This place is about to get real busy for a while."

Jasmine smiled back. "I appreciate the head's up. I'll be gone before anyone arrives. I just want to make sure the mayor is secure and that I get what I'm owed."

Vanessa appeared at Roach's side, walking gingerly, clutching the laptop.

Jasmine looked at her. "Mrs. Pope."

She took a deep breath. "Miss Decker."

"Well… this all got a little out of hand, didn't it?"

Vanessa nodded slowly.

Jasmine took a step toward her. Roach tensed. So did her men. But she simply put a hand on Vanessa's shoulder and smiled.

"We've all been in a relationship where the guy turned out to be a piece of shit," she said. "You and me... we're good."

Vanessa's shoulder's slumped with relief. "T-thank you."

Roach took Vanessa's hand in his. "Come on. We should go."

He nodded once to Jasmine before walking away with Vanessa in tow.

"Hey, Roach," Jasmine called out.

He glanced back.

"I knew I was right about you." She smiled. "If you ever want a job, call me."

He held her gaze for a moment, then looked back and carried on walking.

A few hours later, Roach was standing at Sheriff Bushell's bedside, sipping tasteless coffee from a Styrofoam cup. The hospital was quiet, save for a couple of state troopers patrolling the corridors.

The sheriff hadn't been awake long. The surgery had gone well. He would heal and be fine. Roach had summarized the events of the night before. Bushell didn't say much.

Roach placed the laptop on the bedside table.

"That was in the office," he said, nodding to it. "I figured there might be something useful on there. Figured you might want to see it before the feds do. This is your town, after all."

The two men exchanged a faint smile of respect.

"Appreciate that, Roach," murmured Bushell. He took a deep breath. "How's Mrs. Pope?"

"She's fine. Tougher than she realizes. A few cuts and bruises. She's down the hall being looked at. I think she's mostly just in shock. Can't say I blame her."

"No. That's a hell of a thing, with her husband. Not what you expect to find in a town like Waters Point."

Roach paused. "There are gonna be some big changes around here, Sheriff. You any idea what you're going to do?"

Bushell shrugged lazily. "Ah… same thing I always have. I love this town. I'm gonna keep serving the people who live here. Heh… might need to hire some new deputies."

Roach smiled. "Yeah."

"You looking for work?"

Roach raised his eyebrow. "I'm probably not the best choice to uphold any laws."

"Huh. You got that right."

A cell phone started to ring, breaking the quiet atmosphere of the room. Both men were confused for a moment, then Roach remembered the burner phone he had in his pocket. He took it out and looked at the screen.

"Excuse me, Sheriff," he said, then stepped outside and answered it. "Hank? Are you okay?"

His voice was distant and distorted. "Yeah. I'm fine."

"Where are you?"

"Sitting in a room in the FBI field office, up in Connecticut. The kids are being looked over by a medical team here. I'm gonna wait here until Michael's parents show up. It's been one hell of a year for that family, and I've been right there with them for most of it. I want to make sure they're all okay, y'know."

"Of course. They were lucky to have you on the case. I can't imagine the relief they must be feeling."

"Thank you, Roach. Way I hear it, you did a hell of a job yourself."

"How do you…"

Valentine chuckled, causing a blast of static on the line. "Agents here are buzzing about what happened down there. Said the auction house looked like a warzone. Bodies everywhere. Doesn't take a genius to figure out you had a hand in that."

Roach glanced at the floor awkwardly. "Yeah, well… I just did what anyone else would have."

"You keep telling yourself that… *hero*."

He rolled his eyes. "What are you going to do now?"

Valentine sighed. "After this, I'll probably head back to New York. Take a couple of days off, then find myself another case. Bills don't pay themselves, sadly." He paused. "You know… we did make a hell of a team. You ever thought about becoming a P.I.? I could use a sidekick."

Roach smiled to himself. "That's the third job offer I've had today."

"The third?"

"Yeah. Bushell just tried to deputize me, and before that, Jasmine Decker offered me work."

"Jesus. What did you say to her?"

"Nothing. Bushell got a resounding no, though."

"I bet he did! Listen, you take care of yourself, Roach."

"You too, Hank."

"And just remember, okay? You're a good man. Maybe it's time you forgave yourself and came back to the world."

Roach looked around the corridor and sighed. "I appreciate that. Thank you. But what's happened here has shown me the world hasn't learned a goddamn thing from what it's been through. I have no faith left in people. I'll be okay, but for now, I think I'm better off on my own."

"Fair enough, my friend. If you're ever in New York…"

"Drinks are on you."

Valentine laughed. "Cheap bastard."

"Goodbye, Hank."

Roach ended the call and pocketed the phone, then headed back inside Bushell's room.

"Everything okay?" asked the sheriff.

Roach nodded. "Yeah. The kids are safe. Hank's heading back to New York soon."

"I see. And what about you? Given any thought to what's next?"

Roach stared at the floor for a moment, then looked up and smiled. "You know… I've heard Maine is lovely this time of year."

The two men exchanged a final nod of respect, then Roach left. He navigated the hospital corridors knowing he would never have to walk them again. He stepped outside into the fresh morning and took a deep breath. He looked left, along the road leading back into town, and thought about everything he had been through over the last few days. Then he turned and set off walking to the right, toward the bridge, putting Waters Point behind him forever.

For twenty minutes, he enjoyed the peace. His shoulders no longer carried the weight of someone else's burdens. Then he thought about his conversation with Vanessa yesterday. His mind began to wander. He took a deep breath and swallowed the growing sense of guilt within. Then he reached for the burner phone and dialed a number from memory.

It rang twice.

"Hello?"

Roach smiled at the sound of the voice. "Hey, Becky. It's me."

He heard the muffled gasp down the line. "Oh my God, Will? It's... it's really nice to hear from you. I've been worried."

"Sorry I never called after I left."

"No, don't apologize. We both said things we probably shouldn't have."

There was a moment of silent relief.

"Are you busy?" he asked.

"I can make time to talk," she said. "If you want?"

"Yeah, that'd be great." He smiled to himself. "I've got one hell of a story for your blog."

Post-Credits Scene

The man in the suit placed the laptop on the table and hit the space bar to begin playing the video file that filled the screen. It was black and white but good quality. The video was security footage from the lobby of a building. It showed a man walking in through the doors. He stopped by the security desk, produced a shotgun, and started firing. More security appeared, only to be gunned down without remorse.

The footage then flickered and switched to another camera feed. It showed a corridor filled with armed guards. It showed the man killing them as he made his way through the building. It flickered again. And again. And again. Multiple feeds stitched together to show a violent snuff film.

Finally, it jumped back to the lobby. It was filled with people. There was smoke and chaos and blood. Then two figures emerged, fighting viciously. A man and a woman. After a few minutes, the woman managed to flee. The man gathered himself, then walked calmly toward the exit. The camera tracked him, finally zooming in on his face.

Jasmine Decker leaned forward in her chair and hit the space bar again, pausing the video as Roach's features filled the screen. The time stamp in the bottom corner said April 23, 2020.

A smile crept across her face.

"So, it *was* him," she said.

Her bodyguard nodded. "Our contact in the FBI confirmed it, Miss Decker."

She sat back in her chair, stroking her chin thoughtfully with a manicured finger, still smiling.

"What would you like me to do?" asked the bodyguard.

She stared at the screen for a few moments in silence, then looked up. She was still smiling. "Find him. He could prove *very* useful."

More by James P. Sumner

THE ADRIAN HELL SERIES

vinci-books.com/trueconviction

In a world of killers, trust no one.

When legendary assassin Adrian Hell uncovers a secret that could ignite global war, he has one choice: run. Betrayed and hunted by rival superpowers, Hell must rely on his deadly skills to survive, knowing one wrong move could be his last.

Turn the page for a free preview…

True Conviction: Chapter One

August 20, 2013 – 15:04 PDT

The long, straight highway cutting across the unforgiving landscape in front of me is steaming in the afternoon sun.

Holy crap, it's hot.

I can't really complain. I mean, I'm still wearing my leather jacket. I know it isn't helping, but I'm on a job, and you never know who's watching. Reputation is everything in my line of work. For me, it all rests on the image I portray to the people around me. I've become synonymous with this jacket over the years, so I never leave home without it.

Still, I suppose I could've stayed on the air-conditioned bus for the last four miles. But it's been a long day, and I feel like stretching my legs.

I got the call yesterday. I was in Milwaukee, standing on the balcony of a hotel room fifteen floors up. It was early evening. The temperature had been a refreshing sixty-four degrees.

Inside the apartment, lay on the bed, was a dead man. I

had spent three days tracking him. I finally found him holed up inside the hotel. I knocked on his door. When he answered, I kicked it hard, so it flew open and hit him in the face. I assumed the security chain would be fastened and figured the initial force would've been necessary to gain entry. He stumbled backward and fell over, clutching his bleeding nose, which I had broken. His wide eyes had stared up at me, his face a mixture of fear and confusion.

"Sit on the bed," I said to him.

He didn't move at first, but as soon as I drew my gun and aimed it at him, he didn't hesitate a second longer. Once he was on the bed, I had reached into my pocket and pulled out the suppressor. I took my time attaching it, letting him see what was coming… letting him process the realization that it was the last night of his life.

"W-why?" he asked. "What do you want with me?"

Normally, I keep quiet. Silence forces them to start thinking, to jump to their own conclusions, which leads to fear and submission. It's a standard psychological tactic designed to keep your target distracted, so they don't think about resisting.

Plus, it's more entertaining.

Now don't get me wrong. I never take pleasure in doing what I do. If anything, I find it quite monotonous at times. But it pays well and I'm good at it. It's not always easy, but I try to remain detached. To stay out of my own head. It allows me to see things objectively—every angle, every possible outcome.

I operate by relying on my instincts and preparing for anything.

The man clearly had no idea why I was there, though, so I felt compelled to fill in the blanks for him.

I said, "So, here's the thing. You're a piece of shit who's

spent the last few years abusing your wife. Physically. Emotionally. Completely. And that just ain't right."

He quickly reached the conclusion I was going to shoot him. He went through the motions of begging and bargaining, but it was never going to do him any good.

My cell phone had started ringing just as I took aim at the guy's head. I quickly put my Bluetooth earpiece in and answered.

I said, "Hey, man. Just gimme a second, would you?"

Then I put a bullet right between his eyes, causing an instant explosion of crimson and pink to spray across the wall behind him. His body twitched as it fell back, leaving him lying motionless on the bloodstained covers.

I walked out onto the balcony and took a deep, calming breath as I looked at the beautiful city sprawled out below me.

I then took the call from my handler, and he told me about this job. He said it would be a good payout for easy work.

I took it without more than a second thought.

I got an early start this morning. I hopped on the first Greyhound to Minnesota. From there, I flew down to Las Vegas. There were some delays along the way, but nothing major. Plus, the advantage of being in business for yourself is that you rarely have to rush, so I've tried to relax and enjoy the trip.

But by the time I was on the bus heading here, the traveling, the lack of legroom, and the loud, sweaty people were all starting to annoy me. I could feel the beginnings of a headache, and my stress levels were slowly climbing into homicidal territory. So, when we drove past a sign that announced the city limits were only four miles away, I decided to walk it.

The sweat's running down my face and into my eyes, stinging them as I walk beneath the blistering sun. I squint ahead, seeing the steam rise off the blacktop on the horizon. The faint image of the city and mountains beyond is wavy, like a mirage.

My shoulder's aching from the weight of my bag. I always travel light, but fatigue's setting in.

What I wouldn't give right now for an ice-cold beer.

Heaven's Valley is a basin city in the middle of the Nevada desert, about a hundred and fifty miles north of Vegas. Bordering it to the North and the West are mountains. To the South and the East is nothing but sand. Its reputation is well-known. People say it's easy to lose yourself there. It thrives on the sins of the common man. Drugs, money, women… all there for those who want it.

But one man's Heaven can be another man's Hell.

Me? I've made a career out of being invisible and avoiding places like this. But I've developed somewhat of a reputation in certain… unsavory circles, which means I'm more notorious than anonymous nowadays. It also means I sometimes have to travel to places I otherwise wouldn't.

You see, I'm an assassin. Probably the best operating in North America today. Maybe even the world. I don't know. I say that with no ego. It's just a fact. I've honed my craft over the last eleven years, and I take pride in being this good at it.

I was military—first one through the door during Desert Shield. From there, I was recruited to Langley. But since retiring from doing the government's dirty work, I found it difficult to hold down a job that didn't involve shooting people. Old habits, I guess. So, I've worked hard, and with some help, I've become a legend in the criminal fraternity.

Nowadays, I'm regarded as the only hitman worth hiring if you want a job done right.

Does that make me sound like a bad person? I like to think not. I'm not an assassin like you see in the movies. I won't ever pull the trigger unless I'm satisfied the target deserves a bullet. In my line of work, you deal with a lot of people who do terrible things, so I don't feel bad saying someone *deserves* to die.

On the other hand, I suppose you could argue that, strictly speaking, I kill people for a living. I'm hardly going to win any humanitarian awards.

But think what you want. I'm going to continue taking money off bad people in return for killing other bad people. Once you've worked for the CIA, it's almost impossible to find your moral compass again, so I just listen to my gut and do what I believe is right. So long as I can look myself in the mirror at the end of the day, I'm happy.

So, who am I?

My name is Adrian Hell.

True Conviction: Chapter Two

19:56 PDT

I'm sitting on a stool in the local bar—a small, anonymous place called Charlie's. I'm leaning forward, resting on my crossed arms, nursing a half-empty bottle of Bud. Just to the left of it is a double Johnnie Walker Black, which I like to drink alongside a nice beer. It's just before eight p.m. I'm tired after the walk into town. I headed straight to the first place that looked like it would have a half-decent jukebox and ordered a drink.

A thin layer of dust from the road covers my jeans and boots. The sweat's soaked my white T-shirt through, so I've not removed my brown leather jacket. My shoulder bag is at my feet, resting against my bar stool.

Before sitting down, I'd walked across the bar to the jukebox and cycled through all the crap I've never heard of until I found a couple of good songs to listen to. I'd fed some quarters into the machine, selected my tracks, and then headed back to the bar to order my drinks.

The music isn't too loud, and this place isn't too busy. I close my eyes and listen to the world around me. The clack of the balls on the pool table sounds over my right shoulder, in the dark corner lit only by a neon blue sign advertising a beer I've never heard of. The idle chatter from the table to my left, where three women are discussing work and shopping and men. Two guys are just to the right of me, standing at the bar and exchanging one-line observations about the current state of the government. The bartender is in front of me, wiping down glasses until they squeak.

I open my eyes, examining my reflection in the mirror behind the bar. I take another long pull of my beer and let out a heavy sigh. My ice-blue eyes look like searchlights on the dark landscape of my face, which feels dirty from the hours of traveling. I stroke my chin and throat, feeling the coarse, three-day-old stubble grate on my hand like sandpaper.

I need a shave and a shower.

I rub my hand over my shaved head, briefly massaging my temples. I take a deep breath and feel the strain of a full day on the road slowly leave me.

I smile to myself. I feel comfortable in this bar. Dull lighting, sticky floors, and no pleasantries exchanged between strangers…. Just the music and me. If I ever run my own bar, it'll be exactly like this.

I glance outside as the orange glow of the setting sun casts an impressive, picturesque view through the window. Heaven's Valley is a deceptive place. At first glance, it's a bright, opulent city, filled with opportunity. But beneath the surface beats its true, corrupt, dark heart. Gambling, girls, gangsters… This place has one of the highest crime rates on the West Coast. It's definitely some people's idea of a good time, but it's certainly not mine. Unfortunately, in my line of work, the people who like places like this are usually the people who hire me.

It's not easy doing what I do. You need more than just a trained set of skills. You need certain mental attributes as well. Probably the most important is you have to be comfortable taking a life. It's easy to talk about, but when you're in that moment, staring some poor schmuck dead in the eye right before you pull the trigger—that's something else altogether. I've been doing it over half my life, and it's only been recently that I've found myself feeling more at ease with it.

I don't like seeing nice, normal people suffer. Most of the time, the people who hire me are unsavory at best, but the person or people they want me to kill have usually done something that justifies a bullet. Drug dealers, pimps, corrupt cops... you name it. I can easily look myself in the eye after killing anyone who does something that negatively affects regular, innocent people.

The second quality any good contract killer needs is the right attitude. Not just to carry out a job but to make the job work for you. If you play this game just right, your name can put fear in the hearts of every man in the room, even if you're miles away. Look at me... after a decade of doing this, I'm a legend in the criminal underworld. And to the various law enforcement agencies around the country, I'm a myth—a horror story they tell new recruits to scare them. No one believes anyone as ruthless or as skilled as me can really exist.

Suckers.

Fortunate Son by Creedence Clearwater Revival comes on the jukebox. God, I love this song! The soundtrack of the Vietnam War. The conflict might've been a bit before my time, but I appreciate the music that came about as a result of it.

I'm muttering the words quietly to myself when the music suddenly stops. I look up at the barman with a disappointed and confused expression on my face. He's looking behind me with wide, regretful eyes. He looks at me for a second, then lowers his gaze in a silent apology. He puts the glass he was cleaning down and steps slowly away from the bar.

I sigh. I don't need to look behind me to figure out what's coming next. I take another long sip of my well-earned beer and spin around on my seat. I lean back and rest my elbows on the bar behind me, holding the neck of my bottle loosely in my right hand. Walking toward me are two muscle-bound stereotypes wearing suits—one with the jacket on, open, and one wearing just the waistcoat. They're side by side, staring a hole straight through me and looking really pissed off.

I sigh again.

Why me?

They both look similar. The guy on the left is the smaller of the two, but they're both big guys. I'm a shade over six foot, and they both easily have a few inches on me. The smaller guy hasn't shaved in a few days. He's the one in the suit jacket. His shoulders are back, his chest is puffed out, and I haven't seen him blink once. He's clearly been practicing his intimidating persona, and he's giving it everything he's got as he walks toward me. I suspect he's overcompensating for something, which would make him the mouth.

His slightly taller friend in the waistcoat looks more physically impressive and seems more relaxed. He's clean-shaven and easily the more presentable of the two. He's not as tense, and he's blinking more, so I'm guessing he's the muscle—the confident one who doesn't need to pay much attention to the psychological side of conflict like his friend.

What noise there was in the bar has stopped. There's an audible, collective intake of breath as the people around me stop and stare with a mixture of fascination and fear.

It's good that I don't get self-conscious.

The two angry stereotypes stop three feet in front of me.

The guy on my left cracks his neck. He straightens his jacket and clears his throat. "You put that song on?"

I take a sip of my beer and shrug. "Yeah. You not a fan?"

"That song makes my friend here unhappy. Reminds him of someone he knew."

I turn to his friend in the waistcoat and raise my eyebrows. "Is that right?"

It's the first guy who answers me. "Yeah, that's right, and we don't appreciate a stranger walking in here and causing problems like that for us regulars."

I stare at the muscle a moment longer before turning back to the mouth. "I'm just here for a quiet drink. I meant no offense."

"That may be, but offense was caused all the same. Which leaves you in a bad situation."

You can argue this is a flaw of mine, but I love winding people up just before a fight. And let's face it: this is going to end up in a fight. Not much of one, I'll admit, because these two assholes couldn't beat me if I was asleep. But it'll be a fight nevertheless.

I think a bit of trash-talk is a good thing—if you do it right, you can make people so angry that they'll attack you without thinking. This greatly increases the chances of them making a mistake. And all it takes is one mistake and *Bam!* Goodnight, sweetheart.

Plus, it amuses me.

I smile. "Really? Why? I'm sitting in a bar, drinking a beer and relaxing after a long day. Seems like a pretty *good* situation to me. Granted, it'd be better if I didn't have to waste my breath on you two ass-clowns, but I can definitely think of worse things."

Usually, when people their size confront someone, they would expect them to back down or run off. They definitely wouldn't expect anyone to spark up a conversation or openly insult them.

They exchange a bewildered glance, as if asking each other if they can believe I'd have the nerve to speak to them like that.

The mouth points a finger at me. "You got some mouth on you, asshole. You know that?"

I shrug and nod. "I know. Gets me in all sorts of trouble. What's your name?"

He doesn't expect that, either.

He frowns. "Huh? It's… ah… it's Stan."

"Stan?" I point to his friend. "Does that make him Ollie?"

The muscle in the waistcoat cracks his knuckles. I see his cheeks have flushed red with anger. I thought that only happened in cartoons or something.

"No."

I point at him. "Is your surname Dupp?"

"No, it's not, wise-ass."

They're both getting angrier by the second, and I love it. I honestly can't wait for one of them to make a move for me.

Please don't judge me for how I entertain myself.

I turn back to the muscle—whose name *isn't* Oli, apparently. "So, what do they call you? Big and Dumb?"

Before he has chance to answer, Stan lurches forward and throws a big right hand at my face.

Holy shit, *that* did it! Here we go...

Luckily for me, it's possibly the slowest punch ever thrown, and I see it coming a mile away. In one quick movement, I push myself off my stool with my left leg and step through with my right, kicking Stan's front leg away from him. Just a little tap—enough to send him off-balance but not hard enough to break anything.

Because of the weight he put behind the punch, and the fact his leg's now moving uncontrollably away from him, his own momentum sends him crashing forward into the bar. As he goes down, I side-step away and slam my fist into his left temple. He bounces off the bar, and he's out cold by the time he hits the floor.

Using the momentum from the right hand, I continue to turn my body counterclockwise. I bring my left elbow up and swing it behind me, catching ol' Big and Dumb on the side of the chin as he moves in. It's not the most accurate or powerful shot I've ever thrown, but it does the job of sending him staggering backward because he was completely unprepared for it. As he does, I complete the turn and thrust my right fist into his sternum, just below his rib cage. There's a *lot* of power behind it, and it hits him as sweetly as possible.

When you take that kind of shot, your body instinctively doubles over. Because he's already moving backward from the elbow strike, both movements counter one another, and he just slumps straight down. He lands in the fetal position, making an awful rasping noise as he tries to breathe. He rolls around for a moment before giving up and passing out.

I look first at Stan, then his friend, unconscious at my feet. I step back over to the bar and gulp my Johnnie Walker in one. I reach into my pocket and throw down a twenty before picking up my bag and walking out. My footsteps are loud in the stunned silence of the bar. I stand on the sidewalk just outside Charlie's and take a couple of deep breaths, telling my body I no longer need any adrenaline and to slow my heart rate down.

The tops of the buildings are silhouetted against the setting sun in front of me. I look left and right, trying to decide which way will get me to a motel faster. I have absolutely no idea, so I resort to my age-old philosophy: when in doubt, go left.

I set off walking and take out my cell phone. I dial a number from memory. It rings twice before it's answered.

"Adrian! Great to hear from you, boss! How's Heaven's Valley so far?"

The guy on the other end has one of those annoying voices that always sounds happy, regardless of the situation. However, he's one of the few people on this planet I trust, so I let him off.

I met Josh Winters shortly after being recruited by the CIA to lead a black ops unit that was a joint effort between the U.S. and the British. We quickly bonded and became like brothers, so when I got out and decided to work freelance, he was more than happy to come with me. He's been working with me for the past eleven years, making contacts, finding me jobs, and supplying me with information and anything else I might need. My life is in his hands.

I can tell he's smiling down the phone as he speaks. I shake my head and smile to myself. "I've been in this goddamn town half an hour and I've already been in a fight. I don't like it here."

He laughs. "You *do* have a tendency to make a unique first impression, don't you?"

I laugh with him. "Screw you, Josh. We all set for tomorrow?"

"Yeah, you're meeting a guy called Jimmy Manhattan. This guy, and the people he represents… they're old school, Adrian. So, I say this with all the love in the world, but try to avoid being too… *you*, all right?"

I'm almost offended, but I know what he's trying to say. I've worked for guys like these many times, and they take their code seriously. Disrespecting someone like Jimmy Manhattan would bring a lot of unnecessary trouble down on top of me.

"Fear not, my man. I shall be at my most professional."

"That's what I'm worried about! Call me afterward if you need anything."

"Will do."

I hang up and continue my search for a nice motel where I can grab a shower and some sleep. I find myself humming *Fortunate Son*, which I didn't get to finish listening to in Charlie's.

Assholes.

True Conviction: Chapter Three

August 21, 2013 – 08:06 PDT

I'm walking along a quiet street just off the main strip that runs through the center of the city. The sun is glorious and warm, even at this time in the morning, and it's getting hotter by the minute. A barren, unforgiving desert surrounds Heaven's Valley, so intensely hot sun all year round is commonplace.

I'm meeting Manhattan at nine a.m., so I'm going to get there early and scope the place out. It's an old habit that was drilled into me on the very first day of boot camp—reconnaissance can save your life. Always know where the enemy will come from, and always know how you can get out. Especially in this situation, where I'm meeting someone I don't know or trust. I like to plan my exit strategy long before I make my entrance.

The meeting is in a quaint little family-owned coffee shop called Dimitri's. On the outside, the window frames are a faded brown. The company logo is emblazoned across the glass. To the left is the entrance. There's enough room outside for three sets of tables and chairs, which I imagine are going to be occupied most of the day, given the weather.

I walk inside. I'm surprised at how spacious it is—much bigger than I expected. The layout inside is like a grid, with seating arranged in three rows of three in front of the serving counter that runs almost the full width of the far wall. The rows on the left and right are booths, which seat four people, two facing two. The middle row has round tables with four chairs on each compass point around it.

The café must've just opened. There's an aging guy with short, gray hair setting up the cappuccino machine behind the counter. He turns as I approach and eyes me up and down before turning back to his work. He's probably in his early seventies. His tanned skin is like old leather, and he's got these faded, blue-gray tattoos on his forearms, presumably from time served in the military.

I approach the counter. "Morning. Can I get a coffee, black with two sugars, please?"

He doesn't look around. "Be right over."

I turn and look out at the empty café, trying to decide where would be best to sit and wait. I figure the booth near the window on the right-hand side is best. I walk over and slide across, twisting slightly to my left. I put my back to the wall and rest one knee on the seat, so I can see the entire place in front of me—the entrance, the counter, and the doors behind it, as well as outside through the window. From here, I can see everyone approaching and don't have to worry about anyone coming up behind me. More old habits that have saved my ass more than once.

Some people call me paranoid, but it's not paranoia if the bastards are really after you.

A few minutes pass, then the old guy brings my coffee over.

"You want breakfast?" he asks.

I shake my head. "I'm good, thanks."

He nods once and walks back to the counter. I take a sip of my coffee and gaze around absently. I look out the window and see three men approaching from down the street.

This must be him.

I'm both impressed and concerned that he's prepared enough to show up early like I did. I need to be on my game here.

The door opens and the three men walk in.

Showtime.

The first guy is probably early fifties, wearing what looks like an expensive, light brown three-piece suit. He's a thin, wiry guy but walks with the utmost confidence and grace. He comes across as a man who never rushes to be somewhere. He doesn't need to. He's staring at me but not in an aggressive way. It's more like... curiosity.

Hello, Jimmy Manhattan.

The two guys behind him must be the bodyguards. Manhattan doesn't strike me as the kind of guy who needs hired muscle. They might be here more for intimidation than actual protection. Maybe they—

Shit.

I look closer at the bodyguards.

Yeah... they're my two friends from the bar last night.

Both look like they're suffering from a bad hangover. My face betrays nothing, but inside, I can't help but laugh. Only *I* would manage to get into a fight with the security detail of my next employer.

I don't stand, and I certainly don't extend my hand to greet them. I simply pick up my coffee and take another sip.

The old guy walks over to my booth. "You must be Adrian Hell."

His voice is smooth, and his accent is very... East Coast. Brooklyn, maybe? He's a long way from home.

I nod. "Jimmy Manhattan, I presume?"

"At your service. I see your reputation for being thorough and punctual is well deserved."

I shrug. "Well, you know what they say: the early bird gets the... contract, I guess." I smile. "I see you've brought friends..." I look up at them and address each in turn. "Fred... Ginger..." I hold my hands up apologetically. "No hard feelings about yesterday?"

They both glare at me with evil in their eyes and the hint of a snarl on their lips. But neither speaks or even moves a muscle. They just glance at Manhattan and remain still.

I look back at him and smile. "I see you've got the dogs well trained. I'm impressed."

Manhattan lets slip a half-smile but remains unwavering in his cool, confident demeanor. "And I see the reputation about your mouth is accurate too." He looks over his shoulder at Stan. "Give me and Mr. Hell some privacy, would you?"

Stan and his friend walk over to the counter and sit down facing me. I hold their gaze for a second with my best un-blinking, deadpan poker face, then look away. They don't bother me. The only reason either of them is here is to emphasize Jimmy's importance and to intimidate whomever he's meeting. That won't work with me and everyone here knows it.

Manhattan clasps his hands on the table in front of him. "So, Mr. Hell—or can I call you Adrian?"

He's professional and respectful. I suspect his manner is a practiced act to disarm the other person, get them feeling comfortable and relaxed. That's when he'll reel you in. Again, it's never going to work on me, but I appreciate his friendly approach, and I reciprocate.

I shrug. "I've been called worse than both, so feel free."

I quite like *Mr. Hell* though. I might try using that in the future, see if it catches on.

"Adrian it is, then. Now I represent Roberto Pellaggio, and I'm here at his request to offer you a job befitting your particular set of skills."

He produces a brown, letter-sized envelope and slides it across the table to me. I open it and take out a photograph and some papers. It's a black and white eight-by-ten of a man in a suit walking across a road. He's talking on his phone and carrying a briefcase.

Manhattan gestures to the photograph. "This is Ted Jackson. Until recently, we were working with Mr. Jackson on a business deal to secure some land on the outskirts of the city. Mr. Pellaggio is looking to expand his business portfolio by building a casino there."

I don't look up. I'm engrossed in the picture, taking in every detail. "Go on…"

"A few days ago, with no warning or explanation, Mr. Jackson backed out of that deal. He kept the deeds to the land, as well as the money Mr. Pellaggio had already invested into it."

I look up. "And you want me to make him disappear?"

"Mr. Pellaggio is a respected businessman with a—how can I put it?—well known and formidable reputation. A slight of this kind cannot be tolerated under any circumstances. We must send a clear message."

"I understand. Consider it done."

"There's something else. It's also of vital importance that you retrieve the deeds to that land. Mr. Pellaggio is eager to complete this deal and begin construction of the casino, and that paperwork is the key."

"Not a problem."

I'm more than happy to take this job. It's straightforward and easy money—find a businessman, kill him, and steal some paperwork. Give the papers to the mafia and get my money... I can be out of here in a couple of days. I'm not a big fan of this close, desert heat, so the sooner I can get back to somewhere slightly milder, the better.

Manhattan stands, prompting Stan and his friend at the counter to do the same. "I look forward to seeing more of your work, Adrian." He glances over at his bodyguards. "It comes highly recommended."

I laugh. "Thank you."

"We'll speak again when you have completed the job."

Manhattan nods a silent goodbye, then turns and walks out of the café, followed by his bodyguards. As they walk off, Stan turns to me and flips me the finger. I simply smile and wave back.

God, I wish I'd hit him harder.

08:41 PDT

I wait a few minutes after they leave to finish my coffee. I stand, gather the contents of the envelope up, leave a tip on the table, and head back outside. As I open the door, I'm hit by a blast of heat, as if I've opened an oven that's been cooking for three hours. I was only inside maybe a half-hour, but the increase in temperature is staggering.

The sun is pounding down as I make my way along the sidewalk. I'm wearing a white T-shirt and jeans, minus the leather jacket, with black sunglasses and a baseball cap. I cross to the other side of the street, as it's partly shaded, but it does little to cool me down.

I'm in the center of the business district, and it's busy. Maybe it's because I'm not a local and unaccustomed to the climate, but it baffles me how anyone can walk around in a suit when it's this hot.

I take out my cell and dial Josh's number. It rings twice.

"Hey, boss. How did it go with Jimmy the Glove?"

He sounds as sickeningly enthusiastic as always.

I frown. "Is that what people call him?"

"Apparently."

"Do I want to know why?"

He pauses. "Probably not."

"Fair enough. Yeah, the meeting went fine, despite finding out that Manhattan's hired goons were the assholes that started a fight with me last night."

"You're shitting me?" he says, laughing.

"I shit you not, my friend."

"I bet that went down well?"

"It was fine. He seemed to find it quite amusing, to his credit."

"Only you, boss. So, are you happy with the contract?"

"Yeah, it should be straightforward. It's a property deal gone bad. He wants me to take out the target to send a message, then recover the deeds to some land they were intending to buy from him before he screwed them over. It shouldn't take me more than a couple of days. Will be glad to get out of this place and go somewhere slightly colder—this heat is unbearable."

"Surely, the ice in your veins cools you down?"

I shake my head. "Screw you."

He chuckles to himself. "You need anything from me?"

"Not right now, but I know where you are if I need you. I'll be in touch."

Just as I'm about to hang up, I remember one last thing. "Oh, what do you think of 'Mr. Hell' as my business name?"

Josh begins howling with laughter. Exaggerated and loud. I hold the phone away from my ear until he's finished.

"Oh, dear… Heh… Sorry. Are you serious?"

"Yeah, it's how Manhattan addressed me when we were exchanging pleasantries. Kinda liked it."

"Adrian, you know I love you, right?"

I pause. "Yeah…"

"It makes you sound like a professional wrestler. Who's gay."

I remain silent for a few moments, trying to make him feel uneasy. Although, I know that probably won't work. "Josh, you know I love you, right?"

"Yeah…"

"You're a dick."

I hang up and walk on, navigating the increasingly busy streets.

I think I'll do some recon work for the job, get to know the city a little better. According to the information Jimmy Manhattan gave me, Jackson is attending a meeting this morning, which is due to finish any time in the next half-hour. I'll find where he is and tail him on foot for as long as I can. I'll be able to get a look at his car, any colleagues or security he might have—get a feel for his behaviors and routines. I've also got his itinerary for the next twenty-four hours, courtesy of Manhattan's research, so I'll approach when he finishes work to minimize the risk of exposure and attention.

I walk on through the city, taking in the sights around me. The working day is in full swing, with everyone around me dressed for the office and rushing in all directions. People are carrying bags, or papers, or their morning coffee, weaving in and out of the crowds on either side of the street.

The traffic's just as busy. It's mostly taxis—nose to tail, fighting to get through the next set of lights before they change again.

I come to a large junction, where Main Street meets 9th Avenue. I cross over and turn right, which will lead me to Cannon Plaza, where Jackson is currently in his meeting.

After a few minutes, I come upon the plaza. It has a large fountain in the center and lots of people walking across it in every direction. Jackson's in the building at the far end, which is a tall, unmarked, dark glass structure. It's easily twenty stories high, overlooking the plaza below. I fight my way through the bustle of people and sit on the edge of the fountain facing east, so that the entrance to the building is on my left, about fifty feet away.

After a few moments, a young woman with a child in a stroller sits next to me, smiling politely. I smile back and briefly look at the baby as she rummages in her bag. I've never been a particularly broody guy, and children haven't been on my radar at all since I lost my daughter. But I have to admit, it's one cute little kid. It couldn't be more than eight months old. It's got a bubble of spit on its lips and these big, wide brown eyes looking around in awe at everything. It's nice to see that true innocence still exists in this world.

I turn my attention back to the building, looking out for Jackson. I don't have to wait long. After maybe five minutes, I see him walk out of the building. Just like in the photograph, he looks ever the businessman. He's in his late forties and wearing an expensive-looking gray suit. He's talking on his cell phone as he walks purposefully across the plaza. Handcuffed to his left wrist is a brown leather briefcase. That's interesting... You don't normally see that kind of security measure on everyday people. Not unless he's carrying a large amount of money or top-secret documents. But why would he be?

I'm a details guy and I question everything. Sometimes the smallest detail can have the largest impact. I make a mental note of the observation and move on. I'll mention it to Josh later, see what he thinks.

Jackson's walking fast, like he's running late. It looks like he's alone, so I stand and set off following him, keeping a casual distance between—

Oh... hang on a minute.

I stop after a couple of steps when something catches my eye just behind him. I slow down and watch, double-checking to make sure I'm not mistaken. He's not alone. Walking a couple of paces behind, at roughly the same speed, is a bodyguard.

And she's beautiful.

Grab your copy...
vinci-books.com/trueconviction